Arcane Rites

Cult of the Pajoli

Simon Birks

Arcane Rites
Cult of the Pajoli

First Edition

Visit **http://bluefoxcomics.com** to read more about all our books, comics, and other publications.

For Fraser
Thank you for all the great times,
fun and laughter -
I hope you enjoy the book!

Contents

Welcome to
Arcane Rites

Welcome to this brand-new gamebook series! After many years of trying to create a gamebook (and never really getting past paragraph 100!), here it is – 700 paragraphs worth. I like to think I was saving it all up!

So, what's it all about?

Arcane Rites is a set of gamebooks that follow the exploits of Derilion, a hunter and adventurer known as the Lightbringer to the people of Pegeara, the land she's lived in all her life.

In Cult of the Pajoli, her ward, a young girl by the name of Obishaa, is kidnapped, and she must venture into a hazardous cave system to rescue her.

You must use your experience, stealth, strength, speed, and perception to help you successfully navigate the many chambers and creatures within. Not all are enemies, and it is up to you to choose Derilion's path and actions.

You probably won't make it through on your first attempt (nor second or third), but don't despair! Re-enter the caves and forge a new path toward your goal.

Be aware your actions will affect the outcomes of other encounters later in the book, and even later in the series.

So, without further ado, let's teach you the basics so you can dive in as quickly as possible!

Paragraphs

New to gamebooks? Let us help you. Also known as interactive fiction, a gamebook is a multi-threaded story, which allows the player (you!) to make decisions for the protagonist.

Each section of text (aka paragraph) has a number before it. The first, and starting, paragraph of the book is numbered **1**. The paragraphs that follow it are sequentially numbered but do not follow on. If you tried to read it like a normal book, it wouldn't make any sense.

At the end of each paragraph, you will be faced either with:

a) No choice (Derilion has died)
b) One choice, turn to **n** paragraph
c) Or a series of two or more choices

In the instance of c), you get to choose the next action. Read the paragraph text fully; in places, the book is written with subtle clues as to the possible outcomes of the actions.

Once you have chosen, find the paragraph with the same number as your choice and continue from there!

In some paragraphs you will find objects, test attributes and fight against other inhabitants of the caves. Rules for each are on the following pages.

Attributes

You have 5 attributes, listed below with the appropriate method of calculation. Record the attributes on the adventure sheet.

1. *Health* – you begin the adventure with 30 *Health*. *Health* will reduce as you encounter enemies and traps along the way and is increased by using healing balms when not in battle.

2. *Speed* – designates how quickly you react (and run!) in a given situation. To determine *Speed*, roll 1D6 and add 6 to the score (minimum 7, maximum 12).

3. *Accuracy* – designates how precise you are in aim and movement. To determine *Accuracy*, roll 1D6 and add 6 to the score (minimum 7, maximum 12).

4. *Stealth* – designates how quietly you can move and how well you can hide. To determine *Stealth*, roll 1D6 and add 6 to the score (minimum 7, maximum 12).

5. *Detection* – designates how efficient you are at detecting traps and reading the situation. To determine *Detection*, roll 1D6, and add 6 to the score (minimum 7, maximum 12).

Apart from *Health*, most of the attributes will remain static unless you are injured, impaired or improved during the adventure. Your attributes can exceed their starting level.

Whenever points are *restored* to an attribute, including *Health*, it may not go over the starting value. If the current value is equal to or higher than the starting value, nothing happens.

Testing Attributes

Whilst facing the Cult of the Pajoli, you will find many paragraphs asking you to test one of Derilion's attributes.

To test an attribute:

1. Roll 2D6.

2. If the result is equal to or **lower** than the attribute being tested, the test is successful.

3. If the result is **higher** than the attribute, the test is unsuccessful.

4. The paragraph will let you know what happens as a result of the test.

5. Sometimes, being unsuccessful has hidden benefits.

For example:

You are instructed to test Derilion's *Stealth*, which is currently at 8. You roll 2D6, and the result is 8. As the result is the same as her current total, the test is successful.

If you'd rolled 9 or more, the test would have been unsuccessful.

Combat

These combat rules will cover you for most of the combat you'll encounter in the caves.

1. Whoever has the highest *Speed* goes first. If tied, compare the two *Accuracy* attributes next. If these two numbers are also the same, compare *Health*. If these are equal, then Derilion goes first.

2. The attacker rolls 2D6. If the result is lower than or equal to their *Accuracy*, they have hit the combatant.

3. Subtract the attacker's damage from the defender's *Health*.

4. If the defender has 0 or less *Health*, they have died. If the defender was Derilion, she has died, and you must start the book again.

5. If the defender has 1 or more *Health*, it is their turn to attack.

There is no ability to run away as you are fighting in a cramped cave system.

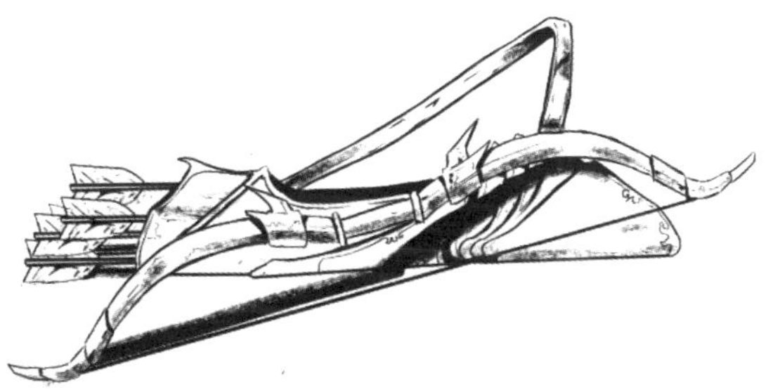

Weapons

Derilion's default weapon is her sword, which has a starting damage score of 2.

Derilion also has a bow and a quiver with arrows in. To determine the number of arrows she begins the adventure with, roll 1D6 and add 6. Record this number on the adventure sheet.

When you are about to begin combat where she can use her bow and arrow, the paragraph will include instructions on how she can use it. Each successful arrow deals 2 damage to the enemy's *Health*.

Depending on the enemy, you may be able to recover some of the arrows. Once again, the paragraph will let you know.

Equipment

As well as her sword, shield, bow, and quiver of arrows, Derilion has two other items where she stores equipment; her belt and her backpack.

1. Belt – this can store up to 5 objects which can be accessed and used quickly. Derilion starts the adventure with 2 healing balms in her belt (**+1w each**). When not in combat, she can use them to heal up to 4 *Health* each.

2. Backpack – this can store many objects.

The total amount of equipment Derilion can carry is limited to 60 weight points.

Weight

Weight limits the number of extra objects Derilion can wear or carry in her belt and backpack.

1. The total weight of all additional objects worn or stored in Derilion's belt or backpack cannot exceed 60 weight points. All objects have a weight associated with them shown in bold in brackets whenever you can pick up or use an item.

2. Derilion's sword, bow and arrow and shield do not count toward her weight limit.

3. If the combined additional weight points go over 20, Derilion's *Speed* and *Stealth* totals are reduced by 1 point until the weight falls to 20 or under.

4. If the combined additional weight points go over 40, Derilion's *Speed* and *Stealth* totals are reduced by a further 1 point until the weight falls to 40 or under.

5. If not in combat, nor about to enter combat, you can discard items to bring the weight points down. You cannot pick discarded items back up.

Items carried at the end of the book can be transferred over to the next book in the Arcane Rites series.

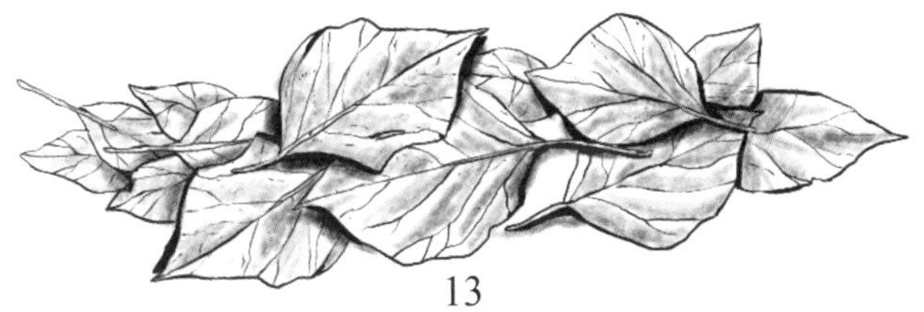

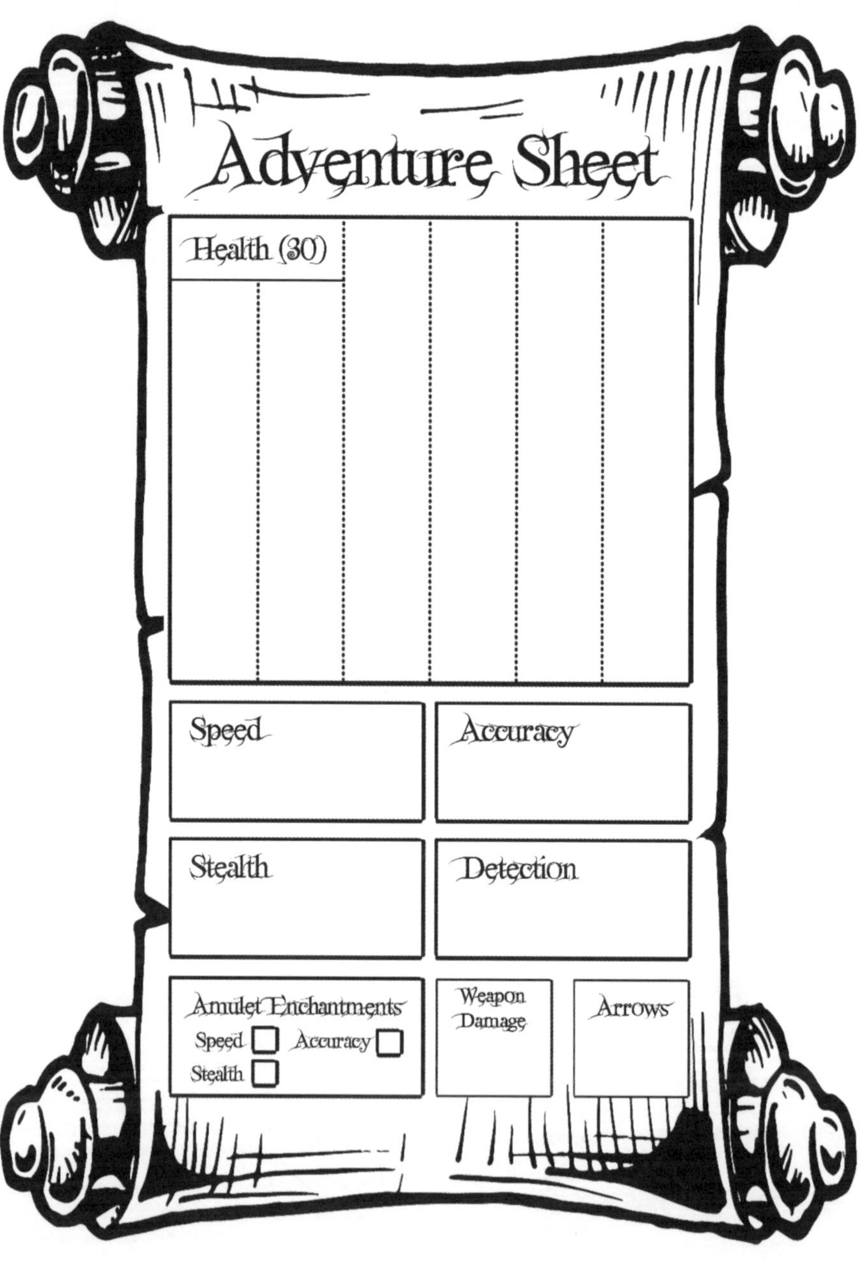

Adventure Sheet
Health (30)
Speed
Accuracy
Stealth
Detection
Amulet Enchantments
Speed
Accuracy
Stealth
Weapon Damage
Arrows

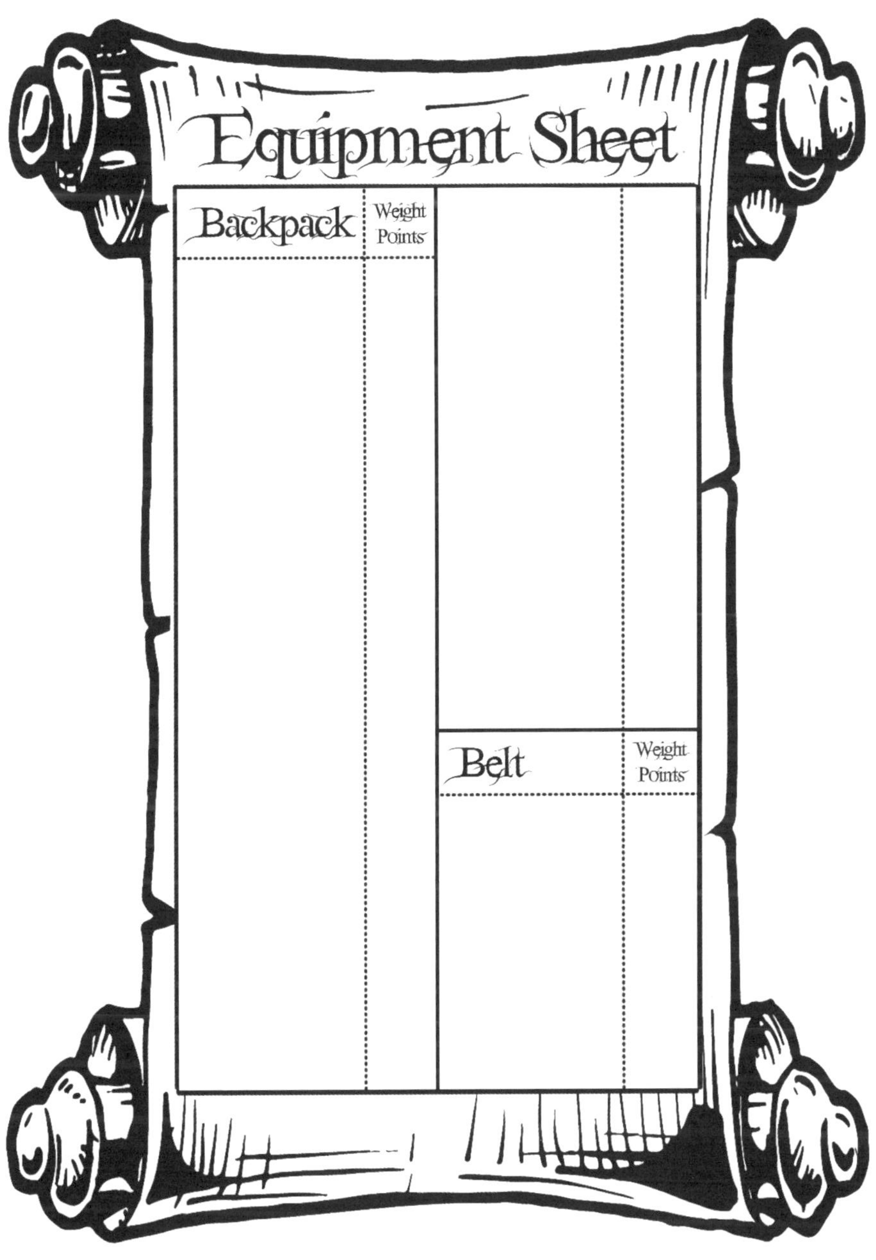

Equipment Sheet
Backpack
Weight Points
Belt
Weight Points

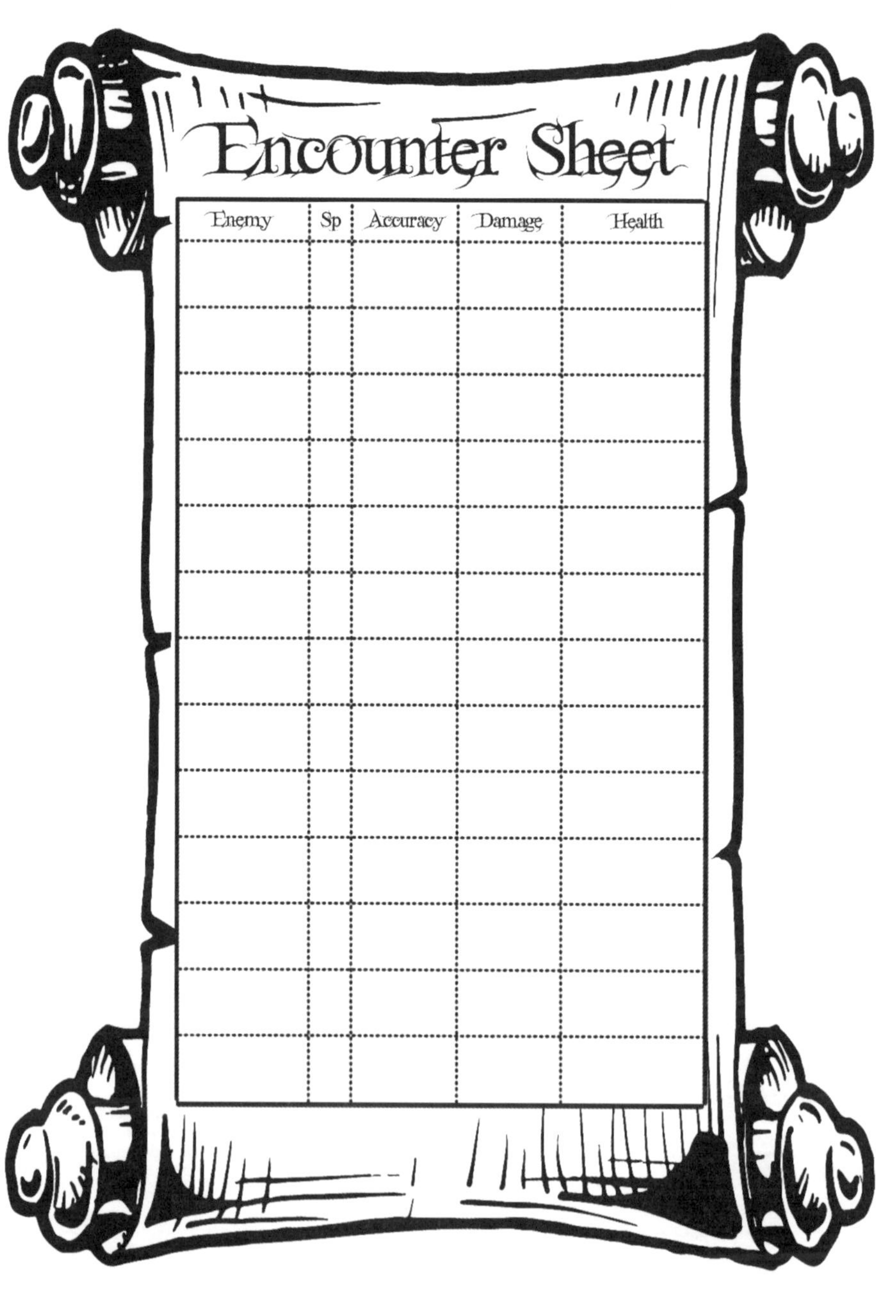

Encounter Sheet
Enemy
Sp
Accuracy
Damage
Health

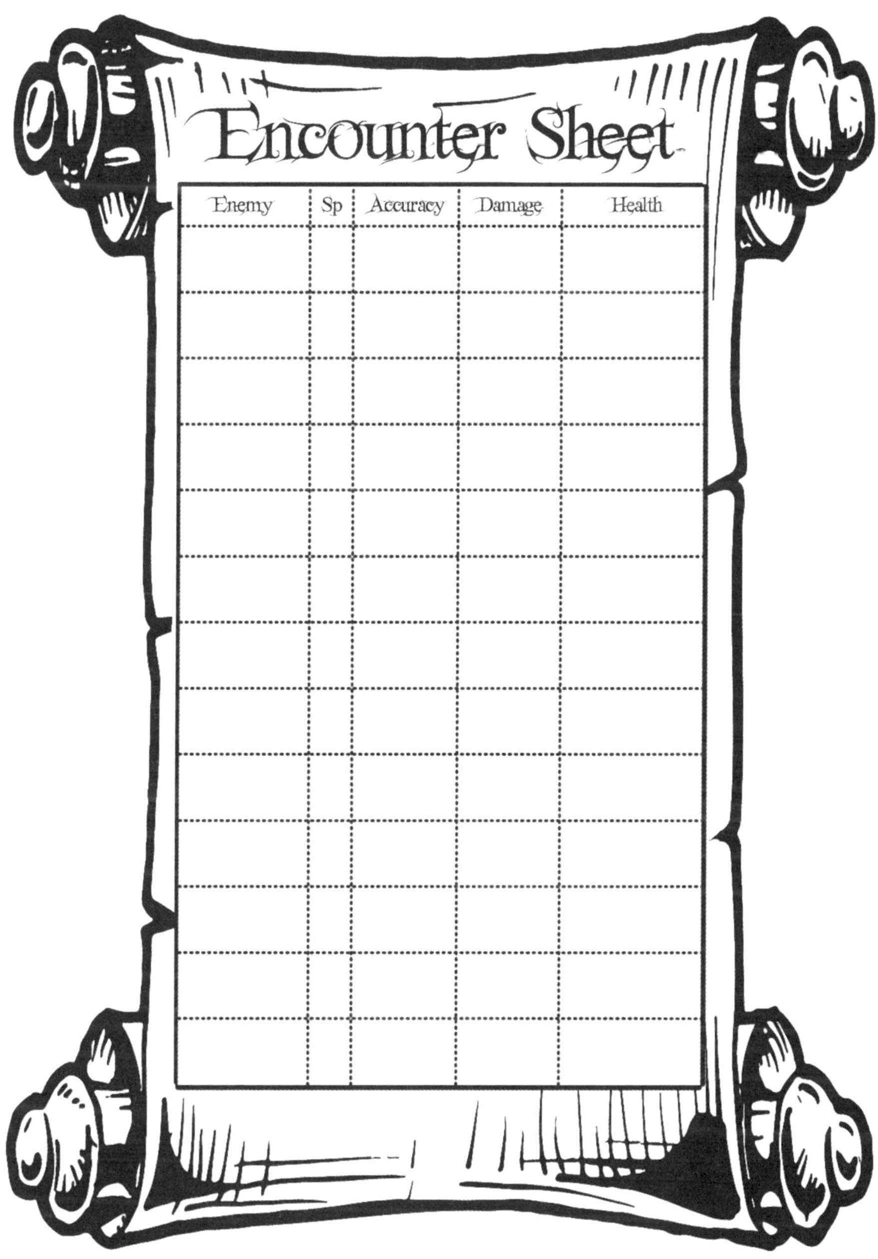
Encounter Sheet
Enemy | Sp | Accuracy | Damage | Health

The Lightbringer

Sitting by the campfire, looking out as dawn breaks over the hills spread before her, Derilion wondered how she got here. Were the gods guiding her or was she the one who'd made all the decisions.

She'd come a long way from the small village where she'd grown up. It was there she'd befriended the woman known as August, who'd lived in the furthest building and kept herself to herself. She had intrigued Derilion, who had manufactured a way of speaking to her, feigning an accident by cutting her leg and limping to August's gate.

The woman had seen through the young girl's lie, Derilion was certain, but, silently, she'd sat her down and expertly dressed her wound using balms and bandages.

"Come back tomorrow, and I'll take another look," the woman had said. It had made the young girl smile, and she'd almost forgotten her ruse and skipped back along the path.

Young Derilion had returned to August's the next day and the next, and over time the woman had taught her many skills, from fire creation to hunting through to fighting. Her parents had been concerned by August at first, but they had come around in the end.

When Derilion had been ready to leave the village, she'd visited August one last time. The woman was still walking, though maybe not as fast as when they'd first met.

"Sit," August had said.

The hunter had sat. August went and dislodged a piece of wall and reached inside it. Derilion sat up a little higher, intrigued. When the old woman brought out her hand, it was holding a shield.

"This is my last gift to you," August said. "Take it."

Derilion reached up and took it. It appeared to be a simple shield.

"This was mine. I looked after it, and it looked after me, you could say. Oh, I can see the look on your face. It's just a shield, you think, and an old one at that? Well, the difference between you and me is something called experience, and I hope you live long enough to gain some. The shield will help. Stand up."

The hunter stood.

"Hold it slightly away from you and speak this word."

August leant forward and whispered into Derilion's ear.

"Volkov," Derilion spoke aloud. To her amazement, the shield burst into flames.

"Keep hold of it," August said. "The flames will not burn you. They do not produce heat, but they will light your way in the dark."

Sat on the hill, Derilion looked down at the shield she knew as Volkov. It had indeed kept her safe on many a perilous adventure, and she had gained valuable experience. She briefly wondered if August was still alive. It was unlikely. Ten years had passed since she'd last seen her.

In those ten years, she'd become known among the villages of Pregeara as the Lightbringer. It was not an accurate name. Whilst she might indeed stand up against unfairness, she did it for money. Life on the road had hardened her. It would harden anyone.

Behind, in the makeshift shelter, Derilion's ward slept, muttering and twisting as if she might be in the throes of a nightmare.

Good, the hunter thought. She needed to understand suffering. To survive in this world was a constant nightmare, a battle every single day.

The Lightbringer returned her gaze to the hills in front of her. Should she move on? The pair of them had only arrived yesterday, but there was something here that made her feel uneasy.

Derilion drained her drink and spat the crushed leaves onto the green grass.

They were both hungry, and her first job of the day was to catch breakfast, or perhaps, at a push, rob someone of their bread. The Lightbringer indeed.

She stood and looked at her ward. Obishaa was her name, a girl of little more than eight years. She wondered how much longer she could keep her alive. Yes, she'd made a promise to her dying father to look after her, but even he must have known it would be difficult. Life on the road was a short one if you weren't lucky.

And yes, her father's death had been the hunter's mistake. He'd been an innocent party on the wrong end of a blade, but it was still her fault. She'd owed him, and now she owed the girl.

"Wake up," the Lightbringer barked at her. Obishaa's eyes immediately opened. Wild eyes, dangerous eyes. She would be fierce if taught how to use that energy. It took a couple of moments before the girl realised who was standing over her, and when she did, she grew drowsy once more.

"Wake up!" Derilion repeated. Obishaa's eyes opened again, and she pushed herself up on one arm.

"I was asleep," she said, dragging a forearm across her brow.

"And now you're not. I need you to hide while I find food."

"Why don't we ever have food?"

"Because you eat it. Now, drink this, and hide."

The hunter handed the girl a cup of warmed herb water and watched as she sipped it slowly.

"I was having a nightmare," Obishaa said. "I couldn't understand it. I think I was underground. I think you were there, too. I can't be sure. I heard a name; Pajoli. Do you know what that means?"

The hunter shook her head.

"It means you should dream less."

Obishaa almost smiled then. Almost. And though she'd never admit it, it made the hunter happy. Derilion hadn't led the best of lives, so perhaps she was destined to look after Obishaa as some retribution. Maybe it was the gods' fate for her. Maybe it was just chance.

"Hide," Lightbringer told the girl. "And hide well."

Obishaa nodded and started to rise. Derilion turned and smothered the fire, before setting off down the hill, bow in hand.

It was a good hour's hunt, and she caught two Jackalopes, which she hoped would feed them for a few days. The hunter turned and headed back to the camp, arriving when the sun was highest in the sky.

"Obishaa," she called softly whilst preparing to skin one of the animals. A minute went by, but the girl didn't reply.

The Lightbringer stopped and listened.

"Obishaa?" she called again. Was it possible she hadn't heard her the first time?

She waited, but still saw no movement of any kind.

Derilion got her sword and made her way to the hiding place the pair had found the previous night. The mug was there, but something about the way it was tipped made the hunter anxious.

She crouched and looked closer. There was a sign of a struggle, and two pairs of adult footprints led away to the south. She'd been taken. Derilion's stomach grew tight.

At least there's a chance she's still alive, the hunter thought. She picked up her rucksack and began to follow the tracks.

Near on an hour later, she was back in the hamlet they'd passed through yesterday morning. Three houses on stilts, crowded in the middle of a clearing. Derilion unsheathed her sword and walked up the nearest set of steps and knocked on the door.

After a minute, the door opened, and an old woman stood in front of her.

"I'm looking for my daughter," Derilion said. "About eight years old. We passed through yesterday."

The woman shook her head.

"Ain't seen no one," she replied, shutting the door.

The Lightbringer tried to keep her temper; resisted putting a hole in the woman's door. Instead, she walked to the next house, climbed the steps, and knocked on the door. This hut had seen better days.

This time the door wasn't even opened.

"What is it?" hissed a man from the other side.

"I'm looking for my daughter. We passed through yesterday. She's eight years old. Have you seen her?"

"Gone missing, has she?" the man asked.

"Yes. This morning."

"They'll have her, then, most likely. No children escape them, not for a long time."

"Escape who?"

"The Pajoli," he replied.

Her heart sank. That was the name Obishaa had heard in her nightmare.

"Who are the Pajoli?"

"An ancient race. They capture the magicked and use them to make the Pajoli stronger."

"Use them for what?"

"No one knows; they're never seen again. Our whole way of life is dying because the Pajoli steals the children."

"Where can I find them?" the hunter asked. "These Pajoli?"

The man laughed a hopeless laugh.

"Oh, that's easy. Do you see the entrance up on the mountain?"

The Lightbringer looked to the mountain. There was indeed a cave entrance in the side.

"I see it."

"That is where you will find the Pajoli. I would advise you not to go, to just forget about your daughter. Make peace with yourself and your loss."

She heard the man's footsteps move away, and Derilion walked down the steps. As she reached the bottom, the front door to the third house opened, and a woman came out.

"I can see you are going on a suicide mission. You're not the first. Let me give you this first; it might help you on your way."

The woman gave Derilion a small parcel with some food in, and a pouch with three sachets of purple powder.

"These are explosives. It's all I have, but they might help you. Throw them hard at your target; they will not ignite if they do not hit with force. Good luck, hunter. The other two think you are stupid, but they have given up. I think you are brave."

She had tears in her eyes.

"Did they take your child?" Derilion asked.

"They took my sister, my Huranee when we were eleven years old. That was a generation ago. I moved back here when I was older, and I live in hope I might see her one day."

"If I hear of her, I will do my best to let you know."

The woman thanked the Lightbringer. Add the 3 explosive powders to her belt.

It took the hunter most of the afternoon to reach and climb the mountain. She rested for a few minutes in front of the cave entrance. She couldn't afford to rest long. Once she had her breath back, she approached the cave slowly, looking for traps. She was mildly surprised when she found none.

The Lightbringer entered the cave of the Pajoli, ready to save Obishaa, whatever the cost.

Now turn to **1**.

Arcane Rites:
Cult of the Pajoli

Simon Birks

1

A few feet in, the entrance narrowed into a passage no more than three feet across. There was the stench of death and decay beyond it, and Derilion stopped, fetched her shield from her back, and spoke the word 'Volkov' into the darkness.

The shield glowed for a moment, and then fire coated its outside, lighting the room before her. Looking around, Derilion saw several fresh tracks of footprints on the wet ground, including one which could have been Obishaa's.

Her heart dipped, and her anger rose. The adventurer's hand gripped her sword tightly, and she stifled a furious scream. How could she have been so stupid to let Obishaa be stolen? Why hadn't she taken the girl with her on the hunt?

Derilion steadied her breathing; this train of thought would do nothing but distract her, and she loosened the grip on the sword. She had to find and save her ward, and for that, she needed total concentration.

Derilion returned her gaze to the surroundings. The walls of the passage were rough, and they reminded her of blast patterns from powerful spells.

She pressed on, the passage opening into a wider, circular, room with smoother walls. However high she raised the shield, it was still too dark to see a way out, and the stench was almost overpowering.

The Lightbringer didn't want to stay there long. She had three options; skirt around the room to the left, (turn to **63**), head straight into the room, (turn to **56**), or make her way around the right-hand side of the chamber (turn to **516**)?

2

Derilion pushed her away with her shield and watched as the woman stumbled and fell backwards into the net.

The woman's body shimmered for a moment, whilst around her the light grew blindingly bright, causing the hunter to shield her eyes. When Derilion could open them again, both the woman and the net had gone.

It had all happened so quickly it was hard for the hunter to understand exactly where she had gone. Perhaps the net had been a doorway through to another place. She could only guess.

Now, she stood alone in the room. Before her was the exit (turn to **466**), and against the wall was a large wooden chest she could investigate (turn to **189**).

3

The hunter approached the left bench, where several bottles of the distilled liquid sat unopened. She removed the stopper from one and sniffed at the liquid inside. It smelt bitter and made her feel lightheaded.

"That'll be enough of that," came a woman's voice from toward the exit.

Turn to **615**.

4

Something struck Derilion in the chest and pushed her back into the wall. Deduct 1 from her *Health*. Instinctively, the hunter raised her shield to protect her face and felt the weight lift from her chest as whatever had attacked her moved away from the flames.

The Lightbringer scrambled to stand-up and got her first look at the creature. It was on all floors and covered in a short grey fur, but its head was almost that of a human's, though with long sharp incisors dripping with saliva. The hunter instantly recognised it – a were-cat.

Did Derilion open any of the tiny boxes? If she did, turn to **104**. If she managed to resist, turn to **408**.

5

Derilion looked in her backpack for something that might help her find the runestone.

If she found any of the following, she can use them:

A stone with concentric circles on it?	Turn to **212**
Bronze metal fragments?	Turn to **52**
Steel gauntlets?	Turn to **12**

Otherwise, she must continue along the corridor, turn to **547**.

6

The water was freezing, making it harder for Derilion to breathe. She kept her head above its surface as the current took her closer to a ledge ahead of her. Did Derilion meet Zalixa? If so, what happened?

Never met Zalixa	Turn to **578**
She freed Zalixa without hurting her	Turn to **61**
She hurt Zalixa	Turn to **83**

7

The hunter took a step back and kicked at the door, just below the handle. To her surprise, the wood splintered easily, and the door snapped open. In front of her was a narrow corridor, with a circular room at the far end. From her vantage point, there appeared to be a golden bow, with an arrow ready to be fired, in the room.

Before she'd had a chance to decide what to do next, the Lightbringer was pulled forwards by an unseen force. She reached out to stop herself, but only managed to scrape her fingers on the rocky walls.

Turn to **697**

8

Derilion showed her the sword.

"A solid weapon. But let's give it a little upgrade." Derilion saw Corzen's lips move, and immediately, she felt the sword become lighter. "That will help you in the caves. Thank you again."

Increase Derilion's *Accuracy* by 1.

Turn to **587**

9

Derilion took a moment to concentrate. She cleared her mind and closed her eyes, making sure the shield was fully covering her head and torso.

She turned her thoughts inwards and let them inhabit her body. Then, when she was truly calm, she pushed those feelings outwards, imagining them filling the space around her.

Roll 2D6 and test for *Detection*.

If the test is successful, turn to **241**. Otherwise, turn to **108**.

10

Derilion slid down the smooth steps trying not to fall over the edge. It wasn't easy, and she took several knocks along the way.

Subtract 2 from her *Health*.

Finally, she reached the bottom, out of breath, but alive. She took a moment to compose herself, then stood and made her way towards the only exit she could see.

Turn to **190**

Derilion kicked a rock beside her foot and watched as it jammed in-between the door and the wall. The door caught on it, and the hunter listened as the sound of metal gears grinding against metal filled the small space around her. When she thought the sound couldn't get any louder, something snapped, and the stone door swung back open limply.

"Well, done," came the voice from behind her. "I thought I was dead for sure."

The Lightbringer turned to see a dwarf sitting in the corner, looking hungry.

"How long have you been here?" she asked.

The dwarf shrugged. "Who knows? A day? A week? Longer? What I *do* know is I've had enough of this tomb." He got to his feet with the help of his axe. "As a token of my thanks, take this. I've got two of them anyway."

The dwarf placed a greenish stone in Derilion's hands.

"Place it on the hilt, and your weapon will stay sharp. And maybe I'll see you on the outside. My name's Gubren. I owe you my life."

The hunter watched as Gubren left and turned right out of the room. She breathed a sigh of relief.

Derilion placed the stone on the hilt, and it bonded with the sword. She watched as the blade, chipped from many a battle, became smooth and sharp once more.

Add 2 to the sword's weapon damage.

The Lightbringer left the room and continued along the corridor (turn to **78**).

12

The hunter put the steel gauntlets on, and they immediately began to constrict on her hands. She tried to pull them off, but they wouldn't move. She hit them against the wall, but still, they tightened. Finally, they stopped, but, try as she might, Derilion couldn't loosen them. She was stuck wearing them.

She attempted to find the runestone, but the gauntlets possessed no abilities to help her.

Deduct 1 from her *Accuracy*. She could still try another object:

Stone with concentric circles on it?	Turn to **212**
Bronze metal fragments?	Turn to **52**

Otherwise, turn to **547**.

13

Derilion continued around the wall to the left, alert for dangers which might come at her through the gloom.

While the shield lit the area in front of her, its glow didn't penetrate the darkness like it usually did, and she couldn't help but feel there was strong magic at work in the cave complex. It would certainly back up the story she'd heard at the three houses.

Derilion instinctively ducked as a scuffling sound came from somewhere above her. Every muscle tensed as she waited for whatever it was to attack.

The scuffling noise stopped, and after a few moments, Derilion decided she should try and detect her next move.

Roll 2D6 to test for *Detection*.

If the test was successful, turn to **371**. Otherwise, turn to **381**.

14

Derilion readied her sword and drove it deep into the woman's back. She took it out, poised to strike again, but saw there was no blood on the blade.

The woman looked up at her, and Derilion realised she was a death maiden, seeking a soul to replenish her own.

The death maiden rose from the floor, ready to fight. Turn to **374**.

15

"All right," the hunter said, standing up and dusting herself down. "I will try once more."

Derilion took the girl's hand. At least she knew what to expect this time around.

Roll 2D6, subtract 1 and test for *Speed*.
Roll 2D6, subtract 1 and test for *Accuracy*.

If both tests were successful, turn to **525**. Otherwise, turn to **497**.

16

"I have a stone with circles on it," the Lightbringer said.

She rummaged in her backpack and produced the stone, holding it out to the woman to take. The woman smiled but stayed where she was.

"That's perfect," she said. "Can you put it in my net for me? My hands aren't what they used to be."

If Derilion decides to put it in her net, turn to **509**, otherwise, turn to **468**.

17

Derilion lowered herself through the hole into the water underneath, and it was just as unpleasant as she'd imagined. There was a small ledge to her right, which she pulled herself onto and rested. She took off her new boots, turned them upside down and watched as the water poured out.

The passage she was now in wasn't high enough to stand, so she crouched and made her way along until, at last, the river retreated underground, and the way ahead opened out into a larger cave.

The hunter looked at her surroundings in awe. There was something which made it resemble a chapel, she thought. The place had a reverence about it.

The floor was laid with coloured tiles, forming two mosaics. One was a picture of the sun and the other of a lightning bolt.

She looked for another exit but couldn't see one. For Derilion to inspect the sun image, turn to **199**. To inspect the lightning image, turn to **326**.

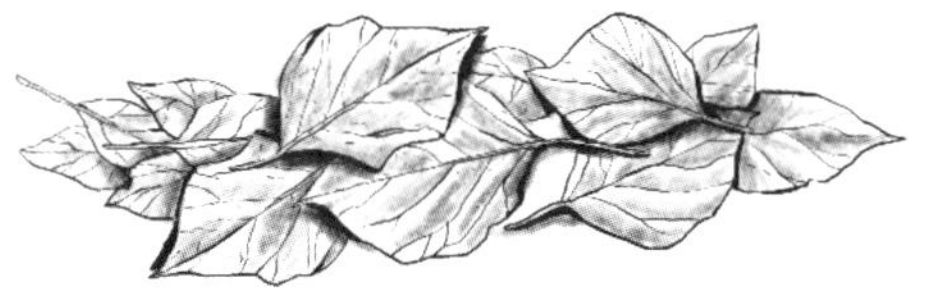

18

Derilion kicked the hex stones into the pool and watched as the water around them turned a brighter blue. The Elemental roared and grew slightly stronger before her eyes.

Add 4 to its *Health*.

Has the hunter kicked four items in yet? If not, she can try another (turn to **633**). If she has, she must face the Elemental (turn to **107**).

19

The hunter didn't stand a chance.

The club struck her midriff, and she fell to the ground. Deduct 3 from her *Health*.

"I'm sorry," the Troll said. "But I'm just not interested in fighting you."

It turned its back and made its way out of the room the same way Derilion had entered. The hunter stood, slightly confused but relieved, and made her way painfully through the other door and into the next room.

Turn to **126**.

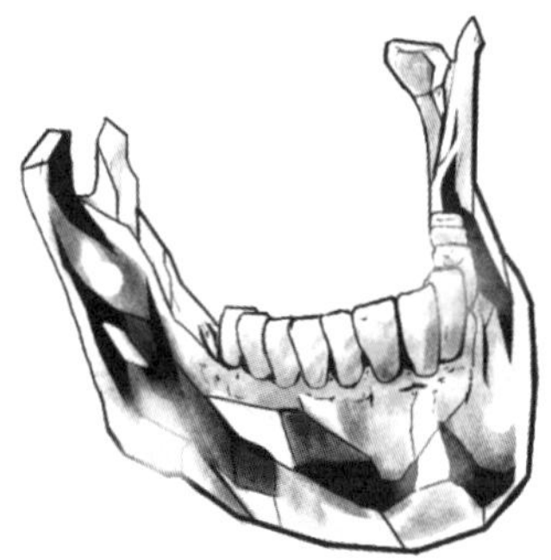

20

Derilion looked behind her. The Lightbringer had the feeling someone was watching her, yet when she turned to look, there was no one there.

Content she was alone, she began rifling through the man's pockets, looking for any valuables they might have left on him.

Turn to **265**.

21

Derilion showed the contents of her backpack to the child, who gave nothing away to indicate she was interested in any of the items.

"Well?" the hunter asked. "There must be something there you could make use of?"

The girl shrugged.

"I'll tell you what," she said. "I'll take two of your items, but you choose. Adventurers like you rarely know the true value of the items you have."

Derilion smiled; the girl was clever.

She looked once more at the backpack. The Lightbringer didn't know if any of the objects were magical.

To give the girl two items, turn to **460**. Otherwise, turn to **387**.

22

Derilion took another arrow, set it up, and aimed at the Otistro. The creature's thrashing made this a harder shot, so she lowered the target to the central body of the beast.

The hunter breathed in, then slowly breathed out as she loosed the arrow. It flew true and embedded itself into the beast.

Immediately, and much to her relief, the Otistro slumped to the floor, dead. She must have hit its heart if such a creature possessed one.

Derilion retrieved her first arrow, but the second was lost.

Turn to **545**.

Derilion headed back to the second coffin and opened it fully.

Inside was an emaciated woman who looked up at the hunter and smiled.

"It's good to see light," she said, trying to sit up.

"Let me help you," the Lightbringer told her. She took the woman's arm and pulled her out.

"Thank you. I'm going to rest here and then try and get out. I see you're wearing an enchantment rune. I can offer you an *Accuracy* enchantment if you need it?"

If Derilion needed the *Accuracy* enchantment, add it to the amulet space on the adventure sheet.

Turn to **689**.

The hunter headed towards the door in front of her. The chamber was cold, and she wanted to be out of it. On her way, she passed by the table. The food smelt delicious, and she was caught between stopping and eating some (turn to **238**) or continuing (turn to **529**).

25

Without speaking, the hunter put her hand into the backpack once more and brought out the potion.

"Very well," the witch sighed, snatching it off Derilion. "I'll let you leave."

Derilion resisted the temptation to slap the girl around the face and moved on into the next room (turn to **165**).

26

The hunter chose the higher path, hoping it'd have better handholds, and for the first few steps, it did. However, about halfway along, she had to place her foot on an almost non-existent outcrop of rock. She looked around for a better option but couldn't see one.

Roll 2D6 and test for *Accuracy*.

If the test is successful, turn to **116**. Otherwise, turn to **598**.

27

There were parts of being an adventurer Derilion wasn't happy with, and this was one of them. She ran her fingers over the dead body, feeling for anything she might be able to use herself, trying not to think that one day she might be the corpse.

The adventurer hadn't been carrying much, though this could be because the hunter wasn't the first person to search them. In fact, from where she was now, she could see another body nearby, its face similarly covered with the corrosive amber substance.

She was about to give up when she found a simple silver ring in one of the pockets. Perhaps it'd belonged to someone special they knew. Perhaps it was just meaningless treasure they'd found.

Derilion can add this to her belt or her backpack (**+1w**).

Feeling sad, Derilion turned to head back to the wall. It was then she heard a scrabbling sound overhead, followed by the screech of what must be the Ambrite, readying to attack.

Turn to **381**.

28

Derilion stopped moving and raised her hand. Unsurprisingly the double did the same.

"Hello," she said and heard it mirrored back to her.

"I have to leave the room," she continued.

She stopped, aware of how talking wasn't helping her very much. She smiled and held out her arms, palms up.

"I mean you no harm," they both said.

She began to walk and tensed as she walked through the doppelganger and back into the normal room.

Her relief was short-lived, however. Stood in the centre of the room, blocking her way, was a far more solid copy of her, sword raised and ready to fight.

Turn to **620**.

29

The hunter made her way to the door, pleased to be leaving the strange girl behind.

She reached out and placed her hand on the doorknob, ready to twist it.

Did Derilion take any of the objects in the room?

If she did take something, turn to **450**. If not, turn to **678**.

30

The powder exploded. Derilion attempted to shield herself against the debris flying at her, but one of the pieces caught her leg, inflicting 2 damage to her *Health*.

She hid behind Volkov and remained there until everything had died down.

When the dust had settled, she looked at the doorway where the vines had been and saw just space. Without needing further prompting, the Lightbringer got up and stepped into the next room.

Turn to **58**.

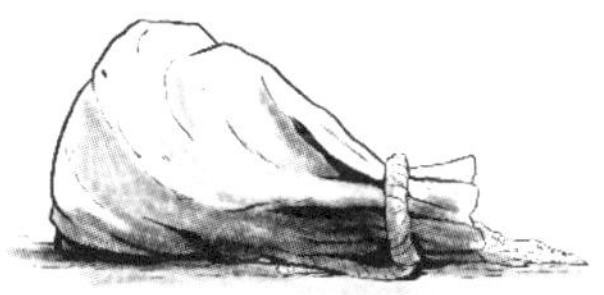

31

As soon as she pressed the tile, one corner of the room began to fill with a light, so bright Derilion had to cover her eyes. After a few moments, the light abated, and the hunter dropped her hand.

In the corner of the room stood a tall, warrior-like woman watching her.

"You brought me back, for that I thank you," the warrior said. "If you help me, I will reward you."

"What do you want?" the hunter asked.

"I have a friend trapped in a vase somewhere here. If you free them, I will help you."

To accept the quest, turn to **308**. To decline it, turn to **331**.

32

Try as she might, Derilion was unable to work out what the problem was. She walked around the room one more time and checked the creature's possessions to no avail.

With nothing else to go on, the hunter had little choice but to go through the door (turn to **147**).

33

"Would you like something in return?" the hunter asked.

Its eyes lit up. "I don't suppose you have anything metal. It's what we use for currency down here."

To give it something metal, turn to **579**. To offer a non-metal object, turn to **268**. To take the key and offer nothing, turn to **353**.

34

The Lightbringer reached in and took hold of the tip of the wand. The woman held it tightly, and Derilion had to pull hard for it to come free.

The hunter held it before Volkov and looked at the carvings, which ran along its length. It was a beautiful object, and she felt sorry for the woman in the box.

She knew she should leave the room (turn to **354**) or, at least, search the other boxes (turn to **45**), but something inside her wanted to return the wand to the woman (turn to **668**).

35

The troll stopped, squinted at Derilion holding her sword, and laughed.

"Do you want to fight me?" it asked. "It's lunchtime, so I'm not really in the mood."

To fight the troll, turn to **514**. Otherwise, turn to **347**.

36

Derilion walked forward into the corridor and stood at the junction where the corridor split. She placed one hand on the wall to the left and the other hand on the wall straight ahead.

She closed her eyes and attempted to find some tranquillity to help her detection.

Roll 2D6 and test for *Detection*.

If the test is successful, turn to **219**. Otherwise, turn to **376**.

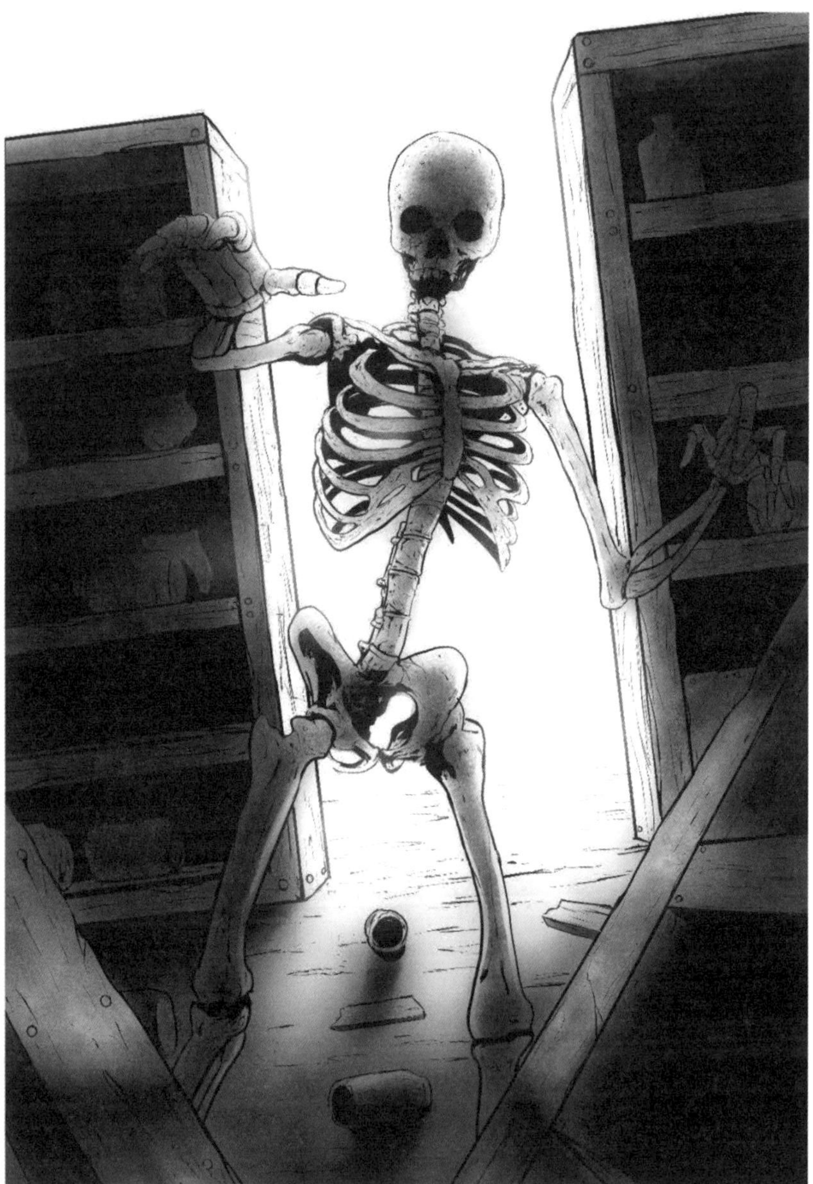

Derilion pushed back with her shield as the Skeleton lunged at her. It worked, the skeleton retreated, and it gave the hunter a chance to gather her wits. She realised she was going to have to smash its bones with her sword if she wanted to defeat it.

	Speed	*Accuracy*	*Damage*	*Health*
Skeleton	7	9	1	8

If Derilion wins, turn to **184**.

38

Derilion abandoned her boots with a hint of sadness but knew it was a small price to pay for her life.

She reached for the handhold and tested it quickly. It felt good. The hunter lifted herself onto the wall, watching as her boots disappeared under the mud. She looked at the bottom of the wall. For some reason, the mud couldn't come up the rock or didn't want to.

Carefully, knowing one slip would be her demise, Derilion moved across the wall and dropped down at a point where the floor was clear.

Turn to **154**.

39

Derilion blocked the skeleton's bite, pushed back on its arms, and struggled free.

She moved away as quickly as she could across the room, trying to put as much space between the pair of them.

When she could go no further, she turned to face the skeleton, knocking into the table which supported the glass ball.

With the skeleton closing in, roll 2D6 and test for *Speed*.

If the test is successful, turn to **157**. Otherwise, turn to **336**.

40

Derilion hit the ground running, not allowing the mud to get a hold on her. It wasn't easy, and a couple of times, she slipped, threatening to go down into the murderous dirt. That would be the end of her, for sure.

She kept her eyes on the ground, and within a dozen footfalls had reached a small step which the mud didn't go beyond. Once safe, she stopped and looked back. Rescuing Obishaa wasn't getting any easier. What trials lay ahead of her?

Turn to **154**.

41

Stepping away from the vines, Derilion searched her equipment for the explosives. She found the small sachets of blue powder, kept one in her hand (**-1w**), and put the rest back.

She knew she'd have to throw it hard at the vines to ignite them, harder than she'd have to if it were a solid wall; the vines would undoubtedly cushion some of the speed.

The Lightbringer drew her arm back and launched the pocket of powder forward.

Roll 2D6 and test for *Speed*.

If the test is successful, turn to **30**. Otherwise, turn to **414**.

42

The hunter replaced the chair on the button and waited, expecting something to be triggered. Nothing happened.

Frustrated at not being able to work it out, she went to the door.

Turn to **147**.

43

The Death Maiden was defeated, but the hunter knew better than to turn her back too quickly. She waited, watching for the tiniest twitch.

Finally, when she was certain she would not get back up again, she turned to the two doors, deciding about which one to take.

To go through the door with the lightning symbol, turn to **410**. To enter the room straight in front of her, turn to **129**.

44

A few moments after looking away, Derilion heard Ashingya scream.

"How dare you not meet my cyes!"

Before the hunter had the chance to look back at the creature, she was thrown across the room and into the wall, taking 3 damage to her *Health*.

If she survived the attack, Derilion scrambled out of the room while she still was able to (turn to **624**).

45

Without warning, one of the small boxes splintered as the hunter walked past, and a dark shadow pounced from it.

Roll 2D6 and test for *Speed*.

If the test is successful, turn to **235**, otherwise, turn to **4**.

46

As the Diamond Elemental approached the hunter, the necklace glowed around her neck, and it began to guide her movements.

Instead of going toward the Elemental, Derilion headed to the pool it rose from, easily dodging a blow from the creature's sword.

As she passed the Elemental, an arc of lightning burst from the amulet and struck the creature in the chest, reducing the Elemental's *Health* to 15, and restoring 9 to Derilion's *Health*.

Turn to **633**.

47

Derilion went left along the corridor. She climbed across a rockfall and stopped to look at it. Carvings and runes covered the rocks, and it appeared to have been a prison of some sort.

She looked up to where the rocks had come from and saw a ledge chiselled into the side. Sitting on the ledge was a small carved wooden animal. Derilion was hesitant about taking it, aware there could be a hex on the carving.

To take the carving, turn to **380**. To leave it well alone, turn to **519**.

48

Derilion knew the most vulnerable time for the creature would be just after it attacked. She stood still, hoping and praying she would survive the initial encounter.

The shield's flame still shone a cone of light around her. Momentarily, she thought about extinguishing it, to put them both into darkness, but what if the creature could see in the dark? She dismissed the idea almost immediately.

If she had to use the shield, she thought, she ought to make sure she got the best out of it. She could either protect her legs (turn to **616**), her body (turn to **575**), or her head (turn to **155**).

49

Derilion moved towards the woman, taking her time, trying to be as silent as possible.

Unfortunately, she caught her foot on some loose rocks on the floor, kicking them out in front of her.

Turn to **76**.

50

"Oh, a hex stone," Othwig said. "It's not my sort of thing. Never mind."

Derilion frowned.

"Do you want anything else?"

"Okay," she said. "One more try won't do any harm."

Bluish leaves	Turn to **463**
Yellowish leaves	Turn to **398**
Explosive powder	Turn to **163**
Moss	Turn to **512**
Something else	Turn to **671**
Nothing to trade	Turn to **484**

51

Whatever she chose was going to be a gamble, but perhaps the information he had was worth the risk.

She removed the necklace and held it out. The man took it.

If the necklace was a fake, turn to **220**. Otherwise, turn to **344**.

52

Derilion threw the bronze metal fragments on the floor (**-3w**) and waited.

Within a few seconds, they began to twitch, before slowly turning in opposite directions, fusing to the floor, and making an arrowhead.

The hunter followed the direction it pointed and stopped in front of the wall (turn to **469**).

<h1 style="text-align:center">53</h1>

The hunter ate the leaves, grimacing from their bitter taste. When she finished, Othwig raised her eyebrows.

"You have the luck of the gods on your side. They are a restorative medicine."

Immediately, Derilion began to feel better. Restore 10 to her *Health*.

"Thank you," the hunter said to Othwig.

"Don't thank me yet. The worst is yet to come for you."

Derilion nodded, turned, and left the chamber.

Turn to **466**.

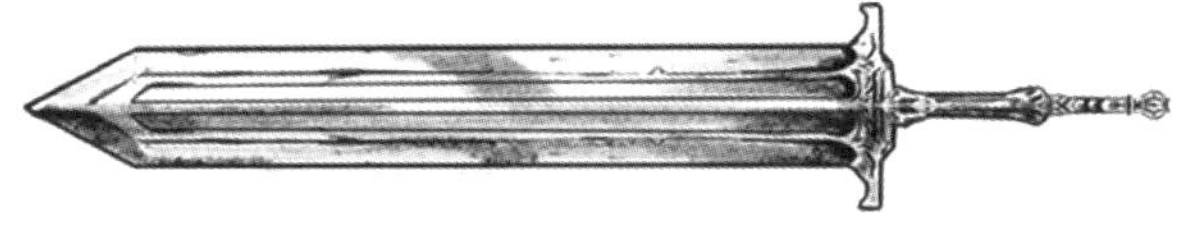

<h1 style="text-align:center">54</h1>

"Oh, right," Othwig said. "Well, I don't want anyone leaving emptyhanded, so how about this."

She went over to the centre bench and took a small phial of liquid from it.

"This is an incredibly effective poison. Not met a creature I can't kill with it, yet. It might come in useful for you."

Derilion took the phial and added it carefully to her belt (**+1w**).

"Thank you," the hunter said, then turned and left the chamber.

Turn to **466**.

<h1 style="text-align:center">55</h1>

Derilion headed for the nearest medium box, put her sword under its lid, and used her body weight to prize it open.

It took a second for the Lightbringer's sight to become accustomed to the darkness inside the crate, but after a moment she was able to make out the outline of a person curled at the bottom. She couldn't tell if they were asleep, unconscious, or perhaps even dead.

She could see if the person was alive (turn to **669**), search the other boxes (turn to **45**) or head for the door (turn to **354**)?

<h1 style="text-align:center">56</h1>

Derilion moved forward cautiously, her boots making a sickening squelching sound in what must have been the blood and guts littering the floor. Fresh blood and guts, her mind told her.

She took a deep breath, bent her knees, and peered closer at the room. In several places around the floor, she noticed hardened puddles of an amber-like resin she'd seen before. A creature she'd heard about, known as an Ambrite, produced such a substance to cover and suffocate their prey effectively.

By the quantity surrounding her, an Ambrite must have been living there awhile, picking off unwary adventurers as they entered.

The Lightbringer took a moment to try and work out the direction the resin had originated from but found it impossible. What she did see, however, was another adventurer, lying prone on the floor of the cave ahead.

Should Derilion skirt right around the wall, (turn to **516**), skirt left around the room (turn to **63**), or take a closer look at the adventurer (turn to **245**)?

57

As she stood there, something struck the hunter's shoulder from above and bounced to the floor. Derilion looked down and saw a small piece of rock.

With dread, she finally understood what the noise was; without the vines, the chamber was going to collapse. She needed to get out now.

Roll 2D6 and test for *Speed*.

If the test is successful, turn to **653**. Otherwise, turn to **400**.

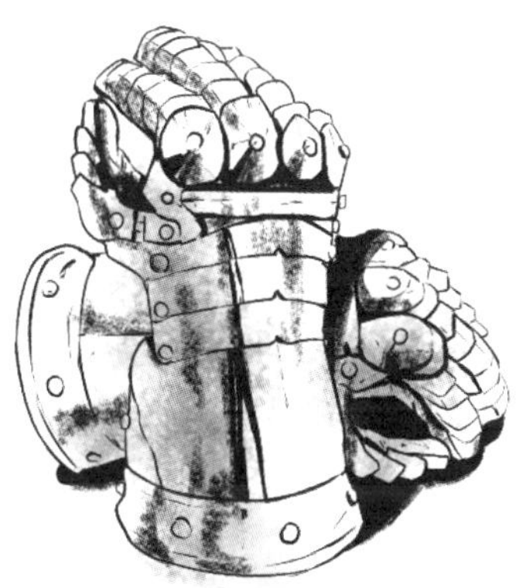

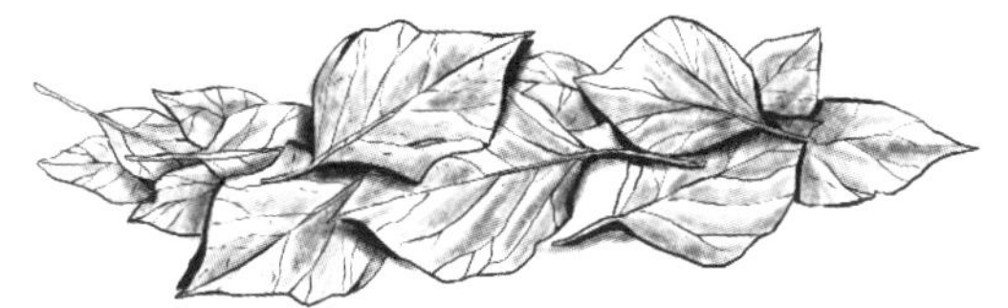

58

The Lightbringer stood just inside the cave. It was larger than the others in the complex, but that wasn't saying much. Against the left wall was a pile of boxes, and against the right was a pile of bones. The only exit she could see was a door in front of her.

The most important thing in the room, however, was the man who knelt at a table, hands clasped as if in deep prayer.

Considering what had just happened with the vines, Derilion didn't see how he couldn't have known she was there.

She stood a few moments more, trying to gauge the situation, trying to pick up on anything that might help her decide. Unfortunately, she sensed nothing, although she thought she could hear a low rumbling noise coming from somewhere nearby.

What should she do next?

Inspect the boxes?	Turn to **236**
Inspect the bones?	Turn to **589**
Talk to the man?	Turn to **306**
Attack the man?	Turn to **386**
Leave the room immediately?	Turn to **221**

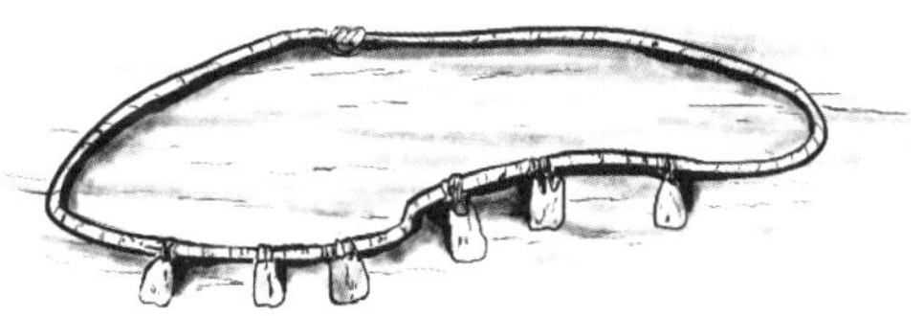

Derilion stepped forward and put her foot on the copper tile. She waited to see if this was the right choice.

"Very well," the voice said. The feel of the blade went, and the hunter turned to see a dark shape behind her. From the floor, copper ran like water up the shape's body and formed a suit of armour around it.

The suit of armour raised its sword in front of its face.

"To the death," it said.

Derilion stood back and unsheathed her sword.

	Speed	*Accuracy*	*Damage*	*Health*
Copper Armour	10	8	2	13

If Derilion defeats the suit of armour, turn to **540**.

60

The hunter used all her stealth to make her way around the busy room, keeping one eye on the creature. She successfully manoeuvred between the pots, being incredibly careful not to nudge any shelves.

She made it to the door, breathed a sigh of relief, and quietly exited, closing it behind her.

The Lightbringer tried the other door but found it locked, though it felt like it had seen better days. She took a step backwards, raised her leg, and kicked the door with all her might.

Turn to **624**.

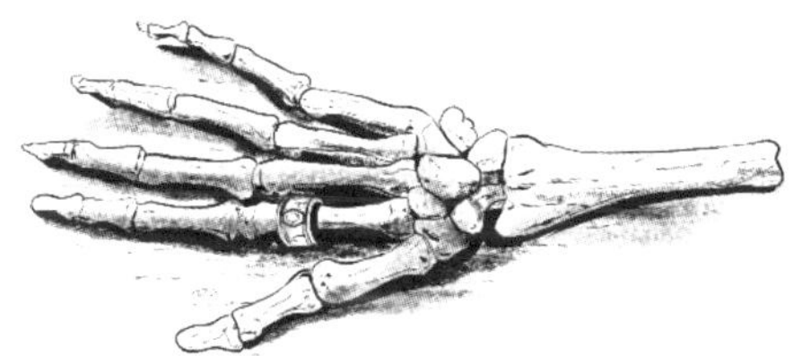

61

Derilion found it hard to float in the quick-flowing stream. Her boots and clothes grew heavy, and her head kept dipping below the icy surface.

Just when she thought she might be in some real trouble, she felt arms close around her waist and lift her till she was above the water once more.

She looked down and could see Zalixa below the surface, helping her. Within a few moments, she was able to scrabble up onto the bank unharmed.

The Lightbringer turned to thank the girl, but Zalixa had already disappeared.

Continue to **197**.

62

The creature looked long and hard at the contents of Derilion's backpack strewn across the floor, but nothing seemed to take its interest.

Slowly, the hunter picked all her belongings back up and put them in her bag.

She knew she was running out of options. She could attack the creature (turn to **401**), wait (turn to **290**) or use some explosive powder (turn to **590**).

63

Derilion kept close to the left-hand wall as she made her way into the chamber, her back to the rock and the shield low to ward off any opportunistic creatures.

As she continued, the rocky wall became smooth and curved inwards. In the centre of the room, something glimmered, reflecting the light from the shield. She stopped, moved the shield in the air in front of her, and saw the light again.

She couldn't see much, and in truth, she was happy she couldn't. The reflection came off the arm of a dead adventurer who wore a golden cuff.

There was an emblem carved onto the cuff, but at this distance, it was impossible to make out.

She can look closer at the fallen adventurer (turn to **245**) or continue around the wall in the same direction (turn to **13**).

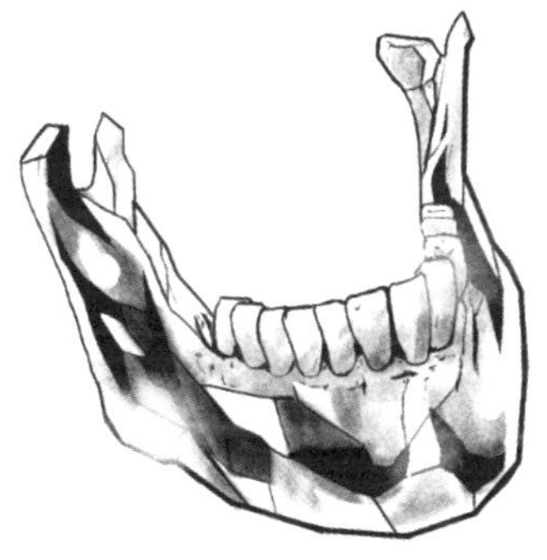

64

The hunter approached the skeleton, being careful not to nudge any of the other ornaments. She was lucky and, after a few steps, stood in front of it, looking at the gap where its jaw should be.

Derilion found the jaw from her backpack (**-4w**) and placed it in the space. Immediately, the skeleton grabbed her arms and tried to bite her.

Roll 2D6 and test for *Accuracy*.

If the test is successful, turn to **39**. Otherwise, turn to **149**.

65

The hunter opened the chest and found herself staring into some part of the night sky she'd never seen before. She was confused. She wanted to look away yet found it impossible to do so.

Just then, she heard a laugh behind her, and something powerful tipped her forwards into the chest.

Derilion fell into the blackness. She half-expected to hit the bottom of the trunk but, instead, she tumbled over and over in the dark, never stopping, never ageing.

Her adventure ends here.

66

Derilion fetched the moss that Grom had given her as quickly as possible, but before she'd had a chance to use it, the woman stepped forward, muttering something under her breath.

The hunter found herself unable to let go of it, and stood there, powerless as the woman approached.

Turn to **512**.

67

Derilion closed her eyes and concentrated on Othwig and the room. She took a deep breath and cleared her mind, hoping maybe the fragrances in the place would point the way.

Roll 2D6 and test for *Detection*.

If the test is successful, turn to **475**. Otherwise, turn to **369**.

68

Derilion watched with dismay as the Otistro batted the powder away with its tongue. It hit the cave wall and exploded harmlessly. The only option she had now was to fight.

Turn to **532**.

69

The further the Lightbringer traversed along the wall, the more her fingertips began to hurt. She stopped and looked at one of her hands and noticed smudges of blood on them.

All along this stretch of the wall she saw tiny glints of light, which Derilion guessed must have been sharp crystals.

Reduce Derilion's *Accuracy* by 1.

Through gritted teeth, she managed to bear the pain all the way to the bank on the other side, where she dropped down onto the ledge.

Turn to **197**.

70

The Otistro slowly began to settle down, its quick movements gradually becoming a rhythmic sway, which Derilion almost thought were worse. Carefully, she retrieved her bow, placed an arrow, pulled back the string, and loosed.

The arrow flew and struck the Otistro in one of its eyes. It screamed and thrashed around wildly.

She had a simple choice; to loose another arrow (turn to **22**), or to fight the wounded creature (turn to **455**).

The hunter picked up one of the small bottles from the left bench.

"Come on," Othwig said impatiently.

Derilion removed the stopper from the bottle and swigged a mouthful of the liquid down.

The room went blurry, and she staggered a little before steadying herself on the rock wall.

Then, as quickly as it arrived, the dizziness went.

"What just happened?" she asked.

"Your senses have been heightened temporarily."

Add 2 to Derilion's *Accuracy* and *Stealth* totals for the duration of the adventure.

"Thank you," the hunter said to Othwig.

"Don't thank me yet. The worst is yet to come for you."

Derilion nodded, turned, and left the chamber.

Turn to **466**.

Derilion took her sword and held it above the man, trying to make as little noise as possible. When she had her balance, she stabbed downwards but was surprised to see him vanish before her eyes. The tip of the sword reverberated off the stone shelf.

She was shoved in the back and fell to the floor. The Lightbringer looked up and saw the man transform in front of her into a large demon with armoured skin, easily twice her size.

"What are you?" she asked.

"For you? Death."

He breathed out a scorching fire that incinerated Derilion within seconds.

Her adventure ends here.

73

The hunter looked down to see a needle harmlessly hit the back of her gauntlet. The door had held a trap, and the creature had known it.

Frustrated, she went quickly through the door without looking back.

Turn to **300**.

Derilion went through the doorway into a corridor, which stretched far ahead of her. She began to walk, and as she did, she noticed a faint smell becoming more pungent with every step. Not only that, but she could hear the sound of an underground stream up ahead.

The walls to either side were craggy, sharp stones jutting out at various angles. Fortunately, it was wide enough that she could avoid them.

After a minute, she came across a patch of wall smoother than the rest. She wondered if she should investigate it (turn to **345**) or ignore it and keep going (turn to **487**).

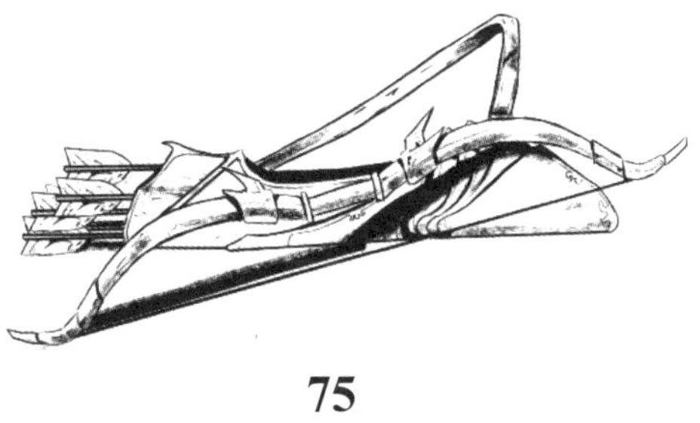

75

Derilion moved onward, once again aware time was not on her side. If the Pajoli were going to use Obishaa, there was no reason why they would wait.

As she worried about this, the noise of a child sobbing pierced the corridor. Derilion stopped and waited. Had Obishaa the strength to escape the Pajoli? Or was this a trap, playing on her obvious emotional ties to her?

The sobbing came again, louder this time, as though the girl was coming closer. Derilion's guilt rose. Should she call out (turn to **420**) or wait to see what happens (turn to **267**).

"Hello," the hunter said. "Don't be alarmed."

The woman stood up straight and looked around at Derilion. She scanned the hunter up and down, turned back to the net, and then back around to the hunter.

"And hello to you," she replied. "I wonder. I'm looking for a gemstone. I don't suppose you have one. Or perhaps you came across some stones with circles on them?"

If Derilion had a golden cuff, she could offer the gemstone from that (turn to **159**). If she has a stone with concentric circles on, she can offer that (turn to **16**). If she has neither or doesn't want to offer them, turn to **396**.

77

Derilion found the lens and held it up to her eye. Instantly, the markings made sense to her.

"Through death, we learn," it read.

It seemed an appropriate statement, even if it didn't help her circumstances.

Turn to **413**.

78

The corridor twisted sharply to the left and then widened. Derilion found she'd been holding her breath in the cramped space and took several deep inhalations before moving on.

The corridor kept going, and the Lightbringer kept moving through it with her shield high, and the sword gripped in her hand. She was almost too preoccupied with fear to hear the soft squelching noise.

The moment she did, she whirled around to see what was behind her. She saw nothing. She looked down at the floor and noticed a thin layer of wet mud that her boots were making footprints in. She didn't remember seeing it before.

She thought it was most likely due to the depth she was at in the caves, but something felt wrong. After a moment, she laughed. She couldn't let this place get to her. How many other caves, dungeons, tombs had she explored? It was the nature of her work. None of them felt normal because it wasn't normal; it was up to her to get used to it.

Still, she could stop to try and detect the problem (turn to **572**), press on quickly (turn to **428**), or press on cautiously (turn to **456**).

79

"I'm on a mission for myself," the hunter said.

"Hah," it laughed. "Your candour humours me. I will let you through if you agree to carry something for me. You see, I'm not allowed to go any further than this room due to some previous misconduct on my behalf. But you can."

Derilion mulled the proposition. At least it was a simple choice; she could either agree (turn to **478**) or refuse (turn to **435**).

80

The rocks whipped by Derilion's head, and she moved quickly to avoid the worst of them, still managing to sustain 3 damage to her *Health* in the process.

As the dust cleared, Derilion scanned the area before her for any sign of the faceless woman.

Turn to **584**.

81

Derilion made her way to the left, keeping a close eye on the demon as she went. It watched her closely but made no move towards or away from her. Perhaps that was what it had wanted all along.

Continue to **47**.

82

"I don't think so," the hunter said to the girl. She was half expecting to have to fight her, but she made no move to attack.

Derilion touched the door to push it open and felt a large jolt of pain shoot through her body.

Subtract 1 from her *Accuracy*.

The girl laughed.

"Always the same," she said. "You think you can just walk through without consequences."

The pain subsided, and Derilion left the room in a hurry.

Continue to **548**.

Derilion travelled a little way along the river without going under its surface. It wasn't easy, but there was a ledge ahead she could use to climb out.

Suddenly, she felt a pair of hands around her waist, dragging her beneath the surface, and when she searched the water below, she saw Zalixa smiling maliciously up at her.

Derilion kicked as hard as she could and managed to struggle free, but only after losing the last four items she'd put in her backpack.

She reached the bank in front of her and hauled herself out of the water, gasping for air.

Continue to **197**.

84

Derilion unsheathed her sword and approached the adventurer, who, in turn, backed away from her.

"I don't wish to fight you," he said.

	Speed	Accuracy	Damage	Health
Adventurer	8	7	1	9

If Derilion defeats the adventurer, turn to **655**.

"You don't tell me what to do," Derilion said, drawing her sword and taking a step toward the Pajoli.

"Are you sure about that?" they replied.

Turn to **302**.

Derilion opened her backpack and retrieved the green potion from inside (**-2w**). Aware the dancer was watching her, the Lightbringer drank the potion and waited to see what would happen.

After a few moments, a dawning of realisation started to form, and it was this; she would never be able to dance well enough.

Derilion smiled at the girl.

"I'm afraid I won't be able to dance again," she said.

The girl did nothing but watched as the hunter stood and made her way towards the door.

Turn to **131**.

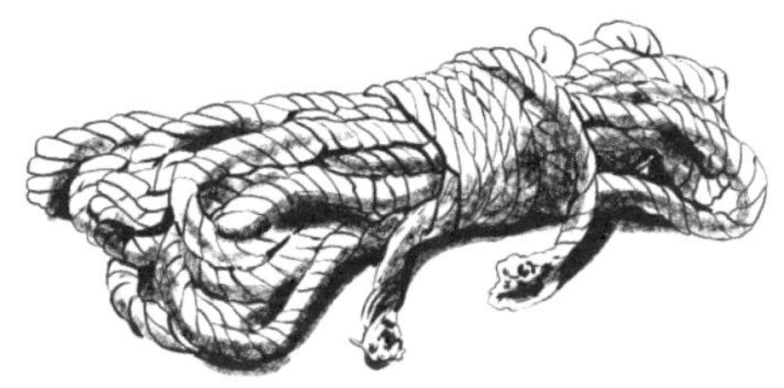

87

Derilion took a breath in, then slowly exhaled. She needed to have absolute concentration. The chamber grew quiet, and she knew the creature was ready to attack.

As gracefully as the environment allowed, the adventurer rolled backwards, half crouched, got her bearings, and rolled again.

The ground before her exploded as an amber substance hit it. This was her chance; the creature had missed and would take a few seconds to attack again.

Derilion looked back and saw what appeared to be an exit behind her. Needing no further encouragement, she took it.

Escape to **251**.

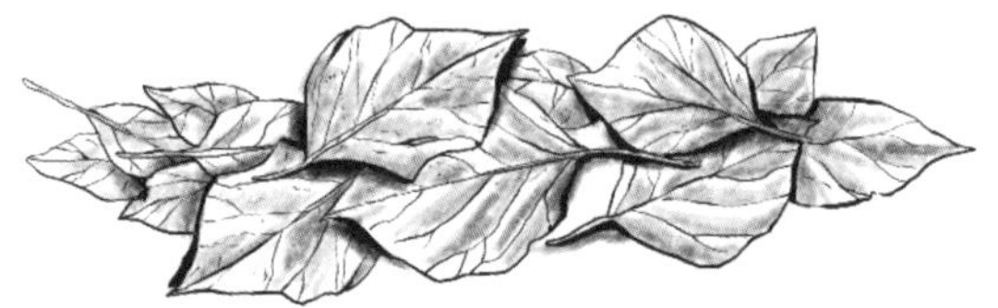

88

Derilion took a further step backwards, closed her eyes, and concentrated. She blocked out the sound of the Diamond Elemental and the warlocks who tried to invade her mind.

She saw a flash, a blue flash the same shade as the pool of water. The flash then turned a shade of red and then black, and Derilion realised the pool was the source of the Elemental's power.

If she could get to the pool, she might have a chance of weakening the creature.

Roll 2D6 and test for *Speed*.

If the test was successful, turn to **314**. Otherwise, turn to **315**.

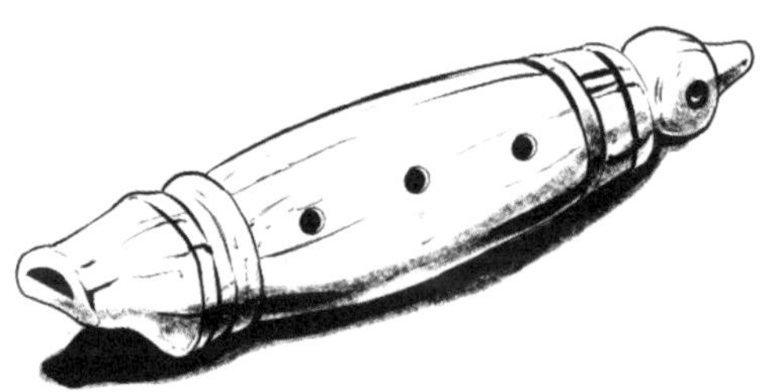

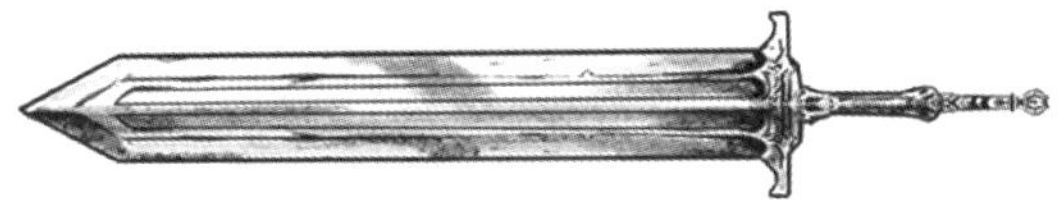

89

Derilion kicked the lead weight into the water and watched as the water around it turned red. The Elemental screamed and withered slightly before her eyes.

Subtract 6 from its *Health*.

If the Elemental has no more *Health*, turn to **137**. Has the hunter kicked four items in yet? If not, she can try another (turn to **633**). If she has, she must face the Elemental (turn to **107**).

90

Derilion found the lower path a lot easier to negotiate, and she was able to progress quickly along the wall. At the end was an opening, onto which she climbed safely.

Continue to **140**.

Derilion entered the next cave hoping for some respite, but as soon as she'd entered, she was struck in the side by a stinging blow. She scrambled as quickly as possible behind some rocks and looked at her side. There was a rip in her clothes, and the skin underneath was red.

Carefully, the hunter looked through the gap in the rocks sheltering her and saw a creature she'd only ever heard of in the dark fairy tales of her youth.

The Otistro stood in the centre of the room, seven feet tall, its elongated head tilting, its four vertical dark eyes searching the room, its long tongue dancing manically in front of it, ready to strike when Derilion next showed herself.

The creature had no arms nor legs, and no way of moving. Its lower half consisted of thick interwoven limbs within which victims were kept alive as they were slowly devoured. The stories said it grew rooted to the floor, growing bigger with each victim, and if not killed young, the creature would grow so large it prayed on humans.

The whole scene was enough to make Derilion turn and run, but she knew she couldn't. Obishaa was somewhere beyond this creature.

With no way of getting past the Otistro, Derilion had to fight. She could attempt to use the explosive powder if she still had any (turn to **247**), use her bow to inflict damage (turn to **70**), or fight it with her shield and sword (turn to **532**).

92

"Is there someone down there?" Derilion called, softly.

The hunter listened and thought she heard someone groan. It could be a trap, or it could be someone in trouble.

To go down the steps, turn to **558**. To take the left-hand path, turn to **171**.

93

Derilion chose to go straight on. Something in her head was telling her perhaps it would be the shortest route, though she knew that was just wishful thinking.

She twisted the handle on the door and was a little surprised when it opened smoothly, revealing a darkened room beyond.

From the little she could see, it looked safe, and the hunter stepped through. Behind her, the door swung shut, and when Derilion turned, she noticed it bore no handle on her side. There was no going back.

The Lightbringer held her shield higher and could see she was now in a low passage. She was not alone. Sitting before her at a makeshift table was a small blue-skinned creature with large eyes. It looked up at her and smiled.

There was something about the creature that unnerved her, but she couldn't quite work out what it was.

"Can I help you?" it asked.

"I'm on a mission to help the Pajoli."	Turn to **382**
"I'm on a mission for myself."	Turn to **79**
Ignore him, and keep going	Turn to **595**
Use *Detection* on him	Turn to **243**

94

The hunter lost her footing completely and fell into the chasm below. With nothing to break her fall, she continued into the blackness.

It wasn't a long drop, but fortunately, it was long enough to break her neck on the floor and spare her from the horror of the creatures below.

95

Derilion put her hand into her backpack, and the first object it found was the glass jaw. It was better than nothing, she thought.

The hunter smiled and held out the jaw (**-4w**).

"My safety for this," she said to them. The male troll narrowed his eyes as if thinking hard.

Slowly, and much to Derilion's surprise, he began to nod.

"Yes, that's something we can add to our collection," he said.

The female troll moved forward and delicately plucked it out of her hand.

"Now, leave here," she said. "And if we see you again, we will not be so forgiving."

They both stepped aside, and Derilion moved swiftly out of the room.

Turn to **698**.

The boy had a burnt arm, and Derilion's thoughts immediately went to Obishaa. If the Pajoli harmed her ward, the hunter knew she would never forgive herself.

Derilion couldn't see the boy's face, but his red hair reminded the Lightbringer of a boy from her village.

Roll 2D6 and test for *Detection*

If the test is successful, turn to **544**, otherwise, turn to **198**.

97

Derilion watched and waited as the troll finished the food. She thought her legs might seize up, stuck as she was in one position.

He got up from the table, checked his wooden club on his belt, and then exited the room via the same door the hunter had entered.

Derilion waited a few moments and then opened the wardrobe. Gingerly, she got out and stretched her legs.

She turned back to the wardrobe and saw two engraved staffs (**+2w each**) on a shelf above the clothes. She could take them if she wanted, before moving onto the next room.

Turn to **126**.

98

"Very well," Derilion said. "I'll pay the toll."

The dancer offered her hand once more, and the hunter took it. Instantly she felt a jolt of pain pass into her.

Deduct 1 from her *Speed*.

The girl shuddered and smiled.

"Thank you," she said. "That was perfect. You may leave now."

Derilion wanted to say something, wanted to get some form of retribution, but she daren't. She didn't know how powerful this girl could be.

She left the room quickly, without looking back.

Turn to **548**.

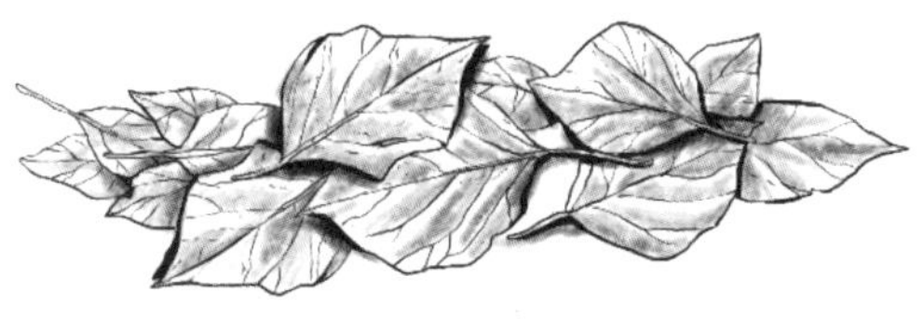

99

Derilion held each type of leaf in a different hand, concentrating on them and trying to remember what she knew of them. After a few moments, the hand holding the blue-tinged leaf felt better, and the one holding the yellow-tinged leaves felt weak.

The Lightbringer can take none, one, or both sets of leaves (**+1w each**).

She had a couple of options open to her, head to the exit (turn to **254**), or investigate the benches (turn to **166**).

100

The hunter dodged past the first two obstacles cleanly enough, but then caught her knee on a table leg, knocking it over. She watched as two vases fell from the shelves and smashed in front of her.

The stone creature watched for a moment and then made up its mind. Slowly it turned and kicked the nearest shelves, sending three of them toppling over.

Derilion saw the pot with Ashingya marked on it topple to the floor and crack open with an ear-splitting boom.

It might have been the creature smiled then, but it was impossible to tell for sure. Either way, Derilion watched as it appeared to melt into the floor. Relieved it had gone, Derilion started to make her way towards the door.

Unfortunately, whatever the Ashingya vase had held was now swirling in front of her.

Turn to **169**.

101

The hunter kept her centre of balance and put an arm on the wall to steady herself. She glanced at the trolls who were thankfully still asleep.

With no other visible exit, she could either investigate the treasure (turn to **335**) or head back along the corridor and choose another exit (turn to **698**).

102

Derilion's sword knocked into a shelf, and a glass phial fell to the ground. The impact cracked the phial and caused a small explosion, causing 1 damage to her *Health*, and knocking over the table holding the ball, which smashed on the floor.

Deciding it was time to leave, the Lightbringer turned to go but heard a noise behind her and turned to face the glass skeleton approaching fast.

Turn to **37**.

103

The door opened, and a troll walked into the room, crouching slightly because of its size.

Derilion sighed, trolls were always unpredictable.

If the Lightbringer had already met a troll, turn to **661**. Otherwise, turn to **35**.

104

The werecat snarled at Derilion and readied to pounce. They were fearless battlers, and the fight would not be an easy one.

The mouse the hunter released earlier began to squeak from the corner of the room, and the werecat immediately turned its head and focused its gaze on the direction of the noise.

The Lightbringer took advantage of the distraction and made her way toward the exit.

Turn to **502**.

105

"Can you hear me?" Derilion called. She didn't want to miss the chance of finding Obishaa.

"I'm... in the wall. They put me in the wall," the voice replied. "I can't believe they put mc in the wall."

"Is that you, Obishaa?" the hunter shouted.

"No, my name is Zalixa. I tried to escape the Pajoli, but they caught me."

Zalixa's voice sounded louder now as if she'd regained some strength.

"What should I do?" the hunter asked.

"If you have explosive powder, sprinkle it on the wall, and I can do the rest. Or perhaps you can dig me out?"

Derilion could use some explosive powder if she had some (turn to **397**) or try and dig Zalixa out (turn to **186**).

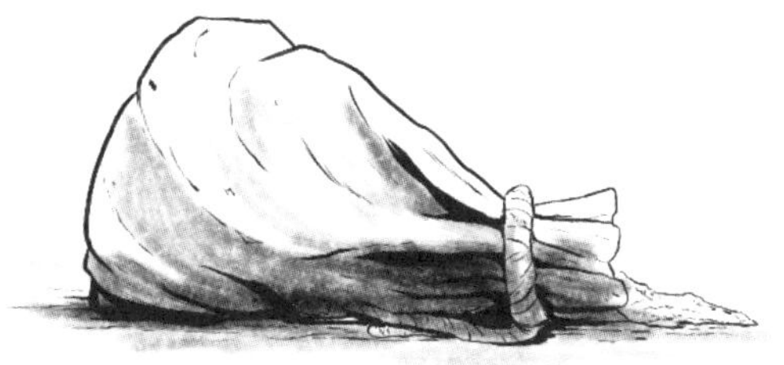

106

Derilion picked up the Ashingya pot and turned it around in her hands. It appeared to be a simple pot, yet the longer she looked at it, the hotter it became.

The hunter tried to put it back, but it slipped from her fingers and fell to the floor, where it cracked with an ear-splitting boom.

As Derilion watched, a swirling mist of dust began to form in front of her.

There was no way out. Whatever Ashingya was, she must face it.

Turn to **169**.

107

Derilion stood in front of the mighty Diamond Elemental. It towered above her, but she knew if she battled hard, she still had a chance. The Diamond Elemental's *Health* is the altered amount.

	Speed	*Accuracy*	*Damage*	*Health*
Diamond Elemental	9	10	3	?

Derilion's blade only does 1 damage to the creature per attack, unless she obtained all three enchantments for the amulet, in which case her sword gets a +1 weapon damage modifier.

If Derilion wins, turn to **137**.

108

Try as she might, Derilion could only see one way to get across the rest of the room; run for it.

Raising her shield to cover her head and upper torso, the hunter sprinted as fast as she could, jinking left and right in an attempt to miss the rocks.

Unfortunately, two-thirds of the way across one of them caught the side of her head, and the Lightbringer fell heavily to the floor, taking 2 damage to her *Health*.

More rocks rained down, hitting her legs and arms, and she knew she was close to blacking out.

She had to do something, or this was where her adventure, and her life, would end.

She could roll to the right (turn to **205**) or roll to the left (turn to **635**).

Derilion walked along the corridor. The walls seemed rougher than the others like something else had made them with simple tools. There were vague footprints in the dust accumulated on the floor, but only one of them seemed fresh.

The Lightbringer stopped at the top of a set of stairs that fell away before her into darkness. She could hear a faint dripping coming from ahead, but the echoes in the corridor made it difficult to gauge the distance.

She was about to take the first step down but stopped. There was another sound, underneath the dripping, of someone, something, breathing.

The hunter was caught between the best action to take. She could call out (turn to **92**), continue down the steps cautiously (turn to **419**), or retreat and take the left-hand passage (turn to **171**).

Derilion picked up the book and studied the cover. There were numerous markings on the front, but none of them meant anything to her. She opened it and flicked through page after page of tightly written text in an indecipherable language.

"You shouldn't touch what you don't understand," the girl said.

Perhaps there was another option.

Use the lens if she had one	Turn to **274**
Investigate the box	Turn to **214**
Investigate the lamp	Turn to **498**
Leave the room	Turn to **29**

111

Derilion approached the bench to the right. The smoke was thick and stung her eyes, so she stopped, not wanting to go any further.

"Carry on," Othwig said. "There's no choice here."

She walked closer, and the smoke seemed to lose some of its potency. Derilion took a deep breath and felt the smoke enter her body. She began to feel hot inside her chest, and her heartbeat quickened.

"What's happening?" she asked.

"It's a healing remedy. You should feel better in a moment."

The hunter breathed again, taking in more of the smoke. The witch was right. After a few moments, she began to feel better.

Restore Derilion's *Speed*, *Stealth*, *Detection* and *Accuracy* to their starting value and restore 5 to her *Health*.

"Thank you," the hunter said to Othwig.

"Don't thank me yet. The worst is yet to come for you."

Derilion nodded, turned, and left the chamber.

Continue to **466**.

112

Derilion made a grab for a more secure handhold but missed. She felt her weight shift, and she toppled backwards into the water.

Turn to **6**.

<h1 style="text-align:center">113</h1>

Derilion left the chair off the button, unlocked the door with the bone key and twisted the handle. Cautiously, she opened the door, expecting to trigger a trap. Nothing happened.

She checked around the door edge just in case she'd missed something, but all appeared safe.

The Lightbringer sighed with relief and stepped through the doorway (turn to **300**).

<h1 style="text-align:center">114</h1>

The hunter took a step back, giving herself enough space to do as much damage as possible. She knew she might only have one chance.

Derilion kicked with everything she had, but as soon as her foot made contact, the vines tried to seize it.

Roll 2D6 and test for *Speed*.

It the test is successful, turn to **521**, otherwise, turn to **448**.

<h1 style="text-align:center">115</h1>

The flames took hold quickly, and the heat given off from them was a welcome respite from the cold of the caves. Derilion stood with her eyes closed and skin prickling.

After a minute, the fire began to die down, until the plant was nothing but charred remains, smoking on the floor.

The hunter thanked whatever gods were looking out for her before stepping through into the room beyond.

Continue to **58**.

116

It wasn't easy, but Derilion managed to make the foothold. She continued along the ledge for a minute more before stepping off into an opening.

Continue to **140**.

117

Derilion spun around as quickly as she could react, but it wasn't fast enough. Something heavy struck the back of her head, and she fell to the floor, dazed.

She raised her shield for protection, but her attacker ripped it out of her hand. As her eyes cleared, she could see a pale-faced man in a long purple robe looking down at her and smiling.

"Yes," he said. "You'll make a perfect subject for my tests."

He retrieved a cloth from his pocket, bent down, and held it over Derilion's mouth. She tried to push him away, but he was stronger than he looked, and she felt herself losing consciousness.

Her adventure ends here.

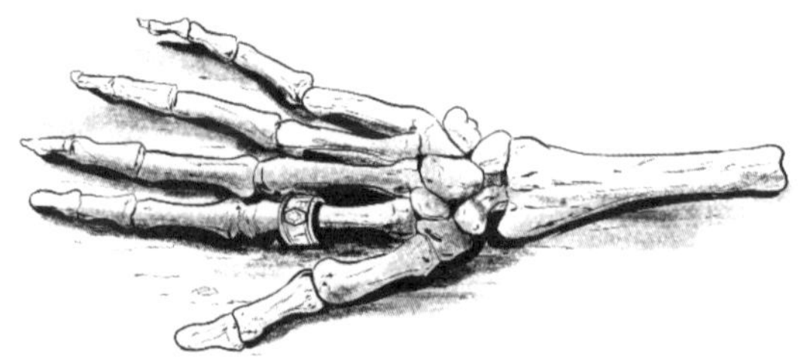

118

"Who are you?" Derilion asked, without moving.

The voice hesitated, as though they hadn't been asked the question before.

"My name is Grom," she replied. "I grew up here."

"How have you survived this long?"

"Oh, the Pajoli are clever. They teach us spells to create food and water early on. A blessing and a curse. I am not their friend."

"I'm looking for my ward," the Lightbringer said. "The Pajoli took her, and I'm trying to get her back. Can you help?"

Another pause. The hunter thought she might have trusted the wrong person.

"Come in, and I will help you," Grom said, at last.

Derilion wondered what was best. She could continue into the room (turn to **319**) or turn and head back to the river (turn to **378**).

119

The hunter looked around the new chamber. It smelled mustier than the others and contained many crates of varying sizes. It reminded her of a storeroom, and as far as she could see, she had it to herself. As she wondered what to do, she noticed an exit in front of her.

Investigate the large boxes	Turn to **304**
Investigate the medium boxes	Turn to **55**
Investigate the small boxes	Turn to **257**
Investigate the tiny boxes	Turn to **138**
Head for the exit	Turn to **502**

120

The hunter made her way quietly to the left wall, and followed it around as well as she could, looking for an exit. Water covered the rocks nearest to the wall making her progress difficult.

Derilion heard a noise from the trolls and glanced behind her to see the male troll turn over in his sleep. Unfortunately, as she turned back to the wall, her foot slipped.

Roll 2D6 and test for *Stealth*.

If the test is successful, turn to **101**, otherwise, turn to **522**.

121

The hunter saw the creature twitch a moment before its tail whipped down to try and strike her.

Roll 2D6 and test for *Speed*.

If the test is successful, turn to **603**. Otherwise, turn to **207**.

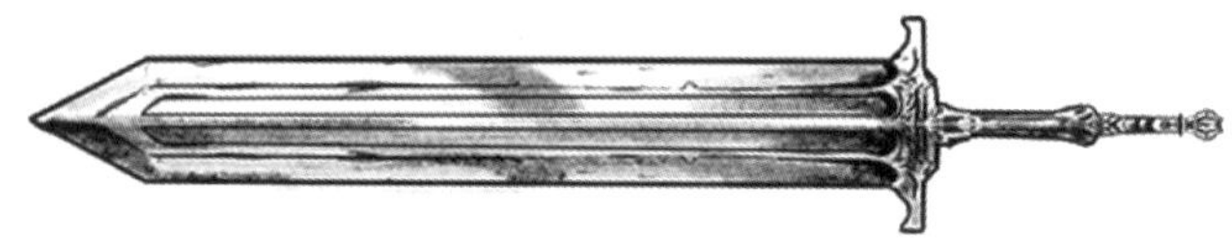

122

Derilion held firm. The Dwarf snarled at her through his beard and advanced.

	Speed	Accuracy	Damage	Health
Dwarf	5	6	2	6

If the hunter wins, turn to **256**.

123

The first couple of steps along the wall were easy, but the next foothold was more difficult and just above the stream. The Lightbringer moved her foot towards it, and almost immediately, a hand broke the surface of the water, grabbed her ankle, and pulled Derilion in.

Turn to **6**.

124

"Yes, that would be helpful," Derilion replied.

Ashingya reached down and took the pendant in her hands. Closing her eyes, she spoke her enchantment quickly, and within a few seconds, the hunter felt warmth emanate from the medallion. Ashingya opened her eyes.

"It is done," she said. "Now, leave here."

Note Derilion now has the *Speed* enchantment on the adventure sheet.

The Lightbringer left the room quickly, not looking back.

Turn to **624**.

125

Derilion closed her eyes and attempted to push her mind towards the creature.

"What are you doing?" it said. "Are you all right?"

The hunter tried her best to ignore it; she needed complete concentration.

"Would you like to sit down, perhaps?" it continued.

It was no use; she was unable to focus. The Lightbringer could either press on (turn to **595**), tell it she was here for herself (turn to **79**) or say she was trying to help the Pajoli (turn to **382**).

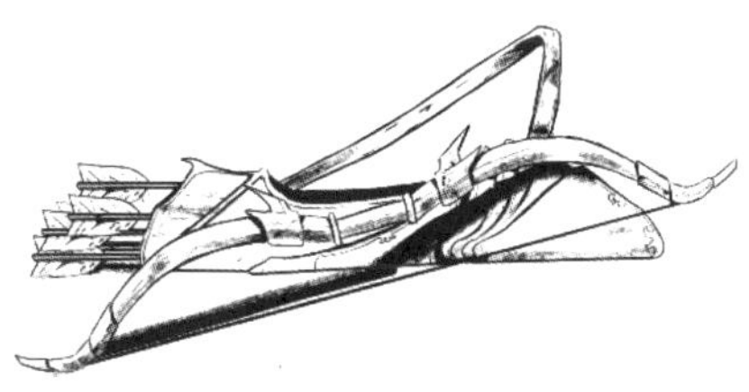

126

Derilion found herself in a long, gently curving, featureless corridor, walking in what felt like circles. After a while, it began to angle down and grew narrower. The Lightbringer hoped it was coming to an end.

At last, before her, stood two ornate doors. One was made of stone, the other, a hard, white material. Derilion looked at it more closely. She didn't want to admit it, but it looked like it was made of bone. The hunter stood and listened at each but heard nothing. The stone door was unlocked, but the white door didn't budge.

If Derilion has the bone key, she could use that (turn to **250**) or she could go through the stone door (turn to **197**).

127

Derilion brought the shield closer to the gem to get a better look. It seemed to twinkle. She kept staring and saw water dripping from beneath it.

The gem was beguiling. The more she watched, the less she wanted to turn away.

Trap, her mind said, but her heart wasn't so sure.

The Lightbringer blinked, unsure what to do next. She could continue to stare (turn to **349**), use her sword to prise the gem out of the wall (turn to **346**), or move on (turn to **587**).

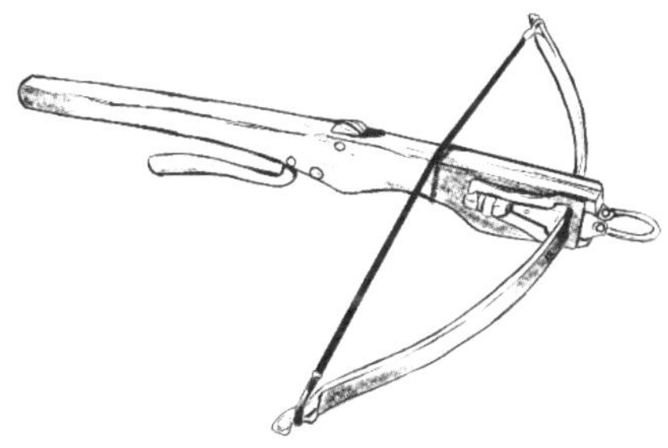

128

Derilion waited. The water continued to come through the walls, yet its level remained the same in the tunnel.

Something didn't feel right.

Roll 2D6 and test for *Detection*.

If the test is successful, turn to **675**, otherwise, turn to **421**.

129

The hunter looked at the room. It was a small living area, with a bed, a bath, and a fireplace.

To the right-hand side of the room was a desk, where a small child sat drawing on a piece of parchment.

The child turned and looked at Derilion with a quizzical expression.

"Did the Maiden ask you to kill me?" she questioned the hunter.

If the maiden did ask Derilion to kill her, turn to **233**; otherwise, turn to **546**.

130

The hunter circled the solidified Cuddower and inspected the area where it had come in.

There was a doorway in the wall, but she couldn't prise it open with her sword.

There was a chance the explosive powder might put a hole in the door. To use some, turn to **681**. To look for something else, turn to **260**.

131

"Weren't you listening? You cannot leave without paying a toll."

"What is it you want?" the hunter asked.

"Nothing much," she replied. "You'll hardly miss it."

Should Derilion leave (turn to **82**), pay the toll (turn to **98**), or attack the girl (turn to **618**)?

132

Derilion approached the woman slowly. She was about the hunter's age and showed no visible signs of battle. She wondered how she came to be in this place.

The hunter noticed a tattoo on the woman's shoulder. A snake rearing up, its forked tongue almost as long as its body.

Roll 2D6 and test for *Detection*.

If the test is successful, turn to **544**, otherwise, turn to **458**.

133

Derilion found the red potion, took it out of her backpack (**-2w**), and drank it while the girl watched, amused. After a few moments, a wave of confidence washed over the hunter, and she felt able to do anything.

She took the girl's hand and matched her dance fluidly.

Continue to **525**.

134

Derilion went over and inspected the pots and vases on the shelves. Most of them were plain, but two of them caught her eye. They had delicate patterns, with words around their base, and stoppers firmly stuck in their necks. The words on the first read 'Ashingya' and on the second, 'Pulreney'.

She felt an urge to investigate further before leaving.

Remove the Ashingya stopper	Turn to **106**
Remove the Pulreney stopper	Turn to **695**
Investigate the kiln	Turn to **612**
Leave the room and check the other door	Turn to **624**

135

The Demon lay dead in front of her. She searched the body but found nothing worth taking. Next, she moved around the hole and saw a set of stairs leading down into the darkness.

Something inside the hunter told her she was getting closer to Obishaa. She hoped she wasn't too late.

Roll 2D6 and test for *Detection*.

If the test is successful, turn to **614**. Otherwise, turn to **430**.

136

The elven hunter lay dead on the floor; Derilion was too late.

She searched her pockets and found 4 gold coins (**+2w**) and a small black arrowhead (**+2w**).

She scanned the bodies one last time and left the room (turn to **74**).

The Diamond Elemental shattered in front of Derilion. Without hesitation, the Lightbringer stepped forward to face the warlocks, raising her sword, and was surprised to see them flinch.

"Tell me where Obishaa is, and I will spare you."

"She's far from here, banished to the Crystalfall."

"Crystalfall is a myth. Everyone knows that," she said.

"It is real. Sit in the empty throne, and we will send you there."

"Do I look stupid?" she replied. "I will find it myself."

"If you wish," they said, irritated.

"One last question," she said. "Why was I here all that time ago?"

"You have magic, Lightbringer, and we wanted to use you."

"I am not magical," Derilion replied.

"But you are. You use detection, yes? That is a skill derived from magic. You have the potential to be very powerful. You might not believe us, but why would we lie?"

Was her detection skill derived from magic? She'd always thought it was just an extension of her senses.

"How do I get out of here?"

"The easiest question yet. Use the door behind us."

Should she go through the door (turn to **352**) or end the warlocks lives (turn to **276**)?

138

Derilion prised the top off one of the crates, peered inside, and saw a mouse scurrying around the edges, looking for a way out. The hunter tipped the crate over gently, and the animal jumped out and made its way to the dark recesses of the room.

She could search different crates (turn to **45**), open the rest of the tiny crates (turn to **310**) or head for the door (turn to **354**).

139

Derilion made her way to the wardrobe as quickly as possible. The footsteps grew ever louder, and she knew at any moment the door would open.

Roll 2D6 and test for *Speed*.

If the test is successful, turn to **175**. Otherwise, turn to **103**.

140

A rusting iron gate stood in front of Derilion, guarding the darkness beyond. She reached out and slowly pushed it open, wincing at the loud, screeching noise it made.

"I hope you weren't trying to sneak up on me," said a girl's voice from the darkness.

"I was not."

"Then what are you doing here?"

Ask who she is	Turn to **118**
Tell her she's working for the Pajoli	Turn to **176**
Tell her she's working against the Pajoli	Turn to **357**
Tell her she's here for the treasure	Turn to **187**
Tell her she's here to kill monsters	Turn to **271**

141

Derilion went across to the other room, tried the handle, and found the door was stuck fast. She could attempt to smash the lock, but something told her it would be better to keep going.

Turn to **253**.

142

The ledge was incredibly narrow. She stepped onto it, looking for good handholds to help her along.

Roll 2D6 and test for *Detection*.

If the test is successful, turn to **424**. Otherwise, turn to **631**.

143

As Derilion left the room, an almighty roar erupted behind her. She ran down the passageway until it ended abruptly in a stone wall. The hunter raised her shield in desperation. She didn't want to be stuck down here.

At the top of the wall was the smallest of holes, rectangular in shape. The hunter didn't know whether she would fit, but she wasn't about to give up. Carefully, she climbed the rocks, slipping her backpack in front of her when she reached the hole and pulling herself through the claustrophobic gap.

She dragged herself along, her only guide was the light from the shield, and the small groove that had been worn over time by others who'd gone this way. Finally, when Derilion could feel the nerves starting to creep in, the gap opened out a little. There was another edge and beyond that a larger room.

The hunter dropped down into the room, hoping there'd be another way out when she finally found Obishaa (turn to **232**).

144

"Not so fast," Derilion heard from behind her.

She turned and saw the man she'd assumed was dead sitting up and staring at her.

"I am Holut, the blacksmith of the Pajoli."

"My name is Derilion," the hunter said.

"There's no need to be nervous," Holut continued. "I mean you no harm. I do wonder, however, if you've come across a carving in your travels. It has magical properties and changes to resemble its current owner."

If the Lightbringer has the carving and wants to give it to him, turn to **543**. Otherwise, turn to **583**.

145

Derilion reacted quickly and dodged the dart, which whizzed by inches from her head.

Angered, she turned and approached the thrones, turn to **276**.

146

Derilion moved quickly to her left and watched as a set of three spikes attached to a metal frame swung into view. It was a crude device, and no doubt meant to weed out the naïve adventurers.

It also made a lot of noise. Enough, in fact, to draw the attention of whatever creature lurked in the darkness of the chamber. Derilion turned quickly, her sword and shield raised to the unknown enemy.

Turn to **381**.

147

Derilion placed the bone key in the lock, twisted, and pulled open the door. As she did, there was a 'Thwip!' sound, and she instantly knew she'd triggered a trap.

If the Lightbringer was wearing gauntlets, turn to **73**. Otherwise, turn to **389**.

148

The girl looked over towards the hunter and sighed.

"I think I'd like you to leave now," she said.

Derilion wanted to argue, but something told her she shouldn't.

Turn to **29**.

149

The skeleton sunk its teeth into Derilion's neck, and she felt the warm blood spurt out. It coated the glass around her as she whirled and fell to the ground. She grasped at her neck, but she knew it was no good.

In her last moments, the hunter knew she had failed Obishaa, and hoped there was another life where she could make it up to her.

150

Derilion reasoned if she used the bottom of the wall, she'd have less distance to fall. Carefully, she manoeuvred to the lower part of the rockface.

If the hunter injured Zalixa, turn to **123**. If she didn't, or never met her, turn to **90**.

<h1 style="text-align:center">151</h1>

Derilion searched for a trap but found nothing amongst the debris strewn on the floor. She stopped, certain she'd heard a noise in the darkness behind her. Perhaps the gloom was a hindrance to other creatures as well as to her.

If that were the case, setting fire to the clothes would probably cause something to attack, so, with this in mind, she decided to investigate the adventurer instead (turn to **245**).

<h1 style="text-align:center">152</h1>

As the Cuddower fell to the floor, Derilion grabbed the arrow from the bow and drove it into its back. The Cuddower roared, and the Lightbringer watched as its body began hardening into stone. Within moments the creature was a statue.

She stepped back, confused but relieved. With the Cuddower dealt with, she now had to look for a way out.

Turn to **130**.

<h1 style="text-align:center">153</h1>

Derilion retrieved the pebble from her backpack (**-3w**). She gripped it tightly in her hand and struck the wall with it. She went to pull away to strike again, but the pebble had stuck to the wall.

The hunter stepped back and watched as it dissolved into the cave surface, which began to glow a dull red.

Within a few seconds, the runestone she'd been looking for appeared through the wall and dropped to the floor in front of her.

Turn to **425**.

154

Derilion saw a rope coiled up on the floor and picked it up.

It was strong and heavy (**+6w**) and would fit in her backpack if she wanted to take it.

The passage onward led down for about fifty feet before turning to the right. The hunter was caught between whether she should be moving fast or being cautious. The mental strain was near-enough exhausting.

As the passage straightened out, she saw a cluster of wooden crates set against the wall.

There didn't seem to be anything special about them, but she knew even the most harmless objects could be a trap in here.

She could search the crates (turn to **279**) or continue (turn to **587**).

155

As soon as the shield covered Derilion's face, she felt something hit it, knocking her back. She looked at Volkov and watched as an amber-coloured sticky residue slid off onto the floor and set hard within seconds.

Derilion thanked the Gods she had chosen the right defence, but now she had to move. It wouldn't be long before it could attack again, and the further she put between herself and the Ambrite, the better.

Swiftly, Derilion moved backwards, and, once more, thanked the gods when she found an exit.

Turn to **251**.

156

Derilion grabbed onto the more secure handhold just in time. She took a moment to catch her breath before continuing left along the wall (turn to **562**).

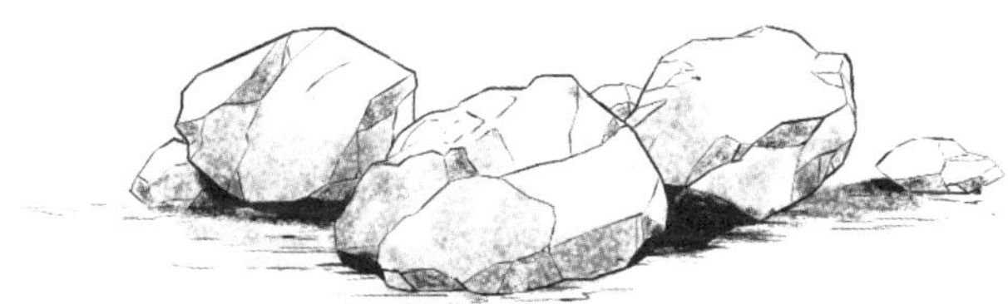

Derilion turned in a blur, almost acting on pure instinct and reached out and down for the glass ball, catching it just an inch above the ground.

She breathed a sigh of relief, then remembered the encroaching skeleton.

Turn to **337**.

158

With her frustration spent, Derilion felt calmer. She reasoned that, however difficult the search for Obishaa was, it was necessary. She couldn't expect to find her immediately; to rescue her immediately. Everything took time.

She placed her hand on the wall and closed her eyes. She cleared her mind and tried to see what thoughts would appear next. It was a useful trick, which generally worked in her favour.

Roll 2D6 and test for *Detection*.

If the test is successful, turn to **301**. Otherwise, Derilion found nothing and turned back (turn to **323**).

159

"I might have something," Derilion said, taking off her backpack and searching the insides.

She found the cuff with the dragon rubies near the bottom and showed it to the woman.

"It's got jewels in it?" she said.

The woman took the cuff **(-4w)**, looked closely at the jewel with disdain, and threw it over her shoulder.

"Nope," she said. "Anything else?"

If the Lightbringer has any stones with concentric circles, she could show her one of those (turn to **16**). Otherwise, she has nothing to give (turn to **396**).

160

Bugs disposed of, Derilion made her way towards the exit. No sooner had she taken a couple of steps, then a dark figure appeared in front of her, blocking the way.

Derilion stopped and waited.

Turn to **307**.

161

Within minutes the corridor opened into a larger room, and Derilion found herself in a vast chamber with high crystalline walls on either side.

It looked beautiful, with the blue crystals emanating light.

There was hardly any shelter in the centre of the room, and experience told the hunter to keep to the sides to avoid an easy ambush.

She had travelled little over halfway into the chamber when her concerns were proven. A rock fizzed past her head, and she dove for the nearest cover.

Roll 2D6 and test for *Speed*.

If the test is successful, turn to **365**, otherwise, turn to **476**.

162

The hunter searched the room, keeping an eye on the girl, who didn't break from reading her book.

The place was a bit of a jumble. Things were stacked on top of each other or hidden in drawers or pushed under furniture.

Derilion picked out three things she'd like to look at closer; a book on one of the shelves (turn to **110**), a box on another (turn to **214**), and a lamp emitting blue light (turn to **498**). Equally, she could leave (turn to **29**).

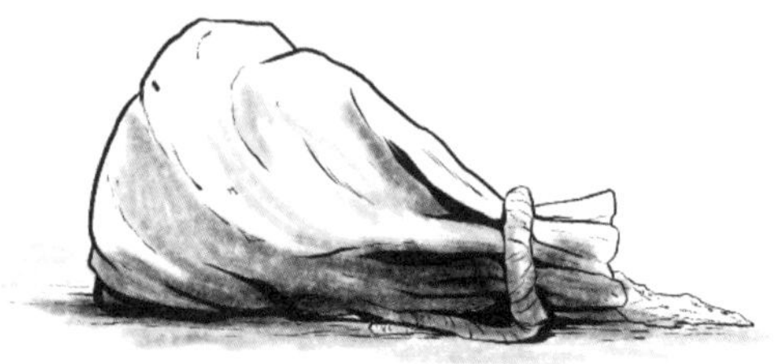

163

"It's been a while since I've seen something so coarse. Explosive powder, yes? How quaint. Yes, that'll help me."

Othwig took it (**-1w**) before Derilion had a chance to react.

Turn to **298**.

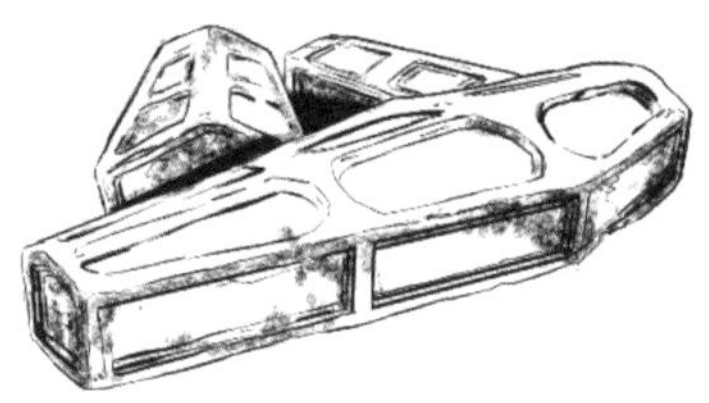

164

The man looked young, with long hair and stubble on his face. He wore overalls and had the palest skin Derilion had ever seen, even for a corpse. His arms rested across his chest, and he looked in deep relaxation.

Roll 2D6 and test for *Detection*.

If the test is successful, turn to **544**, otherwise, turn to **20**.

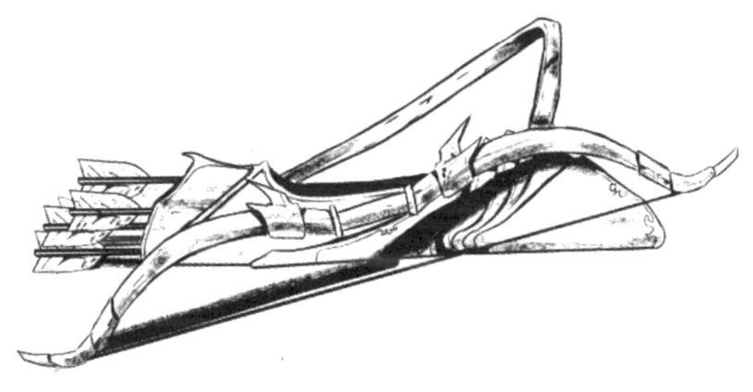

165

The next room holds a bloodbath. Three adventurers lay on the floor, a dwarf, an elven hunter, and an assassin, all bleeding from various wounds.

Derilion scanned the room for their attacker but saw no-one else. She did notice an exit on the far side.

She had several choices to ponder over.

Head to the dwarf	Turn to **494**
Head to the elven hunter	Turn to **394**
Head to the assassin	Turn to **200**
Head to the other exit immediately	Turn to **574**

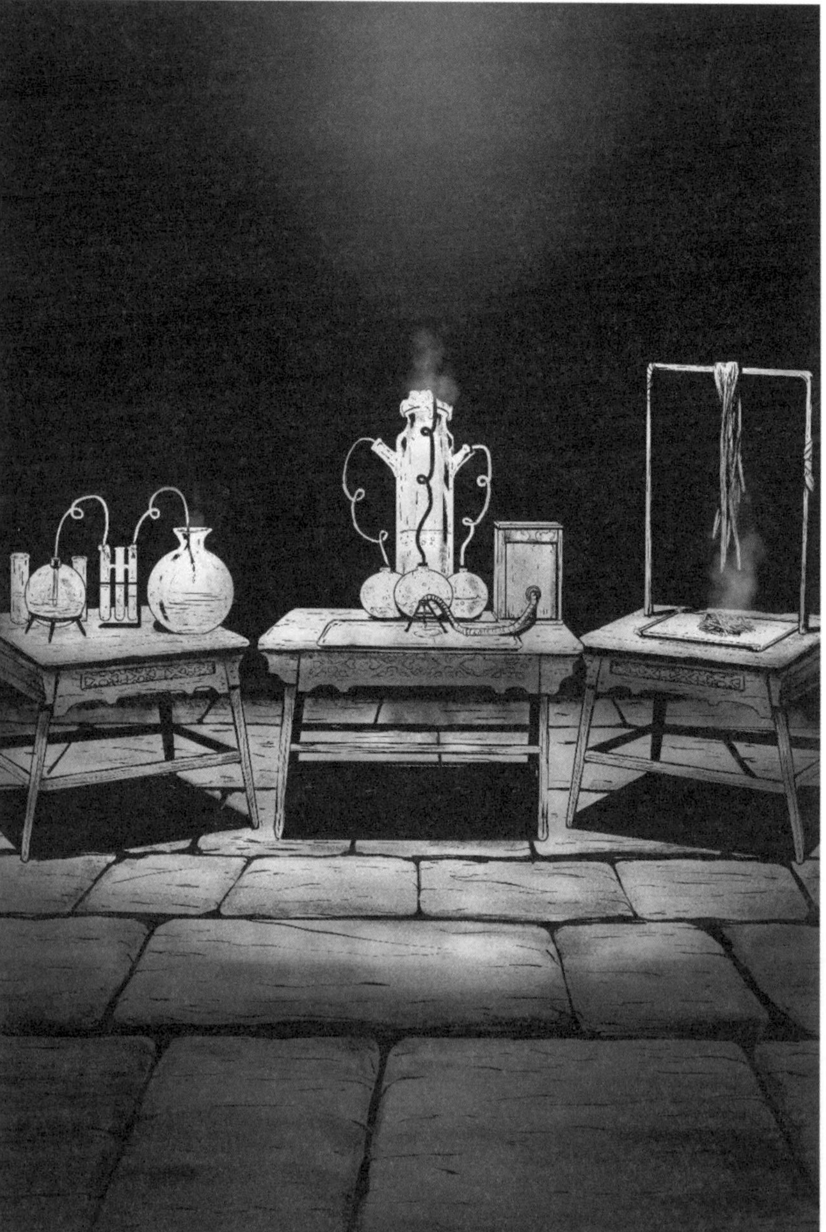

166

There were three benches she could look at, so Derilion took a couple of steps forward to get a better look.

On the left bench, a series of glass tubes bubbled and frothed, until at the end, a steady drip deposited potion into a larger jar.

On the central bench, a tall glass cylinder sat atop three bubbling mixtures. Condensation collected on the side and dripped into a tray at the bottom.

On the right bench, a set of twigs sat in the middle of a metal tray smouldering thick smoke into the air. Hung above the smoke were strips of animal hide.

The hunter took a moment to think over the options.

Check the left bench	Turn to **3**
Check the middle bench	Turn to **180**
Check the right bench	Turn to **690**
Ignore the benches and continue	Turn to **254**

167

Cautiously, Derilion continued, testing every step with as much care as she could. As she moved forward, the number of fallen bodies increased, making it almost impossible to create a path through.

Unfortunately, with all her concentration directed at the floor, the Lightbringer knocked into a low outcrop of rock. To her dismay, she heard the ping of a sprung trap.

Roll 2D6 and test for *Speed*.

If the test is successful, turn to **146**. Otherwise, turn to **239**.

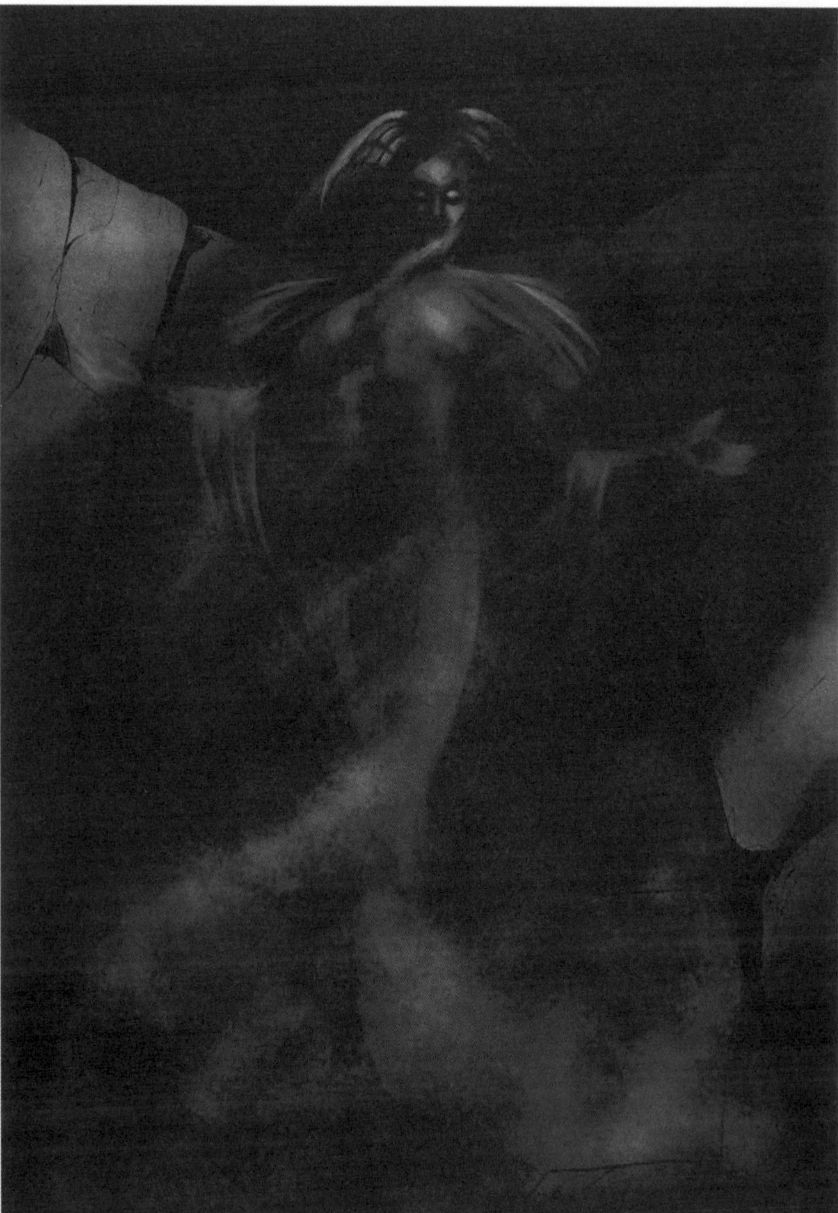

Derilion turned and began to swim back to the body she'd seen earlier. As she swam, the water levels decreased until she could touch the floor with her feet.

When she reached the body, the water was all but gone. Confused, the hunter crouched and turned the body over and instantly recoiled. It had no face.

Something wasn't right.

Roll 2D6 and test for *Detection.*

If the test is successful, turn to **293**, otherwise, turn to **350**.

169

The mist swirled in front of Derilion, forming into a female shape hovering in the air.

Slowly, it circled the hunter, watching and waiting.

"I am Ashingya," the female said.

Had Derilion heard of Ashingya before? If so, she might know what to do. Otherwise, she would have to guess.

Hide her face behind her shield	Turn to **275**
Kneel in front of Ashingya	Turn to **597**
Yell at Ashingya	Turn to **611**
Turn her back on Ashingya	Turn to **683**
Wait and see what happens	Turn to **640**

170

Unfortunately, the scarf only partially covered the mirror and Derilion didn't want to get any closer to adjust it.

She wasn't sure why, but she knew she had to act quickly.

Inspect the nearest mirror	Turn to **582**
Extinguish her torch	Turn to **622**
Speed through the middle of the mirrors	Turn to **573**

171

Derilion moved along the corridor, judging the space in front of her and turning more and more sideways as the gap narrowed. She wasn't normally claustrophobic, it didn't pay to be in her line of work, but this was going to be tight.

She stopped for a moment and gave it one last thought. There was still time to go back if she wanted to (turn to **542**). Otherwise, she could continue (turn to **646**).

172

Derilion unsheathed her sword, but no sooner had she done so, then the demon rose, becoming a darkened shadow once again, filling the room, covering the floor, the ceiling and the walls.

The hunter swung her sword at the shadow, to no avail.

"Do not panic," the demon said. "It is a painless way to go."

The darkness filled Derilion, and when it finally cleared, she was nowhere to be seen.

173

By the time Derilion reached the assassin, she was dead.

She searched her belongings, the only object worthy of taking being a small box of ash (**+2w**).

There was nothing else to do for these people, so the Lightbringer exited to the next room.

Turn to **74**.

174

Derilion shook her head.

"No, there must be another way," she said.

The creature laughed as best it could.

"Do you not understand the Pajoli? Who they are? What they crave? They are creatures who live off others suffering. These caves are built to cause as much suffering as possible; the walls feed off it. That door will not open until one of us dies. I thought it would be me who would revenge them, but now I see you have a greater chance. Good luck."

The Slabac walked towards the hunter for one last attack.

Derilion pushed her sword into the Slabac's chest, killing it instantly.

She searched the Slabac and found two stones with concentric circles (**+3w each**).

Turn to **462**.

175

Derilion sped up as fast as she dared go. She reached the wardrobe and, thankfully, found it unlocked. Not thinking about what she was doing, she jumped in and pulled the door closed behind her.

She hoped whoever was coming was not going to stay for long.

Turn to **255**.

176

"I'm working for the Pajoli," Derilion said. It seemed like a sensible option.

There was a pause. Out of the blackness, a thick rope-like tendril appeared and knocked Derilion off her feet.

"Then you will know my name; Grom. How dare you come here and support those people? Now you will have to face me."

Turn to **432**.

177

Derilion waited for the man to attack her. He looked weak, but she wasn't going to take any chances.

"You don't have to do this," she told him.

"Oh, I know. It's just that I enjoy killing. Why else would I be the mortician?"

	Speed	*Accuracy*	*Damage*	*Health*
Mortician	6	8	1	12

If the Lightbringer wins, turn to **294**.

178

Derilion headed towards the door to the left. She passed the coffins making sure to keep one eye on them. Thankfully, nothing happened.

Even though she'd not long entered, it felt like she had been in the caves for a long time, and the nearer she got to the door, the greater the urgency to leave became.

As she reached it, however, there was a noise behind her.

Turn to **637**.

179

The hunter was eager to leave, and she didn't detect anything wrong with the floor. Until, that is, halfway across, when she stepped on one of the stones. She heard a click and felt herself go down a little.

Roll 2D6 and test for *Speed*.

If the test is successful, turn to **201**. Otherwise, turn to **230**.

180

The hunter approached the middle bench, the glass tube towering above her.

Derilion looked up and saw the top of it was open-ended, and some of the vapour had collected on the cave ceiling. As she watched, a drip fell from the cave roof towards her.

Roll 2D6 and test for *Speed*.

If the test is successful, turn to **329**, otherwise, turn to **593**.

181

Derilion pulled out one of the explosive powders from her belt as quickly as possible, but even as she did so, the woman stepped forward, muttering something under her breath.

The Lightbringer found herself unable to let go of it and stood powerless as the woman approached.

Turn to **163**.

182

The hunter moved almost unnaturally quickly. The troll's club struck the shield and deflected harmlessly away.

"Impressive," he said. "But I'm just not interested."

It turned its back and exited the room via the same door the hunter had entered. Derilion watched it go, then made her way to the door ahead of her and into the next room (turn to **126**).

183

The hunter moved forward cautiously, expecting an attack at any moment. The walls began to narrow, and after a few more minutes of walking the path ended with a circular entrance, through which shone a myriad of light.

Derilion moved through the entrance cautiously and saw a figure hunched over a net laid out on a table in front of them. They seemed focused on it, and the hunter saw the net had many pockets, all but one filled with brightly coloured gemstones.

Something was odd, and the hunter wasn't sure whether she should retrace her steps (turn to **553**), use *Stealth* to sneak up on her (turn to **391**), use *Speed* to attack (turn to **629**) or call out to let her know she was there (turn to **76**).

184

The skeleton collapsed to the floor in a resounding crash, which the hunter assumed would probably attract attention in such an enclosed place as the caves. Without hesitation, she picked up her belongings and left the room.

Turn to **568**.

185

Derilion unsheathed her sword and used its point to press the wobbly stone. Immediately, the wall swung in where she would have been standing.

"Quick," came a voice from inside. "Stop it from closing."

Derilion could either block the door closing (turn to **454**) or do nothing and let it shut (turn to **210**).

186

"I'll use my sword," the hunter said.

"Please, be careful!" Zalixa called. "One slip and…"

Derilion began to pry the rocks out of the wall, as carefully as she could.

Roll 2D6 and test for *Accuracy*.

If the test is successful, turn to **699**, otherwise, turn to **309**.

187

"I'm here for the treasure," Derilion said.

"I admire your honesty," she said, laughing. "My name is Grom."

Slowly, the woman appeared from the darkness. Her arms and legs were thick worm-like limbs, constantly on the move. Her torso and head looked normal. In one of her tendrils she held a moss-like substance.

"Take this. It's a simple stun charm, but I'll doubt anyone will see it coming. Throw it at an enemy's feet as soon as possible."

"Thank you," Derilion said, taking the moss.

"Thank you," Grom said. "Most people run a mile when they see me. Or, at least, they try to."

If Derilion wore the steel gauntlets, turn to **479**, otherwise, turn to **628**.

188

"How did you get so far being this nice?" Zalixa asked.

"I'm not always," she said.

"Good. For the worst is yet to come. I can give you a *Stealth* enchantment for your necklace if you need one."

If the hunter needed the *Stealth* enchantment, she accepted the offer, and the girl performed the enchantment.

The Lightbringer watched Zalixa run towards the water.

Press on to **487**.

189

The Lightbringer walked over to the chest and tried to lift the top, but it was stuck fast.

She put the blade of her sword in the gap under the lid and tried to prise it open, but it quickly became apparent it wasn't going to budge, and the hunter made the decision to leave the room.

Turn to **466**.

190

The hunter stood before a dark, imposing, panelled wooden door, which looked very solid. Derilion put her ear to it, but either the room beyond was silent, or the wood was so thick it blocked out any noise.

There was no turning back, she knew. Obishaa was somewhere behind this door. At least, she'd better be. With more than a little uneasiness in her heart, Derilion took hold of the circular iron handle and pulled the door open.

Turn to **551**.

191

There were many fragile ornaments between Derilion and the glass ball, and the pathway was very narrow in several places.

Carefully, she picked her way past the first few obstacles without incident. She stopped for a moment and looked around to make sure there wasn't a better path through.

Roll 2D6 and test for *Stealth*.

If the test was successful, turn to **533**. Otherwise, turn to **102**.

192

Derilion went over to the plinth. She retrieved the rope (**-5w**), tied one end of it around its base, and the other around her waist.

She went back to the wall, placed her back against one side, and lifted her legs, one after the other, onto the opposite wall.

Slowly she moved along the wall towards the open door. From below, she began to hear scuttling sounds indicating something down there was watching her, waiting for her to fall.

About a third of the way across, the hunter lost her footing, and she fell into the chasm. Fortunately, the rope broke her fall and, more importantly, held her weight. Below her, the scuttling intensified, and Derilion quickly made her way up the rope and led next to the golden bow to get her breath back.

She rested for a moment longer, knowing there was only one choice left. She retrieved the rope and put it in her backpack (**+5w**).

Turn to **503**.

193

The powder hit the woman's chest and ignited in a roar. The woman screamed as flames rose over her body. Derilion couldn't be sure, but it looked as if her victim's arms and legs grew longer as she writhed around.

Finally, the woman fell to the ground, dead, and the hunter moved around her, back out of the door she'd come in.

Turn to **584**.

194

Derilion reached out, removed the glass over the flame, and put her hand into it. It didn't feel cold as she'd first thought. She couldn't feel anything at all.

The room, however, had changed. As the hunter scanned it, she noticed most objects had taken on a blue outline, except for the girl in the chair, who had a red.

The most concerning thing, however, was a red line around the frame of the door, like it bore a hex. The hunter took her hand away from the light, and everything returned to normal.

Turn to **29**.

195

The Frost Sprites looked scared as Derilion approached. They chattered in a language she didn't recognise and tried to shrink back into the corner as far as they could.

It didn't look to the hunter as if they were going to put up a fight, and she was in two minds as to whether to continue attacking them (turn to **299**) or attempt to talk to them (turn to **264**).

196

"Reward me first," the hunter told her.

"All right," the woman replied, unable to hide her annoyance. She looked to the necklace the hunter was wearing.

"I see you have an enchantment necklace," she said. "I can give you a *Stealth* enchantment for it if you need one. Or perhaps some more explosive powder, which I can tell you've encountered already."

Take some explosive powder	Turn to **602**
Take the *Stealth* enchantment	Turn to **561**
Ignore her and leave	Turn to **399**

197

The area Derilion found herself in glowed red and was warmer than any of the previous chambers. Around the room, several torches were alight, burning with a ferocity that seemed supernatural. To one side was a closed stone door with no handle.

In front of her, a large circular hole covered most of the floor. A small path ran around its edge, and from its centre, a low, guttural noise emanated.

She could go around the hole (turn to **649**), drop a torch down it (turn to **564**), or throw some explosive powder down it, if she had some (turn **501**).

Derilion began rifling through the boy's pockets, looking for anything valuable or useful.

Roll 2D6 and test for *Stealth*.

If the test is successful, turn to **688**. Otherwise, turn to **265**.

Derilion looked at the tiles making up the image of the sun and was surprised to see they were made of glass, a surprisingly pretty piece of art so far down in the caves.

The central tile sat higher than the others, and the hunter guessed it might be a trigger for the door or something worse.

She could either press the raised tile (turn to **31**) or inspect the lightning tiles (turn to **326**).

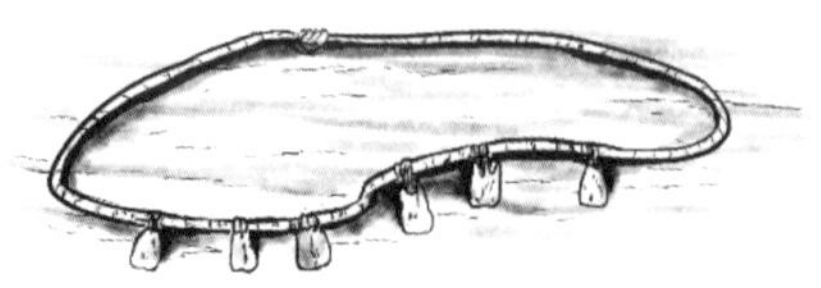

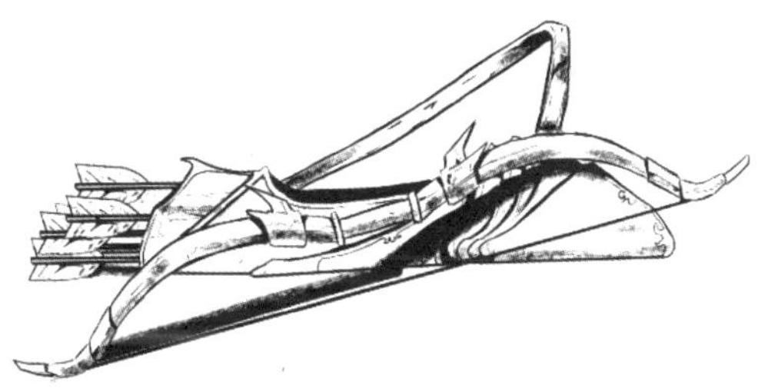

200

Derilion headed toward the assassin, who was looking at the Lightbringer with fear in her eyes.

"I'm not going to…" the hunter began only to be interrupted by the assassin.

"Watch out!" she cried.

She looked behind her just in time to see a crossbow bolt heading toward her leg. She moved out of the way, but it meant the bolt hit the assassin in the shoulder.

Derilion ran to the dwarf and ran him through with her sword before he had the chance to reload.

Turn to **256**.

201

Derilion leapt the moment she felt the stone move and was mid-air before it triggered. The stone flung upwards and would have sent her towards the recently deceased creature.

Unfortunately, the stone she landed on triggered immediately and threw her over there anyway.

Derilion landed heavily beside the creature, losing 2 from her *Health*.

If she was still alive, turn to **426**.

202

From out of the pool rose a Diamond Elemental wielding a large sword. The Lightbringer looked down at her own sword; it was going to be almost useless on this creature.

The Diamond Elemental has a starting *Health* of 24.

Perhaps the amulet might be of some use. If her amulet has all three enchantments, turn to **46**, otherwise, turn to **471**.

203

Derilion kicked the box of ash into the pool and watched as the water around it turned red. The Elemental screamed and withered slightly before her eyes.

Subtract 6 from its *Health*.

If the Elemental has no more *Health*, turn to **137**. Has the hunter kicked four items in yet? If not, she can try another (turn to **633**). If she has, she must face the Elemental (turn to **107**).

204

Derilion took a further step backwards, closed her eyes and concentrated. She blocked out the sound of the Diamond Elemental and the men who tried to invade her mind.

Just when she thought something was coming through, a piercing shriek from the warlocks broke her concentration. She opened her eyes and realised there was no time to lose; she must face the Diamond Elemental as she was.

Turn to **107**.

205

Derilion rolled to the right and dropped into a dip. It wasn't much, but it afforded her enough cover from the bombardment. There was a small rivulet of freezing water at the bottom of the dip, but instead of it causing discomfort, the water felt refreshing.

She moved along the dip quickly, rocks continuing to fly over the top of her, finally making it to the far end of the chamber, where she rested, even though the rock-throwing continued.

As she rested, her body began to tingle, and slowly she started to feel stronger. The water was more than just water.

Restore 5 to Derilion's *Health*. Feeling fitter than she had in a long time, the hunter stood to face her attackers, who turned out to be three Frost Sprites, none of whom were taller than two feet high. As soon as they saw the hunter, they cowered back into the corner of the cave where they lived.

Their cowardice made Derilion angry. She had three choices; ignore them and move on (turn to **226**), try and talk to them (turn to **264**) or attack them (turn to **195**).

206

Derilion kicked the clear liquid into the pool and watched as the water around it turned a brighter blue. The Elemental roared and grew slightly stronger before her eyes.

Add 4 to its *Health*.

Has the hunter kicked four items in yet? If not, she can try another (turn to **633**). If she has, she must face the Elemental (turn to **107**).

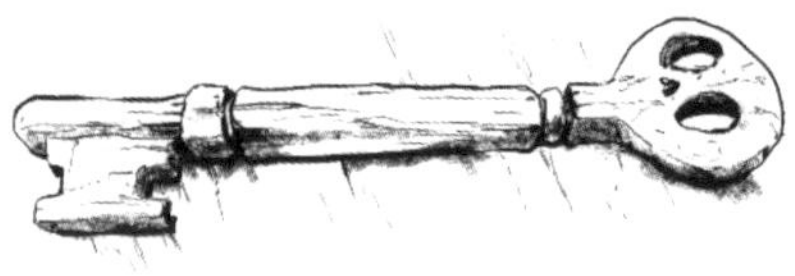

207

Was Derilion wearing metal gauntlets?

If so, turn to **581**, otherwise, turn to **492**.

208

The hunter went to place her hand on the wall but pulled back at the last minute, a feeling of uncertainty washing over her.

"I'm sorry," Derilion said. "Something doesn't feel right."

She waited and watched the letters grow large, spelling out NO on the wall.

"I will leave you here," she continued. "Maybe the next adventurer will help."

Derilion moved on, being careful not to touch the wall.

Continue to **161**.

<h1 style="text-align:center">209</h1>

Derilion moved along the passageway swiftly, picking up a new scent ahead of her. Not only did the fragrance grow stronger the further she walked, but the cave grew warmer, too.

The Lightbringer placed a rag over her mouth in case the air was toxic and continued. After a few minutes, the path widened into a large room with three long tables. On each, various plants boiled in various apparatus.

The hunter scanned the rest of the room, but it appeared empty apart from a chest on the right with its lid slightly open.

The room was quite suffocating, and Derilion was torn between investigating the benches (turn to **166**), opening the chest (turn to **296**) or just continuing (turn to **254**).

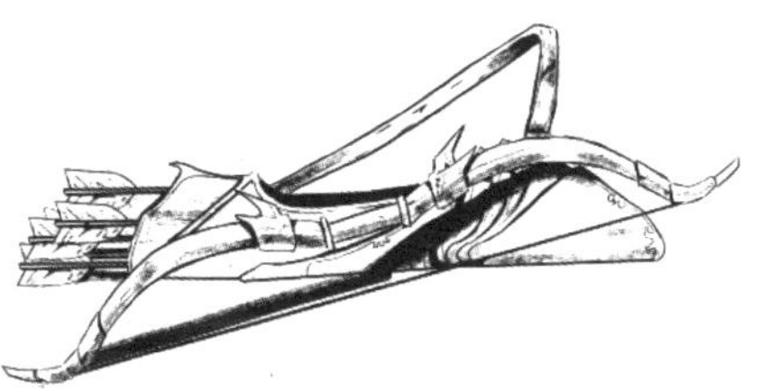

<h1 style="text-align:center">210</h1>

Derilion decided in a split second. For all she knew, the person trapped in the room was there for a very good reason.

She watched as the door swung shut and heard the click of the trap mechanism resetting.

Resolute in completing her quest, she moved past the stone carefully.

Turn to **78**.

211

Derilion grabbed the orange potion from her backpack (**-2w**), knowing there wasn't a moment to lose. She removed the cork stopper and brought it up to her lips.

It tasted bitter, and she very nearly vomited it straight back up. She stopped for a moment, and the feeling of nausea abated.

She rested on the desk, hoping it was indeed antidote to the poison and within a couple of minutes, she began to feel better.

That was too close. The hunter cursed her stupidity at nearly failing in her quest. When she felt strong enough, she stood and stepped through the doorway into the next room.

Turn to **300**.

212

The hunter took out the pebble and cupped it in her hands.

Within moments the concentric circles glowed a deep red. Then the redness pulsed along the pebble's length, showing the Lightbringer a path. She followed it until she stood in front of the wall.

Its job done, Derilion put the pebble back into her backpack.

Turn to **469**.

<h1 style="text-align:center">213</h1>

"Let me go on my way," Derilion said. "I'm not interested in anything you have here."

The hunter began to back away towards the exit.

"You should know that I won't let you leave just like that. Let me give you your choices. You can either trade with me, take one of my three tests, or, if you wish for a quick death, attack me."

Trade with Othwig	Turn to **338**
Attack Othwig	Turn to **358**
Take Othwig's test	Turn to **625**

<h1 style="text-align:center">214</h1>

Derilion moved toward the box. It shone in the light of the shield, making it appear almost alive. She picked it up and realised the pattern on the lid depicted a white scorpion.

As she pondered opening it, the girl stood and walked over to the book Derilion had seen earlier. She glanced at the hunter and smirked.

"Be careful with that," she said, before picking the book up and returning to her seat.

The Lightbringer mulled over her next move.

Open the box	Turn to **434**
Investigate the lamp	Turn to **498**
Leave the room	Turn to **29**

215

"Get out of my way," the woman said.

She pushed Derilion aside and jumped onto the net. Her body shimmered for a second and then vanished. At the same moment, the light grew blindingly bright, and the hunter shielded her eyes. When she could open them again, both the woman and the net had gone.

With the woman gone, the Lightbringer looked around the room. There was a large wooden chest over to one side she could open (turn to **189**) or she could leave the room (turn to **466**).

216

The hunter cleared her throat a couple of times, and the man blinked his eyes open. He looked at her in mild surprise.

"I am Holut," he said. "The blacksmith of the dungeon, which is one of the only reasons they keep me alive."

He stopped and waited for a response.

"My name is Derilion," the hunter said.

"There's no need to be nervous. I mean you no harm. I do wonder, however, if you've come across a carving in your travels. It's a special carving that changes to resemble the owner."

If Derilion has the carving, she can give it to him (turn to **543**). If she doesn't have it, or doesn't want to give it, turn to **583**.

217

The troll looked very upset. He turned to Derilion and took a long hard look at her.

"Now, that's just rude," he said. "How would you like it if I'd eaten some of your food?"

It stood, stretched, and took its wooden club from off its belt, then, almost begrudgingly, advanced on Derilion.

Turn to **514**.

218

The hunter recognised the face in the orb; it was the glass skeleton she'd seen when she'd entered the room. The skeleton was trying to sneak up on her, and she thanked the gods for her fortune. Quickly, the Lightbringer picked up the orb and turned to fight.

Turn to **337**.

219

Derilion pushed all her feelings away, squashed them and tucked them somewhere inside of her, till all she had was silence. She moved her head from one path to the other, slowly, deliberately. She felt an almost imperceptible pull on her and concentrated.

Gradually, the pull began to take shape, and with the shape came two words. Looking straight on the Lightbringer heard a voice whisper '*Stealth*'. Looking to her left, she heard '*Accuracy*'. Which one should she choose?

To take left branch	Turn to **209**
Go straight on	Turn to **183**

220

The adventurer inspected the necklace before throwing it to the floor where it shattered. They sneered at it and then looked towards Derilion.

"A fake? How clever," he hissed. "But now you no longer have it. And they know you are coming."

"Who knows?" the hunter asked.

The adventurer smiled and, in an instant, had vanished. Derilion cursed she hadn't just killed him. She shook her head and moved on, emerging into an area with three paths.

Turn to **639**.

221

Something about the room didn't feel right to Derilion, and she knew she was better out of it. Perhaps that's something she'd learned - it was easier to trust the people who wanted to kill you; at least you knew their mind.

As she moved past the man at the desk, he flicked his wrist, and an invisible force shoved her sideways into the cave wall, causing 2 damage to her *Health*.

With horror, she realised he was not praying but casting a protection spell. Protection from what, she wondered, but in the next instant dust fell from above and Derilion knew the destroyed vine had been keeping the cave from collapsing.

The Lightbringer scampered across the floor and out through the other door, hoping the next room would be safer.

Continue to **143**.

222

Derilion sped through the centre of the mirrors, head down, praying she'd make it unscathed. About halfway through she felt a little strange but decided not to hang around long enough to see what happened.

Move on to **312**.

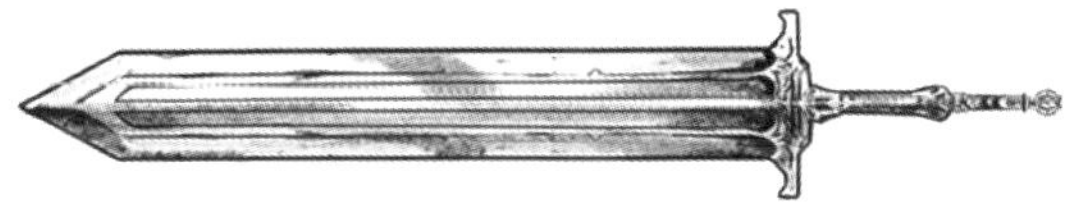

223

Derilion kicked the eye pendant into the pool and watched as the water around it turned a brighter blue. The Elemental roared and grew slightly stronger before her eyes.

Add 4 to its *Health*.

Has the hunter kicked four items in yet? If not, she can try another (turn to **633**). If she has, she must face the Elemental (turn to **107**).

224

As the seconds ticked by the hunter felt weaker and weaker. Whatever poison it'd been, it was potent, and she hardly had enough time to think about Obishaa, and the life she would be forced to lead now.

As her internal organs shut down, Derilion wandered who would find her body, if, indeed, anyone would. She felt like she wanted to cry, and as her last breath escaped her, she saw two boots come through the doorway ahead of her, and she heard the sound of hands rubbing together.

225

"Thank you," the Cuddower said. "If someone recognises it, tell them I am still alive, and give the ring to them – but only them."

Derilion took the ring and put it on (**+1w**).

"Now, leave," the creature said. It muttered some sounds, and a door opened in the wall behind it.

Turn to **443**.

226

The chamber narrowed to a corridor, which, several minutes later, ended in a passage with two doors on both sides, two of them close to Derilion and two further away. It reminded the hunter of some of the prison cells she'd seen in her time.

Then again, perhaps this was where the other witches and warlocks lived.

The options were straightforward.

Try the nearest door on the left	Turn to **626**
Try the nearest door on the right	Turn to **563**
Move on to the doors further ahead	Turn to **253**

227

It was going to be tricky to cross. She stopped for a moment to try and think of something she could do to make it safer. A few seconds spent now was worth her life.

Did the hunter find the rope? If so, turn to **192**, otherwise, turn to **269**.

228

Derilion took her outstretched hand, and in a second, the two of them were dancing. She didn't know the steps though her feet seemed to be moving in time with her partner's.

After a minute or so, Derilion felt herself tiring, and found it difficult to keep up.

Roll 2D6 and test for *Speed*, and 2D6 and test for *Accuracy*.

If both tests are successful, turn to **525**, otherwise, turn to **467**.

229

She knew she had to be careful. The vines were not friendly, and she was their next potential victim.

She paused, watching, trying to see a pattern in their movement. They seemed most active at the top of the doorway, with the roots nearer the ground mostly static.

Derilion crouched and touched her flaming shield to the base of the door. It lit immediately, burning quickly.

If the vines took some explosive powder, turn to **30**, otherwise, turn to **115**.

230

Derilion was unbalanced and couldn't jump clear of the stone before it triggered, sending her flying toward the remains of the creature.

Fortunately, she was able to land well, and only inflicted 1 damage to her *Health*.

If she was still alive, turn to **426**.

231

Derilion emerged from the tunnel, tired but alive. She hadn't gone far into the Pajoli cave system, but this was going to be no easy task. She found a dark corner and rested for a few minutes, listening for any noise which might be another foe.

Fortunately, all was quiet, and the Lightbringer scouted out the next options. To the right, the ground fell away in a gradual descent until she couldn't see the end (turn to **109**). The corridor to the left narrowed significantly; going that way was going to be a tight squeeze (turn to **171**).

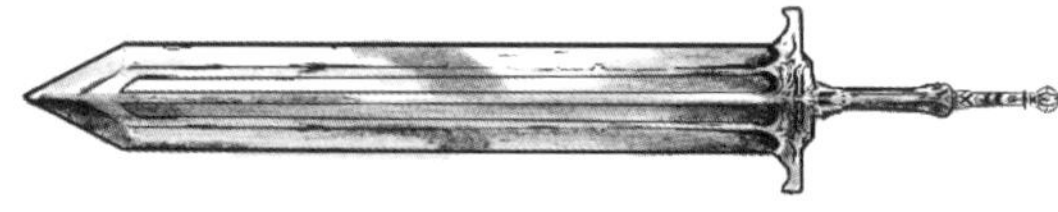

232

A short way along the corridor, Derilion found a pile of bloodstained clothes, dumped in a corner, including a pair of sturdy boots better than her old ones. She put them on, trying not to think about what might have happened to their previous owner.

As she began walking again, she could hear running water nearby, making her nervous. She didn't want to be trapped in here should it flood.

She came to a stop a little way further. The corridor ended abruptly, leaving just a hole in the floor for her to drop down. Through the hole, she could see the water below. It would be freezing, she knew, and if she couldn't get out of it quickly, it could even be a danger to her life.

Still, she had no choice. She had to keep going.

Turn to **17**.

"Yes, she did," Derilion told her, surprised by her frankness.

"Don't be surprised," the girl replied. "You cannot lie in this room. Will you try and kill me?" the child asked.

Derilion smiled. "Anyone who can enchant a room is not someone I want to mess with."

"Very wise. And you do not need to worry, she won't be there when you leave."

Turn to **259**.

234

Derilion kicked the yellowish leaves into the pool and watched as the water around them turned red. The Elemental screamed and withered slightly before her eyes.

Subtract 6 from its *Health*.

If the Elemental has no more *Health*, turn to **137**. Has the hunter kicked four items in yet? If not, she can try another (turn to **633**). If she has, she must face the Elemental (turn to **107**).

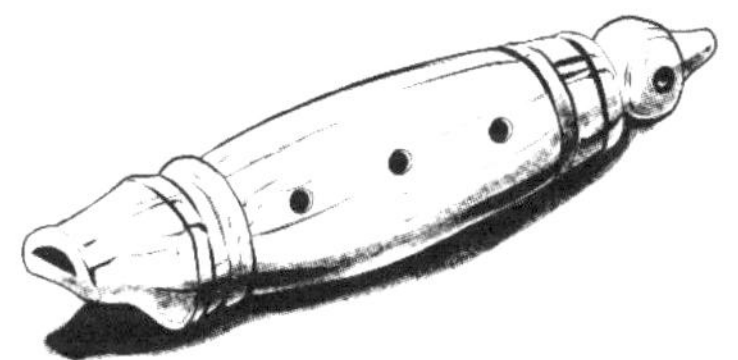

235

Derilion moved her shield quickly, and whatever it was hit it and fell to the floor. Derilion stepped back and got her first look at the creature. A were-cat.

Did the hunter open any of the tiny boxes? If so, turn to **104**, otherwise, turn to **408**.

236

Derilion moved across to the boxes, all the time keeping one eye on the old man, but he didn't move. He wasn't interested in her.

Most of the boxes were sealed, but one was open, and, to her surprise, contained a light, opaque scarf (**-0w**).

When she'd just started hunting, she would have ignored such items, but experience had taught her everything, invariably, had a use, even if it was just to sell it for money.

The rumbling continued to grow. Derilion could try and locate its source (turn to **57**), talk to the man (turn to **586**) or leave the room (turn to **143**).

As soon as she saw the scrolls, her eyes grew hungry.

"Yes. I want those," the girl said, slightly annoyed by her inability to remain calm.

Derilion, always one to spot a negotiation, remained calm.

"In that case, they can be yours if you give me the information, and something else."

The girl raised her eyebrows.

"What?" she asked petulantly.

"What do you have?"

The girl's face screwed up as she tried to think of what to give her.

"I have this healing balm," she said, pulling open a drawer beside her. "It's good for one use and will heal your wounds (+4 *Health*). Will that do?"

"That would be good."

The girl pushed the phial of healing balm (**+1w**) over to Derilion.

"Now, the information," the hunter said.

Turn to **460**.

238

Derilion sat down at the table. There was more food laid out than she had ever eaten at one sitting. Perhaps this was a feast for several people, though she could only see one seat.

She picked up a piece of fruit nearest her and took a bite. Her stomach rumbled, and she realised how hungry she was. She finished it and then ate some bread, after which she tried to rearrange the rolls to make it look like none had been eaten.

Restore 3 to Derilion's *Health*.

Turn to **529**.

239

The attack caught Derilion napping. She moved to her left, toward the centre of the chamber, but not quickly enough. One of the spikes set on a rusting metal frame caught her arm and caused her 2 damage to her *Health*.

The noise piqued the interest of whatever creature was lurking in the darkness of the cave, and Derilion turned as quickly as possible to face the unseen enemy.

Turn to **381**.

240

Derilion concentrated on the leaves, trying to remember what she knew of them. She held each type in a different hand, but try as she might, nothing came back to her. Derilion can take some of each (**+1w each**) and put them in her backpack.

She could now investigate the benches (turn to **166**) or continue (turn to **254**).

241

Derilion thought she could see the ground dipping away to the right, a little way ahead. It might be nothing, but it's all she had.

Raising her shield to cover her head and upper torso, the hunter sprinted as fast as she could, jinking left and right in an attempt to miss the rocks.

Two-thirds of the way across one caught the side of her head, and the hunter fell to the floor heavily, taking 2 damage to her *Health*.

She looked right again and could now see a definite slant to the ground.

Turn to **205**.

242

Derilion had the impression the creature was slow. She might be able to distract it by talking whilst moving closer to the door. She sheathed her sword, took a deep breath and smiled.

"I mean you no harm," she said, arms held out, palms up.

The creature looked at her but said nothing.

"I've got to leave."

The hunter took a step, and the creature mirrored her. Derilion knew they'd both reach the door at the same time. She could try and run for it, use some explosive powder, or continue her walk to the door.

Throw some explosive powder	Turn to **590**
Make a run for the door	Turn to **351**
Continue walking to the door	Turn to **248**

243

Derilion smiled and closed her eyes, pushing out her mind toward the creature. She wanted to know why it was sitting there while most other creatures attacked her.

Roll 2D6 and test for *Detection*.

If the test is successful, turn to **322**, otherwise, turn to **125**.

244

Derilion retrieved the ring and tossed it towards the demon, who caught it in one swift flick of his hand.

"Thank you," it said. "For your kindness, let me advise you to avoid the woman on the floor. She really is no good."

"Thank you," the hunter replied.

"You're welcome," the demon said. "Oh, and you must trust no-one, including yourself."

Derilion was about to question what he meant, but he was gone. She heard a noise from the right-hand passage and decided to head in the other direction.

Turn to **47**.

Derilion ducked and moved closer to the centre of the room, lowering her shield to get a better look at the adventurer. She didn't like the feeling the room gave off. It was far too quiet, the only noises being the ones she was making.

The adventurer was male, tall, and dressed in armour; his face turned away from her. She scanned his body for any obvious wounds, but he looked unharmed.

The cuff was within her reach, and beyond it, a short sword with an emerald encrusted hilt lay on the floor glistening in the light of the shield.

She could turn his body over to look at the face (turn to **594**), reach for the cuff (turn to **277**), head back to the wall and continue (turn to **13**) or reach for the sword (turn to **535**).

246

It was difficult to open the drawer, and Derilion ended up bracing herself on the throne and pulling at it with everything she had. Finally, the drawer opened, and inside she found a pendant with an eye on it (**+3w**).

Turn to **529**.

247

The Otistro slowly began to settle down, its quick movements gradually becoming a rhythmic sway, which Derilion thought was worse. Carefully, she retrieved the powder from the backpack and readied herself to throw it at the creature.

She would have to reveal herself a little to get a good shot, and she didn't want to receive another blow from the Otistro's tongue.

The hunter moved back a little into the shadows, raised herself and threw the powder in one quick motion.

Roll 2D6 for *Accuracy*.

If the test is successful, turn to **320**, otherwise, turn to **68**.

248

As the hunter continued toward the door, she realised the creature was mimicking her; when she moved, it moved.

She smiled at the creature, and after a moment, it tried to smile, too, which, in turn, made her laugh. The creature looked at Derilion for a moment before erupting with its deafening laughter.

The hunter hoped her instincts were correct as she reached the door. The creature met her there, and unsure what to do, did nothing.

Derilion stepped through the open door, still half-expecting it to grab her. When she turned around, she saw the creature waiting at the door, regarding her with simple confusion.

Derilion closed the door and stepped away.

Turn to **624**.

Derilion bent down and inspected the debris. The bones were shattered, with hardly a whole one between them, and most contained the teeth marks of small creatures.

The Lightbringer picked up some pieces of clothing and held them in front of her. The light from the shield showed rips and bloodstains on all of them, and Derilion noticed a similar pattern of holes which indicated a spiked trap. There was bound to be a trigger on the floor or wall nearby.

Off to her left, in the centre of the chamber, Derilion could see a dead adventurer lying on the floor. Whatever her choice, she had to do it quickly, to give Obishaa the best chance of survival.

She could set light to the clothes on the floor to clear the way (turn to **440**), take a closer look at the fallen adventurer (turn to **245**), or attempt to detect the trap (turn to **295**).

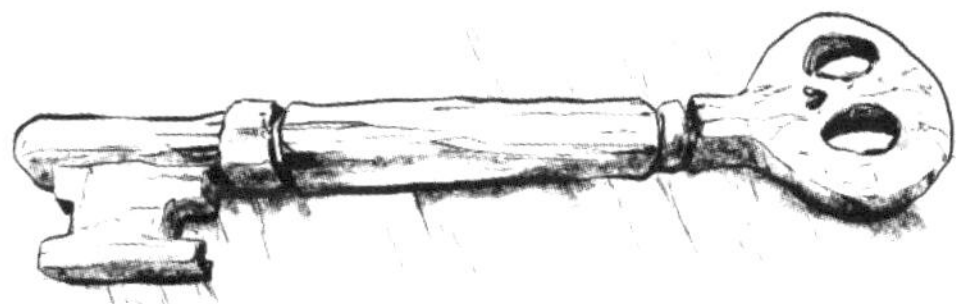

250

Derilion fetched the key she'd been given earlier and placed it in the keyhole. She turned it and heard the click of the mechanism unlocking the door.

She readied her sword and pushed it open. The room beyond was the size of a small cupboard. At its centre was a book on a plinth.

It could be a trap, she knew.

Pick up the book   Turn to **412**
Leave the book and go through the stone door   Turn to **197**

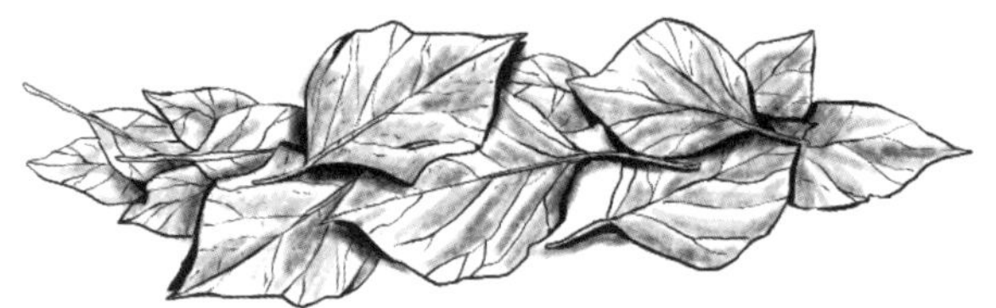

251

The passageway Derilion now found herself in was narrow, but at least she could see its ceiling, which was an improvement. She took a moment to breathe. She had survived the last attack like she had survived all the ones that had gone before, and she was better for it.

Rescuing Obishaa was going to be difficult, maybe even impossible, but she had dealt with the impossible before. She knew it was a case of tackling one problem at a time until there were no more problems left between herself and the goal.

Derilion stopped. In front of her in the softer dirt floor of the passage, the ground had been disturbed. To her experienced eye, it looked as if someone had buried something there.

Search the ground	Turn to **437**
Ignore it and press on	Turn to **75**

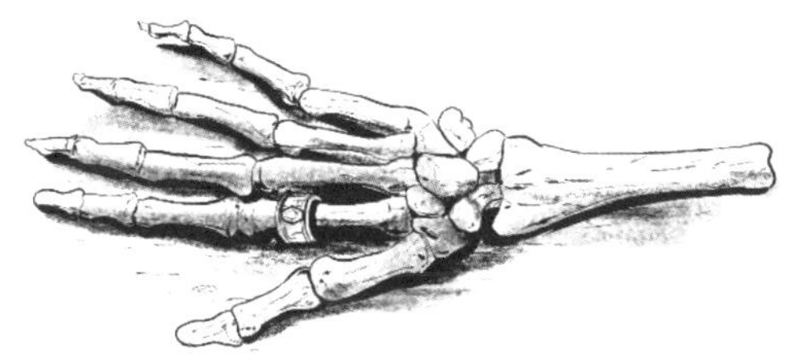

252

This was the way Holut had come, and by the look of it, he was more useful than he looked.

To the right, a large creature lay burnt to a crisp. From the smell in the air, it appeared it'd only recently been set alight. Derilion's stomach rumbled, but there wasn't time to eat.

Before her, clean stones paved the floor.

She could approach the creature (turn to **426**) or cross the stones to the door in front of her (turn to **179**).

253

The hunter headed straight to the next set of doors, not seeing the loose tile on the floor. As soon as she stepped on it, she heard a mechanical trigger and knew she'd just walked into a trap. Three arrows flew at her; one from the left, one from the right, and one head-on.

There was only time to block one with her shield.

Block the left arrow	Turn to **278**
Block the right arrow	Turn to **334**
Block the arrow in front	Turn to **392**

254

The hunter walked past the benches with their various experiments and headed towards the exit. She heard a noise behind her, and a woman's voice spoke.

"Well, we don't often see people in here," she said.

Turn to **615**.

255

The door opened, and Derilion heard someone enter the room. She peered through the slither of a gap where the wardrobe doors didn't quite meet and watched as a troll sat down at the table and began to eat the food.

Roll 2D6 and test for *Stealth*.

If the test is successful, turn to **97**, otherwise, turn to **623**.

256

Derilion went through the dwarf's pockets and recovered a gold watch (**+3w**) and a phial of clear liquid (**+2w**), which she could add to her backpack if she wanted.

Nearby, she could hear the assassin groaning in pain. She could try and help the assassin (turn to **617**), go to the elven hunter (turn to **390**) or head to the exit (turn to **74**).

257

The hunter put her sword under the lid of one of the smaller crates and prised it off without much effort.

Immediately, a dark shadow flew out of the box towards her.

Roll 2D6 and test for *Speed*.

If the test is successful, turn to **235**, otherwise, turn to **4**.

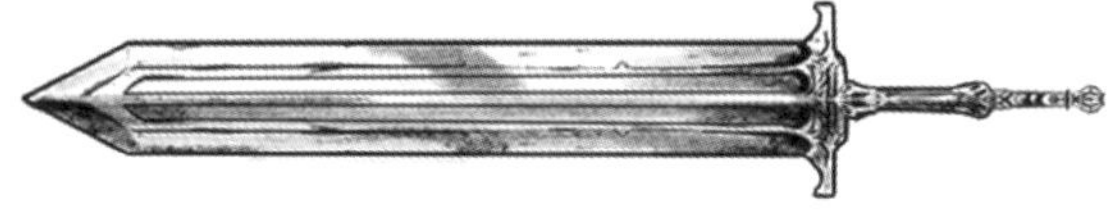

258

Derilion readied her shield just as another projectile flew towards her. It was aimed lower, this time, and the adventurer was able to deflect it onto the wall.

She gripped her sword and the straps of her shield, waiting for the creature to show itself, hoping she would win.

Derilion stood firm and listened as the sound of a crying child grew closer.

Turn to **267**.

"Please, come and sit," the girl said, indicating the chair opposite her. It might be a trap, Derilion thought, but it didn't feel like one.

"Why did the Maiden want you dead?" the hunter asked as she sat in the chair.

"She didn't. I do not die, but she would have wanted you dead, and it always pleases her twisted humour to have me do it."

"But you don't want to kill me, right?" the hunter asked.

"I don't want to kill anyone," she replied, shaking her head. "Which, in this place, makes me somewhat unique."

The girl briefly smiled and then returned to her drawing as if she'd run out of things to say. The next moment she looked back up.

"I expect you're wondering if I have anything you can steal," she said. Derilion almost laughed.

"Why would I think that?"

"Because I'm thinking it about you."

"How about we try trading," the Lightbringer suggested.

"What for?"

"Information."

"All right. What have you got?"

If she has them, Derilion could try trading the golden cuff (turn to **577**), the two parchments (turn to **237**), the glass jaw (turn to **489**) or something else (turn to **21**).

Derilion couldn't see an obvious way to open the door, but equally, she wasn't about to starve to death down here.

There were a couple of options available to her. She could try and pull the arrow out of the Cuddower (turn to **503**) or attempt to traverse the chasm by putting her back against one wall and her feet on the other and making her way across (turn to **453**).

"You tell the truth," the demon said. "For that, I will help you."

The demon recited an incantation, and Derilion saw black smoke start to swirl around her feet. She felt lighter.

"There," the demon said. "That should make you a little stealthier."

"Thank you." Add 1 to Derilion's *Stealth*.

"Now, a troll approaches," the demon said, pointing to the right-hand tunnel. "I suggest you leave that way."

Derilion nodded and set off in the way they suggested.

Turn to **47**.

262

She went to the Otistro and sliced it open, making sure there weren't any more horrors left to creep up on her. The smell was dreadful, but there was nothing else left alive. While looking, she saw some metal fragments (**+3w**) and picked them out.

They were bronze and looked like they may have come from a necklace. Derilion decided whether to keep them and left the room, hoping never to have to see it again.

Press on, turn to **482**.

263

The scorpion (**+4w**) remained still in the centre of the box. It seemed an odd object to keep, but perhaps the girl had some use of it.

Derilion could put it in her backpack if she wished. She scanned the room again. She could investigate the lamp (turn to **498**) or leave the room (turn to **29**).

264

"Stop!" Derilion shouted at them, in a language she hoped they understood.

The sprites looked surprised and dropped the rocks they held to the floor.

"Thank you," the hunter said.

Somewhere in her memory, she recalled sprites were magical creatures and thought they might be able to enchant her amulet.

She crouched and pointed at her amulet.

"Enchantment?" she asked. They nodded at her.

"Accuracy," they said. "For two objects."

If Derilion needed the enchantment, she could give them two items to receive it.

Whether or not she took the enchantment, she bid them farewell and moved on.

Turn to **226**.

265

Before she knew it, the man she thought had been dead flung her to the ground.

"Get out of this room," he demanded. "This is where I live!"

Derilion nodded in agreement and went quickly into the morgue.

Turn to **342**.

266

Derilion approached the closed coffins. There was definitely a noise coming from one or both of them. As the hunter got closer, the sound quietened, and she had an impulse to run her sword through the side of both.

She resisted, and instead, stood still next to the first coffin so she could listen. She heard nothing.

The Lightbringer didn't want to open the coffins, but some inquisitive side of her thought there might be something inside worth finding. Equally, she could head out of one of the exits.

Open the nearest coffin	Turn to **557**
Investigate the second coffin	Turn to **539**
Continue straight on	Turn to **537**
Exit the door to the left	Turn to **178**

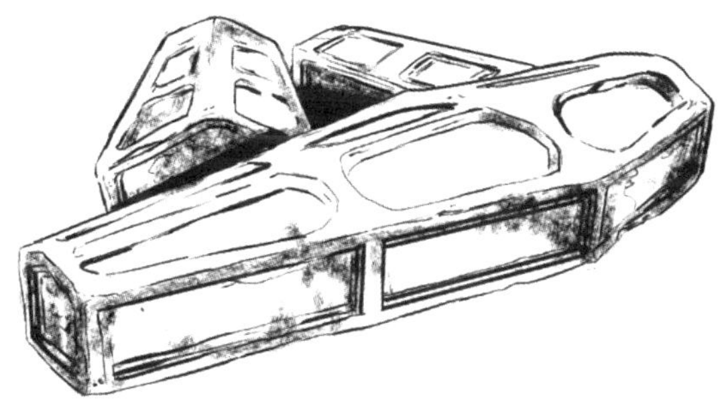

Something struck Derilion's leg. She looked down and saw a sharp spine sticking through her armour, about the length of her forearm. Quickly, she bent and pulled it out, throwing it behind her.

The sobbing sound continued, and out of the darkness, a creature appeared, with a gaping hole where the mouth should be. It stood around five feet and had no other facial features. Its four arms were little more than claws, tethered onto long bones which it used to move.

Spines protruded from its body, and it was these it was firing at her. It opened and closed its mouth in time with the crying child noise. She had never seen anything like it and never wanted to, again.

	Speed	Accuracy	Damage	Health
Lure	5	7	2	8

If Derilion won, turn to **231**.

"Thanks," the creature said, looking at the gift in its hand and unable to hide its annoyance.

It wasn't going to get out of its chair, so Derilion leant forward and took the key.

Turn to **353**.

269

Derilion went to the wall, placed her back against one side, and lifted her legs, one after the other, onto the opposite wall.

Slowly, she moved along the wall towards the open door. From below, she began to hear scuttling noises indicating something down there was watching her, waiting for her to fall.

About a third of the way across, the hunter lost her footing.

Roll 2D6 and test for *Strength.*

If the test is successful, turn to **648**, otherwise, turn to **94**.

270

There was a long way to travel to reach the door, but the hunter didn't think it was impossible. Carefully, she made sure all her belongings were securely fastened close to her body and then began creeping forward.

Roll 2D6 and test for *Stealth.*

If the test is successful, turn to **60**, otherwise, turn to **457**.

271

"I'm here to kill monsters," Derilion said.

"My name is Grom," the voice replied. "Those monsters are here because the Pajoli put them here. It's not their fault they need to eat or defend themselves. Now you will have to face me."

Out of the blackness, a thick rope-like tendril appeared and knocked Derilion off her feet.

Turn to **432**.

Derilion searched the desk. It was old but sturdy, and she had to put a lot of weight behind breaking the lock on the drawer.

Once inside, she found a small triangular wooden box (**+3w**), an orange potion (**+2w**) and a bag of dried fruit (**+2w**), which she could add to her backpack.

There was something else about the desk she couldn't quite see and decided to try and work out what it was. Clearing her mind, she pushed out her senses to see if there was anything there.

Roll 2D6 for *Detection*.

If the test was successful, turn to **621**, otherwise, turn to **32**.

Derilion sucked at the wound on the back of her hand, spitting the blood she drew out onto the floor until she could taste no more blood.

Exhausted, she waited to see if she'd been successful, and after only a couple of seconds, she began to feel dizzy.

Derilion cursed her stupidity, and desperately tried to think of something she might be able to use.

If the hunter found an orange potion, she could try that, turn to **211**, otherwise, turn to **224**.

274

Derilion retrieved the lens from her backpack and held it up to her eye. She looked at the book, and as she did, the words changed on the cover and she could read its title, 'Disassembling Enemies'. She opened the spell book and saw each page was dedicated to a spell. Derilion could add the book to her backpack if she wished (**+5w**) or place it back on the shelf.

Her options were narrowing. She could either investigate the lamp (turn to **498**), investigate the box, (turn to **214**) or leave the room, (turn to **29**).

275

The hunter quickly raised her shield in front of her face for protection. She didn't know who this Ashingya was, and she wasn't going to take any chances.

Turn to **44**.

276

Enraged, the hunter thrust her sword into the nearest warlock and was surprised to feel it hit the stone behind him with no resistance. Derilion reached out and waved her hand in the warlock. They were just magical projections.

"Where are you?" she asked.

"Keeping Obishaa safe," they said. "In Crystalfall."

The hunter lost control of her anger and kicked over the thrones. When the last, empty one, fell, there was a blinding flash of light, and she found herself outside the entrance of the cave.

Turn to **600**.

277

Derilion reached out and touched the cuff. Without warning, a scorpion scuttered from beneath it and stung her hand. She swung at it with her shield, but it had already moved out of sight.

She looked at the small puncture wound, concerned it might be poisonous. The hunter sucked at her hand, spitting the blood she retrieved onto the floor. Beyond that, there wasn't much else she could do. Make a note of the sting on the adventure sheet.

The Lightbringer removed the cuff and placed it over her arm (**+4w**). To her surprise, it fitted. Not just that, it made her feel better. Now she could get a better look at it, and she saw it was engraved with a ruby eyed dragon.

Make a note of the cuff on the inventory and add 1 point to Derilion's *Accuracy* total while she wears it.

Pleased with her find, Derilion headed back to the wall and continued.

Turn to **13**.

278

Derilion twisted to deflect the arrow from the left and watched it glance harmlessly off her shield.

The arrow from the front shattered as it hit her armour, but the arrow from the right went through the hunter's leg armour and hit her thigh. Deduct 3 from her *Health*.

If Derilion survived, she removed the arrow and dressed the wound as well as she could. Deduct 1 from her *Stealth*.

Turn to **568**.

279

Against her better judgement, Derilion searched the boxes but found nothing but splinters. Relieved, she was about to go, when something glittered on the rock wall.

She stepped closer and saw what appeared to be a blue gem embedded in the rocks. It felt like another trap, but perhaps she was getting paranoid.

Looking at her various options, three seemed to stand out.

Inspect the gem	Turn to **127**
Use her sword to prise the gem	Turn to **346**
Proceed around the corner	Turn to **587**

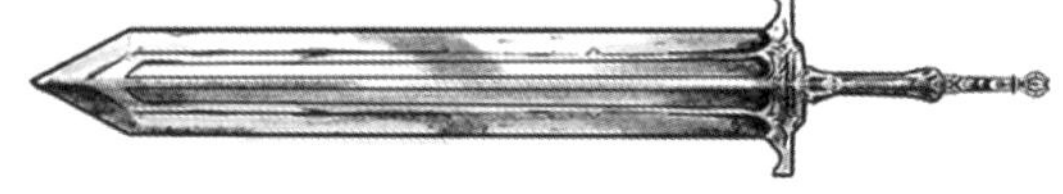

280

Derilion stepped forward and put her foot on the lead tile and waited to see if she'd made the right choice.

"Very well," the voice said. The feel of the blade went, and the hunter turned to see a dark shape behind her. From the floor, lead ran like water up its body and formed a suit of armour around it.

It raised its sword in front of its face.

"To the death," it said.

Derilion stood back and unsheathed her sword.

	Speed	Accuracy	Damage	Health
Lead Armour	8	7	2	9

If Derilion wins, turn to **540**.

281

Derilion searched her backpack for something to use against the creature.

If she picked up the red or the green potion, she could use one of those. Otherwise, if she had a purse of coins, she could offer that.

Otherwise, she must fight.

Drink the red potion	Turn to **292**
Drink the green potion	Turn to **588**
Offer the purse of coins	Turn to **555**
Fight the Cuddowcr	Turn to **485**

282

Derilion inspected the ground as best she could. The more she looked, the more disturbances she found.

Derilion can either search again (turn to **355**) or move on (turn to **480**).

The hunter rolled forward without looking back. Behind her, a heavy object crashed into the ground where she'd been standing.

She turned around and saw a pale man standing by one of the coffins. He wore flowing purple robes and an unhealthy smile.

"Very agile," he said as he looked her up and down. "An excellent subject."

"Subject?" the hunter asked.

"Don't let it bother you," he replied. Derilion saw he was holding two of the crude tools that'd been on the slab. He meant to fight her.

Turn to **177**.

284

Derilion held her breath and swung the sword as close to her hand as she dared. It worked, severing the vines, but she managed to graze her arm, causing 1 damage to her *Health*. She watched in agony as the vines recoiled back into the thick of the door.

Quickly, she bound her hand with some cloth and tied it off.

The hunter thought about her next move quickly.

Try and set light to the door	Turn to **229**
Use some explosive powder	Turn to **41**

285

"I don't need one of those," Derilion told her.

"In that case," she said, "Take this."

The dust swirled before the hunter, solidifying in front of her. As she watched, a replica of the pendant formed in mid-air.

"In case you need to deceive someone," Ashingya explained. "I advise you to wear it instead of the real one."

Derilion took the fake pendant and placed it around her neck, putting the real one in her pocket.

"Thank you," the hunter said, but Ashingya had turned and was heading toward the kiln. She had the distinct feeling Ashingya wanted to be left alone.

Turn to **624**.

286

"Take this gold cuff," Derilion suggested, holding it outstretched in her trembling hands.

The male troll took a step forward and took it (**-4w**). He held it in his palm and slowly closed his hand around it, crushing it.

"Gold is only valuable to stupid adventurers," it said and tossed it over his shoulder. "We have no use for it down here! Such an offer disrespects us."

The two trolls advanced on the hunter, and between them, she didn't stand a hope. Within seconds, the Lightbringer lay dead on the floor, and the trolls were ransacking the rest of her belongings.

287

Derilion approached the stone throne. It looked solid enough, and the seat was well worn, but she noticed a small section at the front sticking out further than the rest.

It appeared to be a secret drawer or compartment.

Try to open the drawer	Turn to **246**
Eat some of the food	Turn to **238**
Leave the room	Turn to **529**

288

As fast as she was able to react, the hunter felt the knife slice through her clothes and pierce her skin, causing 2 damage to her *Health*.

She headed for the door, hoping to outpace the girl.

Turn to **131**.

289

Derilion plunged her sword into the creature and watched it collapse. She was near exhausted and knew she still had a long way left to travel. She had two main options to choose from.

Inspect the Otistro	Turn to **262**
Leave the chamber	Turn to **482**

290

As the hunter sat on the floor, the creature did, too. She waited to see what would happen, and so did the creature. It was an odd stalemate.

After a while, Derilion lay down on her back and closed her eyes. Within a couple of seconds, she heard the creature trying to do the same.

The hunter waited for a few minutes, and when she looked over the creature had gone.

Quietly, she got up and left.

Turn to **624**.

291

Derilion scanned the area as best she could in the poor light. She couldn't see any obvious traps, but that didn't mean there weren't any. There were plenty of places a trigger could be.

The Lightbringer looked around and settled on three possible options. She could set light to clothes (turn to **440**), take a closer look at fallen adventurer (turn to **245**), or press on and hope for the best (turn to **167**).

292

Derilion uncorked the potion and drank the contents in one draft. Immediately, a tingling sensation developed in the tips of her fingers, before spreading up the hunter's arms. With horror, she realised she was no longer able to feel her hands, and she was helpless to stop its journey through her entire body.

She sat heavily on the floor. The Cuddower stopped approaching, cocked its head to the side and looked quizzically at what was happening to her. The Lightbringer waited to die, but it did not arrive. Instead, a feeling of hope washed over her. She looked at the Cuddower once more, and now she was certain she could defeat it with her sword and shield.

The creature watched with faint amusement as she stood and closed in with her sword aloft. Before she'd had a chance to swing her weapon, however, the creature struck her with a fatal blow she didn't see coming.

Derilion fell to the floor, dead before her head hit the stone.

293

The hunter realised the water was nothing but an illusion spell, and she was standing on dry ground, crouched over a dummy made to look like a body.

Such a spell, she knew, required a runestone to be left here, which might be of benefit.

She searched the dummy and recovered a small lead weight (**+2w**), before mulling over her choices.

Search for the runestone	Turn to **5**
Continue along the corridor	Turn to **547**

294

Tired from the fight, Derilion paused to catch her breath. She searched the mortician and found a necklace made from teeth around his neck (**+1w**).

If Derilion opened the second coffin, turn to **23**, otherwise, turn to **689**.

295

Derilion took a moment to collect her thoughts; absolute calm helped her focus. She shut her eyes and concentrated, and when she was as close as she was going to be, she opened them again and inspected the floor.

As an adventurer, she'd spent many years treading the dusty roads, traipsing through forgotten swamps and picking her way through dangerous forests, and knew the makings of a trap when she saw one.

Roll 2D6 for *Detection.*

If the test is successful, turn to **151**. Otherwise, turn to **291**.

296

Looking inside the chest, the hunter saw a plethora of plant leaves carefully stored. She wasn't sure what most of them were, but there were two plants she thought she recognised.

One had a blue tinge to them and the other a yellow tinge.

Roll 2D6 and test for *Detection.*

If the test is successful, turn to **99**, otherwise, turn to **240**.

297

"Oh, dear," the girl said with a smile. Derilion had the distinct impression she'd wanted a fight all along. The hunter watched the witch get up from her seat. The fight was going to be difficult.

	Speed	Accuracy	Damage	Health
Witch	10	10	2	8

If Derilion wins, turn to **445**.

298

Othwig went and placed the item in the chest.

"Now, in return," she said, making her way back to Derilion, "I can enchant your necklace with a *Speed* charm if you need one."

If the hunter needed the charm, turn to **513**, otherwise, turn to **54**.

299

Derilion approached the Sprites, sword raised. As she got closer, they picked up their weapons to retaliate.

The three Sprites have the following attributes, and the hunter must fight each one in turn. She incurs 1 damage to her *Health* for every living Frost Sprite not being attacked each round.

	Speed	Accuracy	Damage	Health
Sprite	5	8	1	4

If Derilion wins, she has the following choices.

Search the Sprites	Turn to **658**
Search their home	Turn to **367**
Ignore them and continue	Turn to **226**

300

The smell of the next room made the hunter feel nauseous. It was a small anteroom for what appeared to be a morgue she could see through an opening in front of her.

Shelves lined the anteroom with a cadaver resting on each one. Many looked like adventurers who had died in the dungeon. While most of the bodies were stripped and dressed in a simple cloth, three of them were still clothed.

Derilion wasn't sure whether to investigate the bodies (turn to **667**) or head into the morgue (turn to **144**).

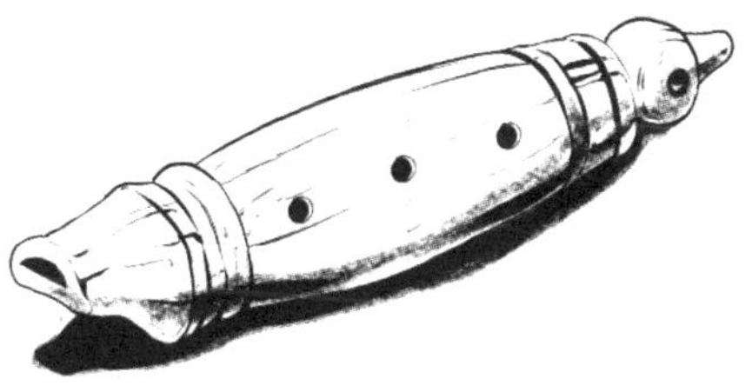

301

Derilion got a glimpse of something, a feeling of an object in the earth in front of her. Using her sword, she dug into the soft ground.

Almost immediately, she struck something metal. She forced the blade underneath and worked it up gradually, revealing a long, hollow, metal tube.

She used some of her water to wash it, clearing off the excess mud to reveal a brass flute (**+2w**), ornately decorated. She put it to her lips and blew, but no noise came out. It was probably thick with mud and sediment inside.

Turn to **323**.

302

"I will never sit on the throne," Derilion told them.

"Very well," the men said. "Then, you will die."

From somewhere within the room came an unsettling rumble. Derilion stood sword drawn, and shield raised. She was not going to give up now.

Turn to **202**.

303

The hunter kept her eyes firmly fixed on the woman as she retrieved one of the powders and held it aloft.

"Stay where you are," she told the woman, who either couldn't hear her or pretended not to. Instead, she turned slowly to face the hunter. Except there was no face there. There wasn't anything. It was like the whole front of her head had been scooped out, and all she could see from the front was the back of the woman's skull.

Derilion found herself both repulsed and deeply fascinated.

"I don't want to hurt you," the hunter said.

The woman started to stand, her limbs unfurling to unnatural proportions.

"Maybe you don't," the woman said. "But I want to hurt you."

Derilion threw the powder at the woman.

Roll 2D6 and test for *Accuracy*.

If the test is successful, turn to **193**, otherwise, turn to **691**.

304

The Lightbringer approached the larger crates, hoping they might have weapons or armour she could use, but when she prised one of them open, it contained an empty cauldron.

She opened another of the larger crates to find a similar cauldron, and she assumed they were all the same. There wasn't anything else of interest about them.

She looked around the room, trying to decide the best move.

Open the medium crates	Turn to **55**
Open the small crates	Turn to **257**
Open the tiny crates	Turn to **138**
Head for the door	Turn to **354**

The hunter approached the middle table, upon which sat a circular glass container with liquid collecting in it.

"Go on, take a sip," Othwig said.

Derilion picked the container up, sniffed it and took a sip.

The liquid burned her mouth and throat. Her face began to bloat, and her throat closed, making it impossible to breathe.

She fell to the floor and looked up towards Othwig for help. The witch just looked down at her, smiling.

"Oh, good," she heard her say to herself. "That looks like the perfect consistency."

Derilion's adventure ends here.

306

The hunter shifted on her feet. She didn't trust the man, but there was no-one else there to help her.

"Hello," she said softly, not wanting to startle him. She knew if she caught someone by surprise, they were more likely to attack than comply.

The man stopped praying and looked at her with no expression.

"Leave now," he growled. "You have done enough harm."

Derilion frowned. She hadn't done anything to hurt this man, yet there was something about his tone which scared her. The rumbling sound continued to grow, and the Lightbringer watched him close his eyes and put his hands together once again.

Talk to the man some more	Turn to **586**
Take a look at the bones	Turn to **589**
Inspect the boxes	Turn to **236**
Investigate the noise	Turn to **57**
Leave the room immediately	Turn to **221**

307

Slowly, the dark figure filled with colour. From the horns on its head and shoulders, Derilion knew it was a demon.

It smiled at her. Demons were cunning creatures, and the Lightbringer knew to be careful. It stayed still, testing the hunter, seeing what her next move would be.

Ignore him and head left	Turn to **81**
Attack the demon	Turn to **643**
Speak to the demon	Turn to **474**

<h1 style="text-align:center">308</h1>

"I will accept your quest."

"Very well," she said. "You will need to prevent my friend Ashingya from attacking you. To do this, always keep eye contact with her. Never look away. Do this, and you will be safe."

"Where will I find the vase?" Derilion asked.

"It will be obvious when you find it."

As she faded from view, a door opened in the side of the wall. The hunter left the chapel before the door closed again.

Turn to **91**.

<h1 style="text-align:center">309</h1>

Derilion used her sword to dislodge the stones in the wall as carefully as possible, not wanting to damage Zalixa.

The first three stones fell without incident, but when the hunter went to loosen the fourth, the blade slipped between the rocks, and she heard the girl scream.

"Zalixa?" Derilion called.

The hunter sped up, hoping to reach Zalixa in time to save her, but when she removed the last stone, the girl fell limply to the ground.

Derilion checked for a pulse and found a very faint one. As she held the girl, she watched Zalixa's body turn to water which flowed down the passage towards the stream.

The Lightbringer could either investigate the wall (turn to **592**) or search Zalixa's clothes (turn to **567**).

<h1 style="text-align:center">310</h1>

The Lightbringer knew what it felt like to be cooped up in a small area for a long time. She opened the remaining tiny crates and watched as the mice found the anonymity of the shadows.

She was about to leave when one of the small crates split open, and a werecat jumped out. Derilion readied to defend herself against the tenacious foe, but it was more interested in the mice, and after glancing at the hunter, it skulked off looking for them.

Derilion decided now would be the right time to leave the room (turn to **502**).

<h1 style="text-align:center">311</h1>

"Hello," Derilion said, staying where she was.

"Look at anything here," the girl said, not looking up from her book. "But don't take anything, however valuable."

The hunter opened her mouth to reply, but the girl put a finger to her lips and hushed her.

To search the room, turn to **162**, otherwise, to leave, turn to **29**.

<h1 style="text-align:center">312</h1>

Derilion went through the doorway into the next room. Something was beginning to nag, but she couldn't put her finger on it. As she entered, she heard music, though she couldn't see anyone playing an instrument. The room was as dark, and shadows played on the walls from the firelight from her shield.

As her eyes became accustomed to the lack of light, she made out a black shape moving quickly towards the back of the room. She wondered whether she should wait and see (turn to **696**) or leave the room (turn to **131**).

313

Derilion kicked the blueish leaves into the pool and watched as the water around them turned a brighter blue. The Elemental roared and grew slightly stronger before her eyes.

Add 4 to its *Health*.

Has the hunter kicked four items in yet? If not, she can try another (turn to **633**). If she has, she must face the Elemental (turn to **107**).

314

Derilion felt daunted by the task before her, but she had to try. The Elemental was quick, and the hunter had grown slower since entering the caves.

She ran, changing direction and hoping to dodge the enemy. However fast she ran the Elemental was a match for her.

Just as she thought it was hopeless, she got a second burst of energy and managed to dodge the raking blade of the Elemental's sword as it swung for her.

She rolled, stood and turned in one fell swoop, ready to face the creature.

At the pool, turn to **633**.

315

Derilion felt daunted by the task before her, but she had to try. The Elemental was quick, and the hunter was exhausted by her exploits in the caves.

She ran, changing direction and hoping to dodge the enemy. However fast she ran, the Elemental was a match for her. Just before reaching the pool's edge, the Elemental caught her with its sword and caused 5 damage to her *Health*.

If she was still alive, she had to face the creature.

Turn to **107**.

316

The hunter placed the bow back into its cradle, hoping it might calm the creature. Unfortunately, it only seemed to bolster its confidence.

Derilion unsheathed her sword, but perhaps there might still be time to talk to it.

Fight the Cuddower	Turn to **485**
Try and talk to the Cuddower	Turn to **672**

317

Derilion wrestled her arms away from the dwarf as quickly as she could, all the while feeling her strength ebb away.

Subtract 2 from her *Health*.

If she survived, the Lightbringer stepped back and watched as he stood, drew his axe, ready to fight.

Turn to **122**.

318

Derilion's hand touched the door, and the water around her vanished. She looked around and saw she had been standing on the floor the whole time, the water just an enchantment.

She felt shaken to have been duped so easily and decided not to hang around. Twisting the rusted handle, she was relieved to find it unlocked and went through into the next room without incident.

Turn to **119**.

319

The hunter took a couple of steps into the room and stopped.

"Closer than that," the voice said. Derilion moved a small step forward. "No closer. Not until you show yourself."

"Very well," the voice replied. "Try not to scream."

Derilion grew concerned about exactly what she was facing. From out of the dark, she heard a slithering sound. Something was getting closer.

She could stay where she was (turn to **580**) or leave (turn to **378**).

320

Derilion watched the powder hit the structure beneath the Otistro, detonating on impact. The creature screamed and fell silent; it must have been its weak point.

Turn to **545**.

321

Derilion waited to see if he'd come over. She didn't know what she'd do if he did, but thankfully she didn't have to find out. She saw him shrug and turn back to the food.

After a few minutes, the troll finished eating, got up and approached the same door the hunter had entered. Instead of going through the door, he locked it and looked at the wardrobe.

"Come out," he said. "I know you're in there."

The hunter sheepishly opened the door and stepped out. Did Derilion already meet the troll?

If so, turn to **661**, otherwise, turn to **35**.

322

Almost immediately, something came through. A bad taste in her mouth, like metal or blood, perhaps both. She tried to probe deeper to find out what it meant, but nothing else came.

She'd have to either speak to him or move on.

She's on a mission for herself	Turn to **79**
She's on a mission to help the Pajoli	Turn to **382**
Say nothing and keep going	Turn to **595**

323

The hunter made her way back along the tunnel to where the bugs had attacked her, and she was pleased to see they hadn't returned. As she approached the centre of the room, a dark figure appeared to step out of the shadows and block her way. She waited to see what would happen.

Turn to **307**.

324

Derilion peered into the glass ball but didn't understand what she was seeing. Was it a face from the past or one from the future?

There was a noise behind her, and she turned just as the skeleton landed a blow. Deduct 2 from the Lightbringer's *Health*.

If Derilion survived, she must fight the skeleton (turn to **37**).

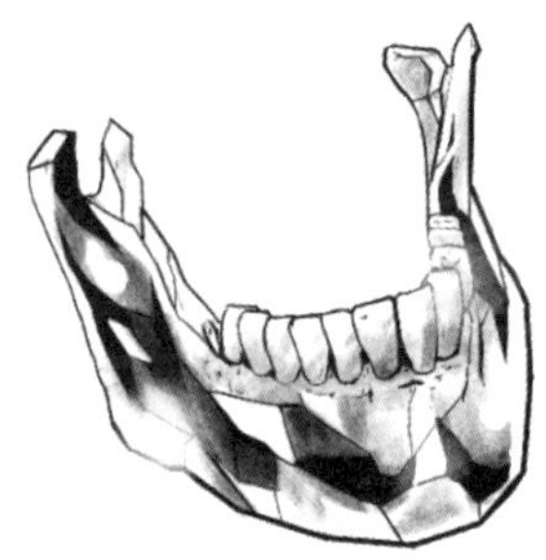

325

The hunter looked at the child and knew she was a witch. Perhaps she was once like Obishaa before the Pajoli got to her.

Whatever her powers may be, Derilion didn't want to test them. She could match most people's strength, but with magic, she was all but powerless. Fortunately, she hadn't opened any of the boxes.

"I didn't open any of them," the hunter said.

The girl looked at her for a few moments before sighing.

"Very well. Do you have a stone with circles on?" she asked.

If Derilion did and wanted to show her, turn to **359**, otherwise, turn to **297**.

The tiles that made up the lightning symbol were filled with bronze, lead and copper metals which made the emblem shine in the light from the shield.

Three raised tiles sat at the centre of the symbol - one each of the three metals. One of them might be her way out of there. Or maybe none of them. As she tried to decide, she heard a voice behind her say "Choose" and felt the tip of a sword in her back.

Press the stone with lead   Turn to **280**
Press the stone with copper   Turn to **59**
Press the stone with bronze   Turn to **427**

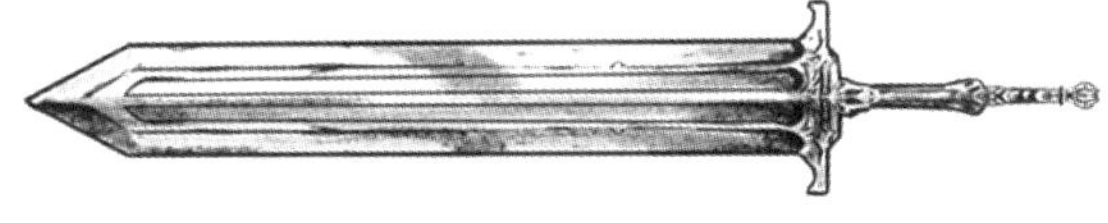

327

The hunter moved along the wall over the stream, gripping onto the thin stone. It was hard going, and her arms began to ache.

Is Derilion wearing gauntlets?

If so, turn to **654**, otherwise, turn to **69**.

328

Derilion moved cautiously through the passageway, keeping low and testing each step with a prod of her sword. She could've been faster but wanted to be safe. Being dead was no use to Obishaa.

After a few moments, the hunter thought she heard a noise off to one side. She stopped and waited.

Turn to **409**.

329

Derilion dodged the drip and watched as it burned angrily on the floor. She was lucky it hadn't landed on her face.

"Well, that's enough of that," said a woman's voice behind her.

Turn to **615**.

330

Try as she might, Derilion could not see any obvious traps. She began to move forward, concentrating on her feet.

Two steps on, her hand brushed against a loose stone in the wall, and before she knew what was happening, she fell backwards as a doorway opened behind her. The hunter braced herself for an impact. Fortunately, she landed on her back, undamaged.

"Quickly," came a male voice behind her. "You must block the door."

Roll 2D6 and test for *Speed*.

If the test is successful, turn to **11**, otherwise, turn to **520**.

331

"Very well," the warrior said. "You are wise to trust no one here. Fare thee well in your coming challenges."

Derilion watched the warrior slowly fade in front of her. Now, she had little choice but to inspect the lightning tiles (turn to **326**).

332

Unsure what it wanted, Derilion upended her backpack onto the floor. The creature watched her possessions hit the ground, seemingly scanning for something specific.

Has Derilion found the blue egg?

If so, turn to **652**, otherwise, turn to **62**.

333

"How can you help me?" Derilion asked.

She waited while the shadows formed new words.

"I can make you harder to see."

The hunter frowned.

"Would it hurt?" she asked.

"No," the words replied. "It wouldn't hurt at all."

The Lightbringer could either accept its request (turn to **499**) or ignore it (turn to **360**).

334

Derilion blocked the arrow to the right, which embedded itself into her shield, and twisted her body as much as she could to avoid the other two.

The arrow from the left glanced across her back. The one from the front hit her shoulder, and due to its age, splintered on impact.

Deduct 1 from Derilion's *Health*. If she survived, she removed the arrow from the shield and pressed on (turn to **568**).

335

Wondering whether she was losing her mind to try such a move, Derilion approached the chests. There were three in all, and carefully she attempted to lift the lids of the first two, with no luck.

The third, however, was unlocked and contained a small blue egg (**+2w**). The hunter had never seen an egg like it.

The breathing pattern changed in the sleeping trolls, and Derilion thought they might be waking up. Not wanting to come face-to-face with them, she took the option to leave the room and head back to choose another route.

Turn to **698**.

336

Derilion moved as fast as she could to catch the ball, given her circumstances. She felt the cool glass touch her fingertips, but that was as close as she got, before it tumbled onto the ground, smashing into hundreds of pieces.

Derilion turned to face the skeleton, who was almost upon her.

Turn to **37**.

The skeleton saw the orb in Derilion's hands and stopped immediately. It waited for a couple of moments and then began to back away as if it was afraid of it. Derilion went to the door still holding the orb, not knowing what to do next.

Fortunately, as she approached, she heard the lock mechanism click and was able to open the door and walk out of the room.

She made sure she closed the door behind her. She can take the orb with her (**+6w**) or leave it on the floor.

She could now investigate the door on the left (turn to **626**) or move on to the next set of doors (turn to **568**).

338

"I'll trade with you," Derilion said, hoisting the backpack from her shoulders and onto the floor in front of her.

"Excellent," Othwig said. "I love it when I can trade something."

The hunter looked through the backpack, trying to decide what to offer.

Moss	Turn to **512**
Explosive powder	Turn to **163**
A stone with circles	Turn to **50**
Yellowish leaves	Turn to **398**
Bluish leaves	Turn to **463**
Something else	Turn to **671**
Nothing to trade	Turn to **484**

339

Something felt odd, but Derilion couldn't tell what. Carefully, she stepped on the first stone, then the second, all the while keeping one eye on the creature, which watched her progress.

When the hunter stepped on the third stone, she heard a click. The stone lifted and threw her across the room in the direction of the creature.

Derilion landed awkwardly, taking 1 damage to her *Health*.

If she was still alive, she must fight the creature.

	Speed	*Accuracy*	*Damage*	*Health*
Creature	6	9	2	13

If Derilion wins, turn to **426**.

340

Derilion thought about her next move. She had no way to know what she had done in the past to cause this punishment.

She figured if the Pajoli were this frightened of her, then perhaps she should be even more afraid.

"Sorry," Derilion said. "I cannot trust you."

The woman's voice in her head started to plead, but Derilion stepped away, and it reduced to a whisper and then nothing at all.

The hunter couldn't help everyone, she knew. She was there for Obishaa.

Turn to **587**.

341

The chamber grew quiet, and Derilion knew the creature would attack. She took a breath and rolled backwards as best she could. Something pierced her shoulder, and she almost cried out with the pain.

The adventurer reached behind her and felt the end of whatever had punctured her flesh. She clenched her teeth and pulled. It came out easily enough, but the pain nearly made her faint.

Still crouched, she took a couple of steps backwards and looked at what had punctured her. It was a shard of yellow crystal, like the end of a broken stalactite (+3w).

An amber-like substance hit the ground in front of her. Derilion needed no other warning and turned and ran.

Within a few feet, she found an exit.

Turn to **251**.

<h1 style="text-align:center">342</h1>

The morgue seemed to have a different atmosphere. The noise sounded dulled, and the air was heavy. She wanted to leave.

She stood where she was and looked around. Over to her left, against the wall, sat a wooden chest. Next to it, an elevated slab had crude tools laid out ready for an autopsy.

Nearby to her right, two closed coffins huddled against the edge of the wall. There were two visible two exits; one straight on, and one to her left.

Derilion thought over her choices, trying to ignore the feeling she was being watched.

Investigate the chest	Turn to **610**
Investigate the coffins	Turn to **266**
Investigate the slab	Turn to **470**
Exit straight on	Turn to **636**
Exit to the left	Turn to **178**

<h1 style="text-align:center">343</h1>

Derilion moved backwards, away from the crying noise, which continued to grow, to taunt her, as she retreated.

Another projectile whistled through the darkness, this one finding its target. The adventurer called out as the spine embedded itself into her thigh. Pain radiated out from the wound, even as another spine hit her shoulder, throwing her head up.

She wanted to escape, but now the crying was louder. The hunter tried to see where the creature was, but her vision was blurry. She saw a shape approaching, but just as it was coming into view, one last spine buried itself into her left eye, and she fell backwards, dead.

344

The adventurer inspected the necklace before throwing it to the ground. As it hit the floor, lightning arced from the centre, hitting Derilion in the chest, knocking her backwards and somehow paralysing her.

She watched the lightning hit the adventurer, but instead of harming him, it made him younger.

"You," he said with disdain. "Are an adventurer so foolish she does not deserve to live."

He reached down and gripped the hunter's body, crushing the air out of her, ending her life with Derilion helpless to respond.

345

Derilion inspected the wall. The rocks here, while similar, seemed less natural. She put her hands to the stones and tried to dig one away. It was difficult, but not impossible.

As the Lightbringer rested, she heard the faint sound of someone calling out. It was impossible to make sense of what they were saying, but whoever it was, sounded in trouble.

Derilion wondered whether she should talk to the wall (turn to **659**) or ignore it and press on (turn to **487**).

346

Derilion stepped up and placed the blade of her sword by the top of the gem. She paused; certain she'd just heard a voice coming from nearby.

The hunter waited, listening to see if the voice would come again. When all was silent, she placed the blade to the gem once more. The voice returned louder.

"Leave me alone!" it shouted directly into her head.

Derilion stepped back, and the voice was no more.

Confused, and a little scared, the hunter decided it was time to move on.

Turn to **587**.

347

"No," Derilion said. "I've had enough fighting for one day."

The troll shrugged.

"Good," it said, and went and sat at the table. It surveyed its food hungrily.

Did Derilion eat some of the troll's food?

If so, turn to **217**, otherwise, turn to **641**.

348

Derilion retrieved the rope and placed it over a boulder as she slid past.

It held, and the hunter came to an abrupt stop. She looked over the lip of the steps. She should have enough rope to lower herself down safely.

Carefully, she went over the edge, and, one step at a time, descended to the floor below without incident.

She tried to dislodge the rope, but it was stuck fast around the boulder, so she left it where it was (**-5w**) and headed towards the only exit she could see.

Continue to **190**.

Derilion took another step closer and watched the flickering and the water, and an odd notion occurred to her. The gem was *crying*.

That wasn't just any water, they were tears, and the flickering, the twinkle, was the blue of an iris, moving.

"How can I help?" the hunter asked.

The words 'wash me' came into Derilion's mind. The Lightbringer retrieved her water and a cloth, and carefully washed the gem, clearing the years of grime that had built up.

Derilion stood back and gasped. She could see the eye behind the gem. Instinctively, the hunter used the cloth and began to wash around the eye. The grime was far thicker here as if the crying had been the only thing keeping it from being completely covered.

She saw a face emerge. A woman, no older than thirty years, was looking back at her. She was smiling. Derilion kept washing the cave wall, finally revealing a woman encased in the blue gem-like substance.

"My name is Corzen. I can be free if you'll forgive me," the woman spoke into the hunter's mind.

"Forgive you for what?"

"Past transgressions. Simple forgiveness will free me. That was my curse."

Derilion took a moment to decide the best option.

Forgive Corzen	Turn to **576**
Deny Corzen	Turn to **340**
Ignore Corzen and move on	Turn to **587**

350

The hunter was at a loss to understand what was happening. She began to panic and headed as fast as she could to the end of the passageway.

The water returned, and once again, she had to swim to move forward.

Turn to **682**.

351

Derilion realised speed might be her best ally in this situation. She stopped for a moment, waiting for the perfect opportunity. She didn't have to wait long. She watched as the creature blinked slowly and took her chance.

Roll 2D6 and test for *Speed*.

If the test is successful, turn to **481**, otherwise, turn to **100**.

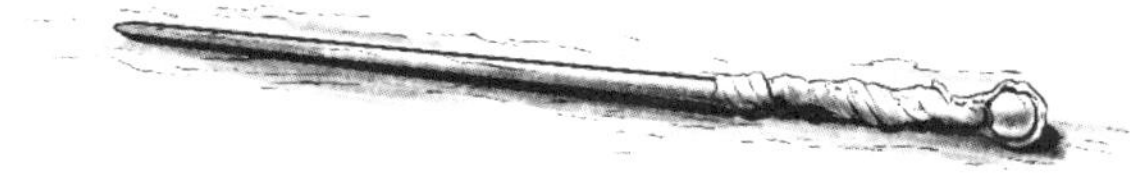

352

Derilion walked past the thrones keeping an eye on the warlocks. She searched for the door was unable to find it, hidden or otherwise.

As she looked, her foot pressed against a loose tile and she heard a 'thwip'!

Roll 2D6 and test for *Speed*.

If the test is successful, turn to **145**, otherwise, turn to **384**.

353

Derilion placed the key in the lock, twisted, and pulled the door towards her. Immediately, she heard a 'Thwip!' sound and attempted to pull her hand away.

Was Derilion wearing gauntlets?

If so, turn to **73**, otherwise, turn to **389**.

354

Derilion had had enough of the room and wanted to leave. There was something about the number of crates that unnerved the Lightbringer. She put one hand on her sword and advanced towards the door in front of her.

Turn to **45**.

355

Again, the adventurer scanned the floor in hope for a clue directing her towards the real patch of ground.

Roll 2D6 and test for *Detection*.

If the test is successful, turn to **526**, otherwise, turn to **480**.

356

The arrow pierced the Cuddower's skin, and it reared backwards in pain. Derilion tensed, expecting it to rush towards her, but instead, its skin began to thicken and turn a pale grey. The creature's movement stiffened, and Derilion realised it had turned to stone, a fierce expression sculpted on its face.

Turn to **130**.

357

"I'm here to find my ward. The Pajoli took her."

"That's not something you should be saying out loud down here," she replied. "Fortunately, I am on your side. Come on in. My name is Grom. I can help you."

Continue to **319**.

358

Derilion didn't have much time to choose the best attack. She'd have to use a weapon or something she'd stored in her belt.

Use moss, if she has some	Turn to **66**
Use explosive powder, if she has some	Turn to **181**
Unsheathe her sword	Turn to **585**

359

"I do," the hunter said. She found the stone in her backpack (**-3w**) and put it on the desk in front of the witch, who looked a little disappointed.

"Right," the girl continued. "How about a green potion? I've heard they're quite rare."

If Derilion has the potion and is willing to give it to her, turn to **25**, otherwise, turn to **297**.

360

Derilion shook her head. "I don't trust you."

The shadows whirled.

"Few do."

"I tell you what," the Lightbringer said. "Become my sword's shadow, and you can still travel with me."

"All right," the words read. "Place the sword tip against the wall."

The hunter placed her sword on the stone. Within a few seconds, the shadow had formed into its shape on the wall.

On Derilion's next successful combat, the shadow will leave the sword and consume the victim immediately, killing them outright. At that point, the shadow will remain with its victim.

Now, turn to **161**.

361

Off to the right sat a large bulbous creature looking intently at Derilion as she entered the room. It clearly thought of her as its next meal.

As if to emphasise this, the hunter noticed a pile of human bones nearby, picked clean. She waited to see if it'd do anything, but it remained still.

The floor in front of the hunter consisted of white stone slabs, roughly a foot in diameter.

Roll 2D6 and test for *Detection*.

If the test is successful, turn to **693**, otherwise, turn to **339**.

362

Derilion kicked the moss into the pool and watched as the water around it turned a brighter blue. The Elemental roared and grew slightly stronger before her eyes.

Add 4 to its *Health*.

Has the hunter kicked four items in yet? If not, she can try another (turn to **633**). If she has, she must face the Elemental (turn to **107**).

363

Derilion watched as the arrow glanced off the Cuddower's toughened skin, hitting the wall behind and falling to the floor.

The creature smiled and advanced toward her. With the chasm blocking any escape route, the hunter knew she had to fight.

Turn to **485**.

364

The hunter reached out to try and push open the door, but no sooner had her hand touched the leaves, then the vines began to coil around it. Derilion gasped and tried to pull away, but her hand was stuck fast.

Derilion's mind span. She had to act fast, but she was too close to the vines to use the explosives.

Chop at the vines with her sword	Turn to **684**
Try and set the door alight	Turn to **373**

<h1 style="text-align:center">365</h1>

Derilion dodged the first rock and two more which swiftly followed it, both hitting the floor where she'd stood a moment before.

There was still a long way to go to reach the end of the chamber, and the Lightbringer couldn't see where her assailants were hiding. Not wanting to incur any more damage, she decided she should use one of her attributes to cross.

Use *Stealth* to cross	Turn to **493**
Use *Speed* to cross	Turn to **599**
Use *Detection* to find the best route	Turn to **9**

<h1 style="text-align:center">366</h1>

Derilion dropped like a stone, and a projectile whizzed over her head. She turned and saw the Dwarf holding a crossbow. He threw it to the ground in disgust, stood and drew his axe, ready to fight.

Turn to **122**.

<h1 style="text-align:center">367</h1>

The hunter crouched and entered the place where the Frost Sprites lived, hoping to find something of use, but there was barely anything there. A few old bones from a recent meal, the smouldering remains of a fire. Against one wall was a chest which contained a scrap of material with an Axe Emblem (**+1w**) on it. She thought she recognised it but couldn't remember where from.

Under the cloth are a pair of steel gauntlets (**+4w**), which looked more useful.

Turn to **226**.

368

"Yes, that would be good," the hunter said.

The girl stepped forward and took hold of the amulet. She spoke a few words under her breath, and the amulet glowed.

After a few moments, she stepped back.

"All done," she told Derilion.

"Thank you."

The Lightbringer smiled, turned and walked out of the room. She crossed the previous room and exited through the other door.

Turn to **404**.

369

"Well, that's interesting," Othwig said. "Perhaps that's why you're here, after all."

Derilion opened her eyes.

"What do you mean?" she asked.

"Oh, it's not for me to say. Wouldn't want to get into trouble with anyone."

Derilion looked at Othwig, trying to work out what she meant.

"Come on. I haven't got all day. Take the test. You know you want to."

Take the test	Turn to **625**
Pull out her sword to attack	Turn to **585**

370

Derilion moved towards the woman, taking her time, trying to be as silent as possible. She avoided some loose stones on the floor and finally stood close enough to strike.

Derilion raised her sword and brought it down, but it went straight through her body as if she was a ghost. The woman turned and smiled at the hunter.

Turn to **396**.

371

The Lightbringer closed her eyes and pushed out her senses to try and see if she could pick up on anything. Nothing happened at first, but then slowly the word Ambrite appeared in her mind.

If it was an Ambrite waiting for her in the darkness, it wanted her close enough to use its suffocating residue to smother her.

The creature would most likely aim at her head to cover her nose and mouth, so she raised her shield and stepped forward to face the creature (turn to **155**).

372

Quickly, Derilion made her way around the wall of the chamber, thankful not to encounter any further obstacles. At first, she couldn't find a way out and thought she might have to turn back. Finally, however, and with some relief, she found it.

The Lightbringer hesitated for a moment, wondering whether she should search for more doorways, but it was then she heard the creature moving again, and, wasting no more time, she
stepped through into the passageway beyond.

Turn to **251**.

373

Derilion pressed Volkov to the door and watched as the vines burst into flames. She kept trying to pull her arm free, but the thick coils held her fast.

The flames reached her arm, and she did her best not to cry out. Finally, after the flames had caused 3 damage to her *Health*, they released their grip on Derilion, and she fell away.

If she was still alive, turn to **115**.

374

Derilion readied herself to fight the Death Maiden.

"How are you going to defeat me?" her opponent asked, sneering at her. "I'm already dead."

Roll 2D6 and test for *Speed*.

If the test is successful, turn to **518**, otherwise, turn to **490**.

375

Derilion dodged the Cuddower's club, the speed of her reaction surprising even herself. The Cuddower over-balanced and the Lightbringer tripped it, grabbed the arrow from the bow, and plunged it into its shoulder.

The Cuddower screamed, and, before her eyes, began to solidify. She watched with a morbid fascination as slowly its flesh turned grey, and it came to a standstill in front of her.

Turn to **130**.

376

The hunter tried to concentrate but felt nervous about the tests yet to come. At the point where she was about to give up, something came through. Not much, but from the path straight on, she 'felt' light, and from the path to the left, she detected the smell of something cooking.

The feelings went as fast as they came, and the Lightbringer couldn't be sure they had ever really been there to begin with.

Straight on   Turn to **183**
Take left branch   Turn to **209**

377

The hunter looked at the child and knew she was a witch. Perhaps she was once like Obishaa, but the Pajoli had changed her.

Whatever her powers may be, Derilion didn't want to test them. She could match most people for Strength, but with magic, she was all but powerless. She looked through her backpack and found enough items (-**?w**) to give the child.

"Just a couple more things," the girl continued without looking up. "Do you have a stone with concentric circles on?"

If Derilion has such a stone and wants to give it to her, turn to **359**, otherwise, turn to **297**.

378

Derilion turned to leave.

"No!" the girl screamed from behind her.

The hunter felt something thump into her back, and she was knocked to the ground.

"How dare you run away from Grom!" the voice continued.

Derilion stood and turned to face the girl.

Turn to **432**.

379

Try as she might, Derilion couldn't reach the door, and finally she had to open her mouth. She felt the water rush in and was powerless to fight it.

She twisted and turned in the water, but nothing was going to save her, and she died in the corridor, alone.

380

Derilion reached up with her sword and knocked the carving off the ledge, catching it before it hit the floor (**+2w**).

She could see it better now. As she watched, its facial features began to change, and within a few seconds, it resembled Derilion.

Not knowing what it meant, the hunter had to decide whether to take it with her and then head on.

Turn to **519**.

Derilion waited to see if the creature would come close enough so she could take a swing at it. It continued to screech but remained hidden in the darkness above.

The Lightbringer knew all the while it remained there it put her at a disadvantage. She remembered the woman from the village had given her some explosive powder; that might bring the creature down to her level (turn to **604**), or she could wait for a chance to strike (turn to **48**).

"I'm on a mission to help the Pajoli," Derilion said.

"Is that what you're doing?" the creature asked. "I'm afraid they're not worth helping."

"Can I go through?"

"If you have some metal," it replied. "Do you have some metal to give me? A coin will do."

If Derilion had an item made from metal, she could give it to him (turn to **579**), or she could just ignore the request and keep going (turn to **595**).

383

Derilion watched as the woman continued to moan. It sounded as if she was in a lot of pain, and after a couple of moments, the hunter made up her mind to show her compassion.

"Can I help you?" she asked.

The woman looked up. She was deathly pale, and the moment Derilion saw her face, she knew she was not injured; this was a Death Maiden, and she was in search of a soul to take.

"You can," the Death Maiden said, smiling. "If you choose to fight the creature in the room beyond, I will take its soul instead of yours."

Fight the Death Maiden	Turn to **374**
Fight in the next room	Turn to **674**

384

Derilion moved as quickly as possible, but she just hadn't expected a trap. She felt a dart lodge in her shoulder, causing 1 damage to her *Health*.

If she was still alive, she turned and headed toward the warlocks.

Turn to **276**.

385

While it might not have been the safest way to proceed, the hunter was aware of how long Obishaa had been with the Pajoli. She looked at the path in front of her and decided to take a run at it.

Roll 2D6 and test for *Speed*.

If the test was successful, turn to **459**, otherwise, turn to **416**.

<h1 style="text-align:center">386</h1>

Derilion drew her sword and took a step towards the man. Immediately, the air changed. The Lightbringer had felt it before; it was the feeling created by magic.

Carefully, she reached out towards him and wasn't surprised to feel a barrier resisting her reach. The man wasn't praying, after all, but casting a spell of protection. But why?

The rumbling noise grew louder still, and the knot of worry tightened in Derilion's stomach.

Turn to **57**.

<h1 style="text-align:center">387</h1>

"You're not much of an adventurer, are you?" the girl scoffed. "Fortunately, you do have something I could use anyway. Some of your blood. If you want the information, that is my price."

"Very well," the adventurer replied and held out her hand.

The child took a pin and a small glass container.

"It'll only hurt a little," she said, pricking Derilion's index finger. "Five drops will be plenty."

When she'd collected the blood, she handed the Lightbringer a cloth to wrap around the cut.

"Thank you," the child said. "I shall have fun with that."

Turn to **460**.

388

Derilion continued to wait, and the water kept tumbling down the side, but the level rose no higher. She had an idea and slowly swam towards the place she'd come in. The water level dropped the further back she went, and by the time she'd reached the door,
the corridor was almost dry.

Something wasn't right with this passage, and she thought she might know what.

Turn to **675**.

389

She felt a sharp pain across the back of her hand and looked down to see a pin sticking out of her index finger, and red drops of blood dripping down onto the floor. Aware she might have been poisoned, Derilion sucked at the wound on her hand as quickly as possible.

Roll 2D6 and test for *Speed*.

If the test is successful, turn to **591**, otherwise, turn to **273**.

390

Derilion went straight to the elven hunter, who beckoned her closer. The Lightbringer placed her ear next to the elf's mouth.

"Poison in the well," Derilion thought she heard. She wanted to ask more, but the hunter went limp in her arms. She checked the elf for a pulse but found none. When she checked her pockets, she found 4 gold coins (**+2w**), and a small black arrowhead (**+2w**).

She could now either go to the assassin (turn to **173**) or head to the exit (turn to **74**).

391

The woman was concentrating on the net, muttering to herself. There was a good chance she didn't know the hunter was there.

Roll 2D6 and test for *Stealth*.

If the test is successful, turn to **370**, otherwise, turn to **49**.

392

The hunter raised her shield to block the arrow coming towards her from the front, which, fortunately, shattered harmlessly on her shield. The arrow from the left glanced off her back. Unfortunately, the one from the right went through her armour and embedded its tip into her shoulder.

Derilion suffered 4 damage to her *Health*.

If she was still alive, she removed the arrow and dressed the wound as best as she could.

Turn to **568**.

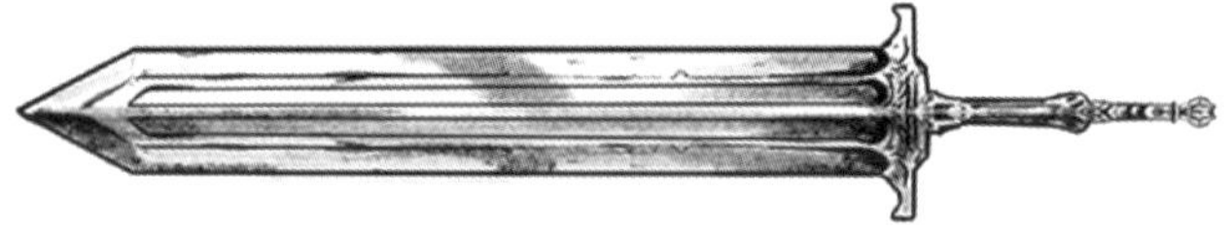

393

Derilion decided to attack the reflection.

Not only were all their attributes the same, but they were able to block one another's swing every single time. The harder the hunter attempted to hurt the reflection, the harder they defended.

Derilion wasn't sure when she lost track of time, but the two of them continued fighting like that, forever.

Derilion headed toward the elven hunter, steering clear of the other two as much as she could. As she neared, she heard a 'thwip' and felt a thud in her leg and looked down to see a crossbow bolt sticking out of her thigh.

Reduce her *Health* and her *Speed* by 1.

She pulled the bolt out, crossed to the dwarf, and ran him through with her sword before he'd had the chance to do any more damage.

Turn to **256**.

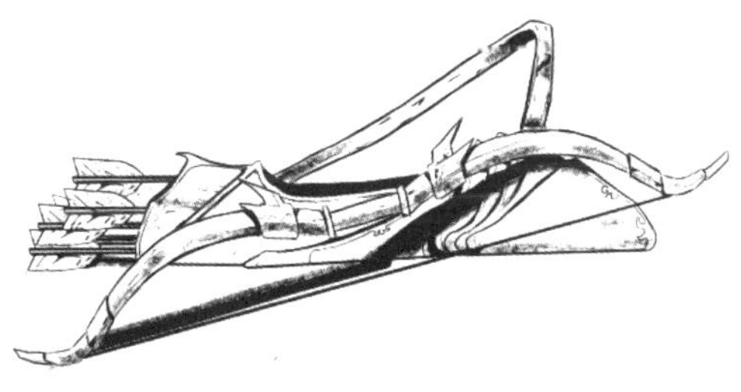

395

It was a very tight space, but the hunter managed to squeeze herself between the throne and the wall. It was comfortable if she didn't want to breathe too deeply.

She heard the door open and watched as a troll entered the room and sat down in front of the food. It ate hungrily, and all the while Derilion was certain she'd be discovered at any moment.

Thankfully the troll was too hungry to notice the intruder, and after a few minutes, got up and left via the other door.

Derilion got out from behind the throne and went through the door ahead of her.

Turn to **126**.

396

"Well, I was looking for a test subject."

Without warning, she grabbed Derilion's hand before she'd had a chance to move.

"Don't worry; it'll be fun."

Was Derilion wearing gauntlets? If so, turn to **407**, otherwise, turn to **511**.

397

Derilion retrieved a pouch of the explosive powder (**-1w**). She opened it carefully and sprinkled the contents along the wall.

"I've done it," she called, stepping away.

She watched as the powder started to fizz and then exploded in multiple tiny explosions.

The wall fell away, and Zalixa stepped into the corridor.

Turn to **188**.

398

The witch laughed.

"These are mine already!" she snorted. "For your cheek, I will give you a choice. Eat the leaves or take my test."

Eat the yellowish leaves	Turn to **638**
Take the test	Turn to **625**

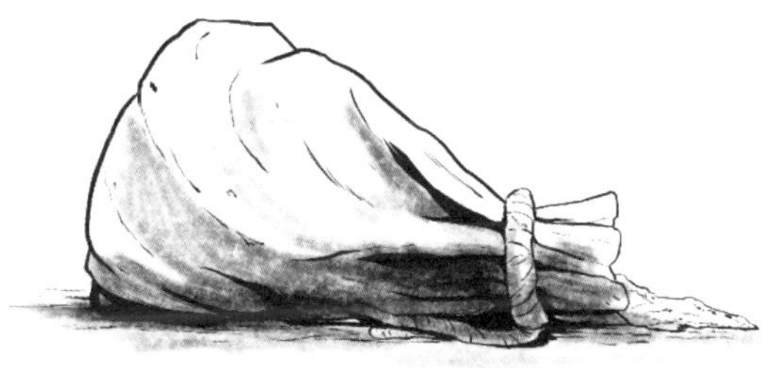

399

The hunter went to leave, but she'd underestimated the power of the witch. The moment she'd turned her back on the woman, Derilion felt a jolt in her back which knocked her to the floor.

Deduct 2 from the Lightbringer's *Health*.

The hunter, ever resourceful, picked up a hand of dust from the floor and threw it into the eyes of the woman, who staggered back disorientated.

Derilion had to act now.

Push her off with Volkov	Turn to **2**
Run her through with Derilion's sword	Turn to **444**

400

Derilion launched herself towards the exit as the shower of boulders increased. One grazed her shoulder, while another landed directly in front of her. She jumped to avoid it, but as she came down on the other side, she lost her footing and fell sprawling to the ground. She looked up just in time to roll away from a large boulder, though it caught her leg, making her sustain 2 damage to her *Health*.

She didn't have time to cry out, she knew, so the hunter gritted her teeth and scrambled the rest of the way, through the door to the passageway beyond.

Continue to **143**.

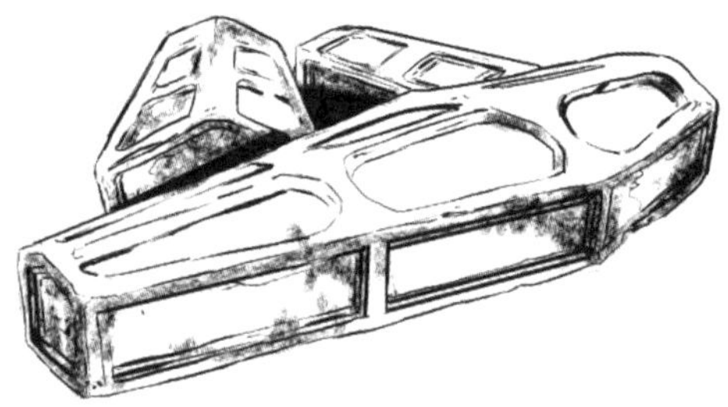

401

Frustrated at her predicament, Derilion raised her sword and struck at the creature.

The blow deflected off its tough surface, and a few moments later, it swiped its arm towards her, connecting and sending her flying backwards into the wall.

Her adventure ends here.

402

Whatever information he had it wasn't worth the amulet.

"I think I'll keep it," the hunter said.

The adventurer shrugged.

"Have it your way. But you won't rescue her, you know. You're already too late."

The Lightbringer felt the anger and the pain rise in her, and it took everything she had not to strike him with her sword.

"What do you mean?" she asked through gritted teeth.

The adventurer smiled and, in an instant, had vanished. Derilion cursed she hadn't just killed him. She shook her head and moved on, emerging into an area with three paths.

Turn to **639**.

403

Derilion rushed at the woman, sword aloft, not caring what noise she made.

Almost immediately, the woman turned and held up her hand. Derilion slowed and then stopped as the air suddenly became thick around her.

"That's better," she said. "Best not be too hasty."

The woman smiled, then returned to her net. The air became normal once again.

Turn to **76**.

404

The hunter walked through the door into a smaller room which housed four mirrors angled into the centre. Derilion glanced at the mirrors before going any further, and noticed they reflected a distorted version of the room.

It'd be difficult not to appear in one of their reflections as she crossed the room, so she took a moment to think over her options.

Cover mirror with the opaque scarf	Turn to **441**
Look closer in the nearest mirror	Turn to **582**
Extinguish Volkov, and pass by the mirrors	Turn to **622**

405

Derilion attempted to dodge the Cuddower's club, but it caught her shoulder and knocked her backwards towards the chasm.

The hunter desperately thrust her hands out to stop her and managed to grab an outcrop of rock.

Reduce Derilion's *Health* by 2. If she was still alive, she must fight the Cuddower.

Turn to **485**.

406

Derilion nodded.

"I did. What of it?"

"There's a tax to pay," the girl replied. "One item for each type of box opened. There are no exceptions."

If the Lightbringer wanted to pay her the tax, turn to **377**. Otherwise, turn to **297**.

407

Derilion began to feel light-headed, but somehow the gauntlets were interfering with the spell they were trying to cast, giving the Lightbringer enough time to fight back against the woman, pushing her away.

The woman looked confused and disorientated, and Derilion realised she had the chance to attack.

Push her with Volkov	Turn to **2**
Run her through with her sword	Turn to **444**
Leave the room	Turn to **399**

408

Derilion faced up to the werecat. Its head was level with her knee, and its mouth held an array of sharp teeth. It wore a hungry look on its face while it slunk around the wall in front of her. It was waiting for a moment to attack.

	Speed	*Accuracy*	*Damage*	*Health*
Werecat	8	8	2	6

If the Lightbringer wins, turn to **524**.

409

An adventurer stepped out in front of Derilion. He looked like he'd seen better days, with ripped clothes, thin physique and unkempt beard. The hunter looked for a weapon but couldn't see one. He held up his hands, palms facing her, in a gesture of calming.

"Listen," he whispered. "I've got something to tell you."

It was a strange request, and Derilion was unsure whether to fight him (turn to **84**) or see what he had to say (turn to **523**).

410

Derilion chose the door with the lightning symbol. Tentatively, she reached out and touched the handle. Nothing happened. She twisted it, but the door didn't budge. It was either locked or stuck fast.

The hunter only had one option, after all.

Turn to **129**.

411

Derilion took a step back towards the exit, but the woman moved quicker than expected and blocked the hunter's route back to the corridor.

"I tried," the faceless woman said. "I really tried. But I'm so hungry."

She turned to look at Derilion, though with what, the hunter couldn't be sure.

"Who are you?" asked the Lightbringer.

"What does it matter?"

Turn to **596**.

412

Derilion leant into the room and picked up the book. It looked familiar to her, but she couldn't place why. She guessed a lot of books look similar and suspected that was all it was.

She tried to open it but couldn't. The pages were stuck together somehow, though she suspected magic. She could either put the book back (turn to **666**) or take it with her (turn to **565**).

413

Derilion focused on the tools by the slab. All of them looked as if they could do significant damage. She picked one up and felt the weight of it in her hand. They were in good shape considering these caves saw their fair share of the dead. As she investigated, she heard a noise from behind her.

Turn to **637**.

414

As soon as she'd thrown it, Derilion knew it wasn't going to work. She watched frustrated as the powder hit the leaves and fell to the floor. The vines stretched out and picked up the powder, and within a few moments, the sachet had been pulled back out of sight into the mess of vines.

There was now only one obvious choice left to the hunter. She had to try and set the vines alight.

Turn to **229**.

415

Derilion took a step toward her. "I can help you leave," she said.

The woman either couldn't hear her or pretended not to. Instead, she turned slowly to face the hunter. Except there was no face there. There wasn't anything. It was like the whole front of her head had been scooped out, and all she could from the front was the back of the woman's skull. Derilion found herself both repulsed and deeply fascinated.

"I warned you," she said.

Turn to **596**.

416

Derilion began to run through the corridor, trying to be as careful as possible. She was rightfully nervous, and after a moment saw a shadow move nearby, so stopped to see what it was. There was no point running into a sharpened blade.

Turn to **409**.

417

The rocks whipped by Derilion's head, and she moved quickly to avoid taking the worst of them, still managing to sustain 1 damage to her *Health*. With all her focus taken on the debris, she was unable to keep an eye on the faceless woman.

As the dust finally cleared, Derilion scanned the room for any sign of her.

Turn to **584**.

418

Derilion abandoned her boots but knew it was a small price to pay. She reached for the handhold and tested it quickly. It felt good. The hunter lifted herself onto the wall, watching as her boots disappeared under the mud.

She wanted to get away from this as quickly as possible, so moved swiftly along the wall. Unfortunately, about halfway across, her hand slipped, and she had no choice but to land on the floor. She felt her feet hit the mud.

Roll 2D6 and test for *Speed*.

If the test is successful, turn to **40**, otherwise, turn to **660**.

The hunter reached the bottom of the stairs, the stench of death growing with every step, till she had to cover her mouth and nose to stop her from being violently ill.

About four foot in front of the stairs a figure lay barely moving in the filth on the ground. Derilion went to them, knowing they were too weak to pose any threat, and knelt.

"Can I help you?" she asked.

The figure barely managed to look up at her.

"Leave me. I am close to death," they said. "Just… be careful of the vines. They are alive."

Derilion noticed a door nearby and looked at the vines which grew on it. As she did, the figure breathed one last deep breath, closed their eyes and laid still. Slowly, their palm opened, and something rolled across the floor into the darkness.

The hunter followed the object's path and retrieved it from the shadows. It was a round stone with circles running across it (**+3w**). She had never seen anything like it but thought if the figure had held onto it so much, it might be worth something.

Derilion searched the body but found nothing else of note. Finally, she stood and approached the door very slowly.

Turn to **680**.

420

"Obishaa!" Derilion called in little more than a whisper. Her heart was in her throat. It could be a trap, but if it wasn't, if it was the child, she didn't want to attract nearby creatures.

The sobbing sound floated towards her again.

"Obishaa?" the adventurer said, stepping forward. "It's Derilion. I'm here to get you back."

The crying came again, and even though something didn't seem right, Derilion stepped forward once more.

Almost immediately, something flew past her right ear and shattered on the cave wall. The adventurer tensed. It was a trap, and she had to move, right now.

Roll 2D6 and test for *Speed*.

If the test is successful, turn to **258**, otherwise, turn to **343**.

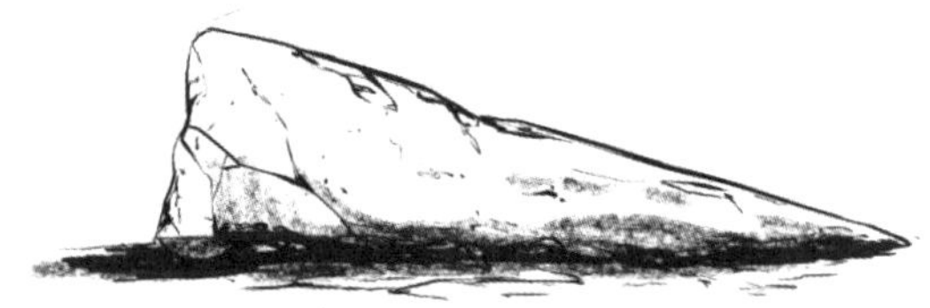

421

Derilion concentrated on the water around her, trying to figure out what was happening. Her feet were now soaked, and still, the water came. It was no use. She couldn't work it out, and she decided to press on before the water rose any higher.

Turn to **656**.

422

Derilion examined the rest of the room, in particular, a small section of the shelf which housed one red potion (**+2w**) and one green potion (**+2w**) which she could take. It wasn't obvious to her exactly what they were.

She now had two options available. She could go for the glass ball (turn to **191**) or use the glass jaw (turn to **64**).

423

Derilion chose the door to the right and found it unlocked. She twisted the handle and pushed the door inwards.

The room beyond was light. Not only that, it was inhabited. A girl sat behind a desk reading, talking to herself as she scanned the pages.

The Lightbringer looked around the walls but couldn't see any other exits to the room.

Speak to the girl	Turn to **311**
Search the room	Turn to **162**
Leave the room	Turn to **29**

424

Derilion began moving along the wall. It was hard going, and she nearly slipped with the first couple of steps but managed to steady herself in time. As she reached for the next handhold, she noticed it was loose.

She stopped and searched the wall for another place she could use. It was a little further away but a lot safer, so she took it and continued.

Turn to **562**.

425

Derilion picked up the runestone (**+3w**). It was purple and surprisingly light for the strength it possessed. It was roughly pentagonal, and she couldn't make out if it were natural or made by hand. She decided whether or not to keep it and went through the door ahead of her.

Turn to **119**.

426

The creature lay dead. The lowness of the cave roof made the smell more intense, and Derilion fought hard against throwing up. Off to one side were the pile of bones, and next to them, a pile of clothes had wisps of smoke coming from them. Something was glinting within the clothes.

Investigate the pile	Turn to **534**
Leave the room	Turn to **165**

427

Derilion stepped forward and put her foot on the bronze tile. She waited to see if this was the right choice.

"Very well," the voice said. The feel of the blade went, and the hunter turned to see a dark shape behind her. From the floor, bronze ran like water up its body forming a suit of armour around it. The armour raised its sword in front of its face.

"To the death," it said.

	Speed	*Accuracy*	*Damage*	*Health*
Bronze Armour	9	7	3	11

If Derilion wins, turn to **540**.

428

Trusting her senses, Derilion picked up her speed through the corridor, hoping she'd have time to react to any threats should she need to.

It was tough going, with the mud underfoot taking a lot to get through, but she went fast and before long reached a step that took her out of the mud. As she did so, the unsettling feeling died away, and she was able to slow down once again.

Turn to **154**.

429

The hunter had an idea. Could it be a coincidence the boy had had a lens on him? She found it and held it up to her eye and smiled as she saw the runes become letters she could understand.

The runes read, Live Always. Derilion didn't know what it meant but smiled at the irony of the message.

Turn to **446**.

430

Derilion started down the stairs, unhappy at not being able to see where it led. The shield wasn't giving out much light, and she didn't have enough hands to carry one of the torches.

She focused on the steps in front of her, not wanting to slip. Unfortunately, her hand pressed a loose stone on the wall, and immediately the stairs fell away beneath her.

Did Derilion find a length of rope?

If so, turn to **348**, otherwise, turn to **10**.

431

She began to move through the space between the mirrors, head down, as quickly as she could. Halfway through she suddenly felt like she had too many legs, which made her stumble and fall to the floor.

Before she'd had time to react, she felt pulled in all four directions towards the mirrors, and however much she attempted to scramble free, the hold was too strong.

Finally, unable to escape, Derilion felt her body pulled apart. Her adventure ends here.

432

Light shone from overhead and Derilion could see the girl behind the voice. She stood in a pool of water, with long worm-like tendrils swirled from where her arms should be.

Derilion must fight Grom. She had six tendrils which the Lightbringer must battle each turn.

	Speed	*Accuracy*	*Damage*	*Health*
Grom Tendrils	7	8	1	5

Once Derilion has managed to kill one of the tendrils, turn to **442**.

433

The hunter took a step back and to the side and then knocked on the door, ready for an attack.

Nothing happened. Derilion knocked once more, but if an enemy was waiting on the other side, they were patient.

Turn to **7**.

434

Derilion opened the box. Inside she saw the fossilised skeleton of a scorpion, its tail high, ready to pounce.

Was the hunter stung by a scorpion earlier in the caves?

If so, turn to **121**, otherwise, turn to **263**.

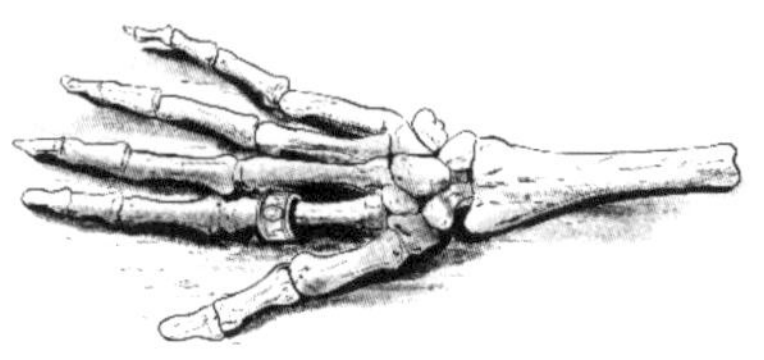

435

"No, I have enough to carry," the hunter said.

"Very well," the creature replied and returned to his reading.

Derilion watched the creature and thought perhaps she should say something else.

"I'm on a mission to help the Pajoli."	Turn to **382**
"What are you doing here?"	Turn to **571**
Just keep going	Turn to **595**

436

Derilion searched the creature's pockets and found a small key made from bone. She looked around the room, but the only keyhole she could see was the one in the door.

She wanted to go through it, but maybe there was something in the desk that could help her.

Search its desk	Turn to **272**
Go through the door	Turn to **147**

Derilion placed the shield on the floor, and using its light, began to dig with her hands. The top layer came away easily but revealed nothing.

She continued to dig, trying to concentrate her efforts in one place so as not to waste time. Still, she found nothing.

In her frustration, she searched the floor around her and noticed several more patches of ground which appeared disturbed, likely done to put people off the scent.

Derilion could either waste time inspecting each patch or try and detect some other clue.

Roll 2D6 and test for *Detection*.

If the test is successful, turn to **282**, otherwise, turn to **75**.

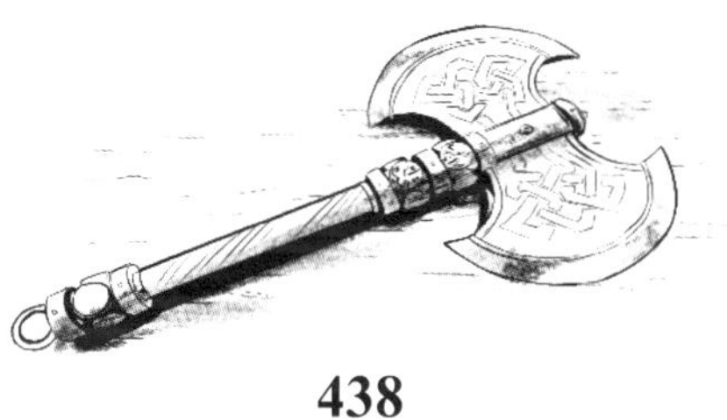

438

Derilion wrestled her arms away from the dwarf before he could do too much damage.

Subtract 1 from the Lightbringer's *Health*.

Derilion stepped back and watched as he stood, drew his axe, ready to fight.

Turn to **122**.

439

Derilion entered the cave. Incense hung in the air, while crude furniture sat awkwardly in the space ahead. After a few steps, she came to a lip where the ground fell away, and she could see two trolls sleeping over on the far side.

Three chests were next to the trolls. If past experiences were anything to go by, they would contain their treasure.

Check out the treasure	Turn to **335**
Search for another exit	Turn to **120**
Return to the previous room	Turn to **698**

440

Derilion bent and put the shield's flame to the clothes. At least setting light to them should clear some of the debris, she thought.

In less than a second, the dry fabric caught and with a 'whoomph' the clothes began to burn. The heat of the fire in the small chamber pushed the hunter backwards.

Almost immediately, there came a scrabbling sound above her, and she turned, sword in hand, ready to battle whatever monster hid in the darkness (turn to **381**).

441

The hunter approached the nearest mirror carefully, going around the outside so as not to be reflected. When she was as near as she was happy to get, she retrieved the scarf and threw it.

Roll 2D6 and test for *Accuracy*.

If the test is successful, turn to **556**, otherwise, turn to **170**.

442

"Stop!" the girl said. She threw something down at Derilion's feet, which knocked her back to the floor.

It took her a second to get her bearings, and by the time she stood, the girl was gone. Confused, the hunter turned and made her way carefully back to the stream.

Turn to **676**.

443

Beyond the door was a narrow passage snaking away into the darkness. After everything she'd been through Derilion was naturally cautious.

She knew her strengths and thought one of them might come to her aid, now.

Detect for traps	Turn to **472**
Speed through it	Turn to **385**
Tread carefully	Turn to **328**

444

Derilion took the chance and put her sword through her. The woman's eyes opened wide in surprise.

"This wasn't how it was supposed to end," she said. "No-one has the net but me." The woman moved her arm towards the net, and it disappeared. Derilion stepped back and watched the woman fall to the floor, dead.

The Lightbringer looked around. There was a large wooden chest she could inspect (turn to **189**) or she could move on to the next room (turn to **466**).

<h1 style="text-align:center">445</h1>

Derilion searched the witch's body and found any items she gave her plus two concentric circle stones (**+3w each**) and a green potion (**+2w**), then exited through the door (turn to **165**).

<h1 style="text-align:center">446</h1>

With the unopened chest in front of her, Derilion went through her options.

Open the chest	Turn to **65**
Investigate the slab	Turn to **470**
Investigate the coffins	Turn to **266**
Exit to the left	Turn to **178**
Exit straight on	Turn to **636**

<h1 style="text-align:center">447</h1>

Derilion rushed towards her sword aloft, as fast as she could. She had only taken two steps when the hunter felt a painful twinge in her thigh, causing her to slow.

Turn to **76**.

<h1 style="text-align:center">448</h1>

Derilion tried to get her boot out of the vines, but the more she struggled, the tighter the grip on her leg became.

She dropped her shield and tried to chop at the vines with her sword, an action which would normally work. This time, however, the weapon did no damage to the plant.

Derilion watched on in horror as the vines crept along her leg and up her torso. She attempted to tear them away with her hands, but the vines snared her wrists, pulling her in. Derilion knew she had failed her ward.

449

Derilion kicked the Blue Egg into the pool and watched as the water around it turned red. The Elemental screamed and withered slightly before her eyes.

Subtract 6 from its *Health*.

If the Elemental has no more *Health*, turn to **137**. Has the hunter kicked four items in yet? If not, she can try another (turn to **633**). If she has, she must face the Elemental (turn to **107**).

450

As she touched the handle, a jolt went up and through her body, throwing her backwards. Derilion lay on the floor, unable to move and watched as the girl got up and walked over.

"I told you not to take anything," she said. "I'm not the bad person here."

She picked up the book Derilion saw earlier, flicked to a page and recanted the spell. The hunter's molecules started to loosen and drift apart. It wasn't painful, as Derilion had been dreading, but it killed her just the same.

Her adventure ends here.

451

The Slabac walked towards the hunter for one last attack. Derilion sidestepped it and pushed her sword deep into the creature, killing it instantly.

The Lightbringer searched the Slabac and found two stones with concentric circles (**+3w each**).

Turn to **462**.

452

Derilion didn't want to chance kicking the wrong thing into the pool. She knew it was a risk, but she'd come so far, she didn't want to leave anything to chance.

She closed her eyes and focused.

Roll 2D6 and test for *Detection*.

If the test is successful, turn to **644**, otherwise, turn to **569**.

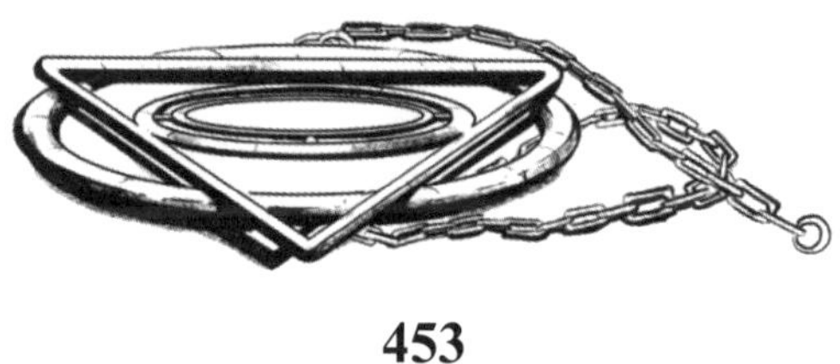

453

Derilion looked at the walls across the chasm. They were certainly narrow enough for her to attempt to cross them. The issue was there was no room for failure. The yawning darkness below sucked the wind from her lungs.

She looked back at the statue-like Cuddower. Perhaps removing the arrow would be a good thing.

Pull the arrow out	Turn to **503**
Head out over the chasm	Turn to **227**

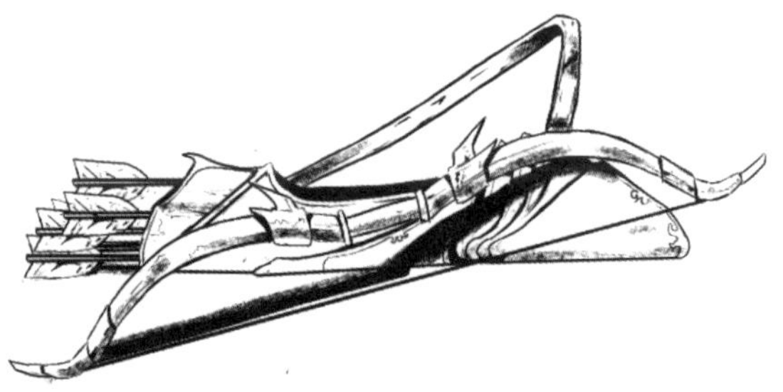

"Well, done," came the voice from the room. "I thought I was dead for sure."

She looked in to see a dwarf sitting in the corner, looking hungry.

"How long have you been in here?" she asked.

The dwarf shrugged. "Who knows? A day? A week? Longer? What I do know is I've had enough of this tomb."

He got up with the help of his axe.

"Thank you," he said, "And as a token of my thanks, take this. I've got two of them anyway."

The dwarf placed a greenish stone in Derilion's hands (**+3w**).

"It will keep your weapon sharp. And maybe I'll see you on the outside," the dwarf said. "My name's Gubren. I owe you."

The hunter watched as Gubren left and turned right out of the room. That could have been a lot worse. Derilion stopped a moment and used the stone on her sword. It did, indeed, sharpen the blade even more.

Add +1 to her weapon damage.

When she finished, the Lightbringer left the room and continued down the corridor.

Turn to **78**.

Derilion stepped forward, Volkov raised against an attack. Fortunately, it appeared the Otistro couldn't see her or was in too much pain to care.

While it wasn't actively in the fight, the Lightbringer needed to avoid its tongue.

	Speed	Accuracy	Damage	Health
Otistro	7	5	1	8

If the hunter won, turn to **545**.

456

The hunter pressed on, cautiously. Each step she took taking more effort than the last.

Derilion looked down and saw with horror the mud beginning to creep up her boots. She almost laughed; first, the vines and now the mud? Was there anything that wasn't alive in these caves?

She could see a small ledge in front of her where the mud stopped. It was going to be quite a jump, but she had no other choice. Derilion tensed her leg muscles and jumped forwards with everything she had.

Roll 2D6 and test for *Accuracy*.

If the test is successful, turn to **40**, otherwise, turn to **660**.

Derilion began to make her way around the room, keeping one eye on the creature at all times. Clumsily, the hunter knocked one of the shelves, and she watched, almost in slow motion, as a vase fell to the floor and shattered.

The creature turned and looked toward the smashed vase. The Lightbringer saw that its head resembled a bull, with thickset shoulders and large scales covering the rest of its body. It remained still, staring where the vase fell.

There was a chance she could make it to the door first if she were quick. Otherwise, there was the explosive powder, if she still had some, or perhaps she could think of something else.

Explosive powder	Turn to **590**
Make a run for the door	Turn to **351**
Think of something else	Turn to **242**

458

Derilion began rifling through the woman's pockets, looking for anything valuable or useful.

Roll 2D6 and test for *Stealth*.

If the test was successful, turn to **549**, otherwise, turn to **265**.

459

Derilion raced through the corridor, on the lookout for anything that might come at her. There was no way she could see everything, but her knowledge as a hunter kept her sharp. Thankfully, she made it through without incident, emerging into an area with three paths branching off.

Turn to **639**.

"This place is a prison for children like me, for would-be-witches and would-be-warlocks. There have always been the magical born to this place, and it didn't take the Pajoli long to find us and carve out this cave complex to concentrate our energy for their own good."

"But if you're a witch, can't you just leave?" Derilion asked. The girl laughed a hopeless laugh.

"I can't. None of us can. They shackle us and other creatures here using spells made with the energy they drain. We are stuck in these rooms, while they feast on our power."

"If you're stuck in this room, how do you know all this?"

"Other adventurers, more knowledgeable ones, have told me. They've come in search of treasure or magic, or something else entirely. Some tell stories of gold and jewels hidden in the caves, but do you know what? I don't think there is any treasure. I think they're just rumours spread by the Pajoli to bring outsiders here to test our skills. Hone them, as such."

"The Pajoli took someone close to me. Do you know where she might be?"

"There is a room, the deepest cave I ever went, where they keep you when they first take you. This is where they break our defences and make us susceptible to draining our power. There the Pajoli sit on thrones before a pool of the bluest water and watch us bound and gagged. You'll need strong magic to reach her if you intend to travel there."

"Strong magic?"

"Take this," she said, showing you a dull steel amulet. "It needs three enchantments cast upon it, one *Speed*-based, one *Stealth*-based, and one *Accuracy*-based. I will cast one, but the final two you must convince other witches and warlocks to help, which is no easy task."

"What will they want in return for the enchantments?"

"Anything, maybe everything. That is what you risk being here."

Derilion chose one of the three enchantments and told the girl.

"Very well," the girl said. "It will be done."

She stood and placed the amulet around the hunter's neck.

"Now, sit still. We don't want any accidents."

The girl closed her eyes, and Derilion saw her mouth working silently, forming words and enchanting the amulet. She thought she felt a tingling feeling in her chest where the amulet sat, but she might have been imagining it.

After a minute, the girl opened her eyes and stepped back.

"There, it is done. Farewell, adventurer."

She returned to her writing, and Derilion left the room without looking back. Mark the enchantment on the adventure sheet.

Turn to **607**.

<h1 style="text-align:center">461</h1>

Corzen looked at her and smiled.

"I cannot blame you," she communicated. "Wariness will save you here, for sure. But if you won't let me help you, I'll offer you a little advice. The Death Maiden's staff works just as well on her."

"Thank you," Derilion replied.

"You're welcome. Now, I must leave."

Corzen turned and left the way Derilion had entered.

Turn to **587**.

<h1 style="text-align:center">462</h1>

There was only one exit to the room. As the hunter approached it, she heard it unlock. The Lightbringer entered the next room, cautiously. This one was well lit, too, though the light came from three pools of luminescent water.

Off to the left was a throne made of stone, with a wardrobe next to it. In the centre of the room sat a table with food laid out, and a door ahead of her.

The food looked fresh and untouched, so there was a good chance someone would be back to eat it.

Eat some of the food	Turn to **238**
Check out the throne	Turn to **287**
Search the wardrobe	Turn to **508**
Leave through the door	Turn to **24**

Othwig laughed.

"These are mine already!" she snorted. "For your cheek, I will give you a choice. Eat the leaves or take my test."

Eat the bluish leaves Turn to **53**
Take the test Turn to **625**

464

The Insect Demon smacked into Derilion, knocking her back against the wall, causing her 2 damage to her *Health*.

The Demon roared, and Derilion ran back to get a better footing for the attack. The Demon stared at the Lightbringer, a murderous look on its face.

She knew this was going to be her hardest enemy yet.

	Speed	*Accuracy*	*Damage*	*Health*
Insect Demon	8	9	2	13

If the Lightbringer wins, turn to **135**.

465

Derilion spread her arms wide and laid down her sword.

"I mean you no harm," she said.

The female troll laughed.

"You meant to rob us," she said. "It's only because you are so clumsy that you didn't."

"You are right," Derilion answered. "I am here to save my ward, and I thought you might have something of use. I no longer wish to rob you."

"It's lucky you don't," the male troll replied.

"Go on your way," the female continued. "But if we see you again, we will not be so forgiving."

Derilion nodded and returned to the previous room (turn to **698**).

Derilion walked through to the next room. As soon as she set foot in it, the light from her shield disappeared, leaving her in complete darkness. She turned to try and go back but could only feel rock wall behind her.

"Derilion, are you there?" said a voice from the darkness. One she recognised.

"Obishaa?" the hunter said. "Where are you?"

"I don't know. I can't see you," the girl replied, fear in her voice.

"Don't worry," the Lightbringer told her. "I'm here with you. I'll find you."

"They said they'd let me go when you arrived, but I didn't believe them. I think they're going to kill me."

Derilion felt sick to her stomach.

"No, it won't happen. I won't let it happen."

She walked forward to where the voice was coming from and fell into an opening in the floor.

Turn to **500**.

467

It was only a matter of time before Derilion tripped over her own feet and fell. She lay on the floor looking up at the girl, who didn't look amused.

"You can leave now, or try once more? I won't be so forgiving if you fail again. Perhaps you have a potion that might help?"

Drink a red potion	Turn to **133**
Drink a green potion	Turn to **86**
Dance again	Turn to **15**
Leave the room	Turn to **131**

468

"No," the hunter told her, feeling she could get something out of the situation.

"Huh, I could kill you where you stand," the woman said. "Don't tempt me."

Derilion got the stone from the backpack and instinctively took a step closer to the woman. She backed away, unable to hide her fear.

"What is this?" Derilion asked her, pointing to the net with the jewels.

"Why should you care?" she replied. "Very well. It's a door to somewhere else. I don't know where, but I've always known about it. They said I was mad, but I wasn't. I need one more gem, and the hex stone you're holding will work just as well. Put it in the net, and I will reward you well."

Put the hex stone in her net	Turn to **509**
Refuse to put it in her net	Turn to **196**

469

The hunter put her hand to the wall. It was tough, but with enough force, she thought she'd be able to dig into it. There were a few items she could use if she had them. Equally, she could keep going.

Use her sword	Turn to **601**
Use explosive powder	Turn to **531**
Use the stone with concentric circles	Turn to **153**
Keep going	Turn to **547**

470

Derilion made her way to the slab, passing the chest on the way. Time seemed to drag in this room, and though she'd not long arrived, she was keen to leave.

Fighting against these feelings, the hunter reached the stone slab and saw strange markings she didn't recognise carved into its top.

If she found the lens, turn to **77**, otherwise, turn to **413**.

471

Derilion held the amulet hoping that even though it didn't have all three enchantments, it would be of some use. Unfortunately, nothing happened, and the Diamond Elemental paced in front of her, ready to battle.

Whilst it stayed there, she could try and detect her next move.

Roll 2D6 and test for *Detection.*

It the test is successful, turn to **88**, otherwise, turn to **204**.

472

Derilion began to detect for traps. One of the biggest issues, she knew, was the vast number of different types there could be. Slowly, she checked the floor, the walls and the ceiling above her, inching along the corridor carefully.

It took a long time, but there was little else could she do.

Turn to **409**.

473

The Lightbringer moved her hand along the wall in front of her feeling for traps. She kept her breath shallow, listening for any tell-tale clicks or whooshes. The wall facing her was clear of traps, but the one behind her contained a wobbly stone about a foot ahead.

She could try and trigger the trap (turn to **185**) or continue past it (turn to **78**).

474

"What are you doing here?" Derilion asked.

"I am on my way out. The sorrow drew me here, and now I have had my fill. I suggest you leave, too. It will not end well."

"Turning back is not an option for me. I'm here to find my ward."

The demon looked at her with blackened eyes.

"That is your business. Do you have a silver ring in your possession? If so, I will exchange it for information."

If Derilion has the ring and is willing to part with it, turn to **244**, otherwise, turn to **491**.

Derilion sensed Othwig was about to speak and raised her hand to quiet her. She didn't expect it to work, but it did.

The hunter concentrated on the smells, and almost immediately got the sense of dread from the woman. She was someone to be feared, far more powerful than her stature would make anyone believe.

There was something else too, something about the sides, but she couldn't discern anything more than that.

She opened her eyes and weighed up her options.

"Come on, I haven't got all day," Othwig said. "Take the test. You know you want to."

Take the test	Turn to **625**
Pull out her sword	Turn to **585**

While Derilion dodged the first rock, two more swiftly followed and both hit their target, causing the hunter 1 damage to her *Health* each.

There was still a long way to go to reach the end of the chamber, and the Lightbringer couldn't see where her assailants were hiding. Not wanting to incur any more damage, she decided to use one of her skills to cross.

Use *Detection* to cross	Turn to **9**
Use *Speed* to cross	Turn to **599**
Use *Stealth* to cross	Turn to **493**

Derilion opened the door slowly with her sword. The room beyond looked deserted, despite being filled with shelves of what looked like ceramic pots and vases. She waited a moment listening, but heard nothing, so stepped into the room.

The ground beneath the hunter's feet softened, and she looked down and saw the floor was covered in a thick layer of dust. The Lightbringer could see the room better now she was stood in it. Not only were there shelves of ceramics, but there were at least a dozen misshapen tables which housed many more ornaments.

A potter's wheel sat in the middle of the clutter, and towards the furthest corner was a kiln, radiating heat.

Investigate the potter's wheel	Turn to **570**
Investigate the kiln	Turn to **612**
Investigate the pots	Turn to **134**
Choose the left door	Turn to **624**

"All right," Derilion said. "I'll help you."

"Excellent," the creature replied. It opened a drawer in its desk and brought out a triangular, wooden box. "Take this," it said. "It might help you, but it'll definitely help me."

The hunter took the box, and the creature moved its chair back, stood and unlocked the door with a key made from bone.

"Thank you," it said, as it pushed the door open.

Derilion nodded and went through the doorway to the next room.

Turn to **300**.

479

The girl looked at Derilion's hands.

"I can take those gauntlets off for you if you'd like," she said.

"That would be good," the hunter replied.

She put her hands out and listened as the girl recanted a spell. Mercifully, she felt the gauntlets loosen and shook them off.

"Thank you."

Restore 1 to Derilion's *Accuracy*.

Grom bent down and picked them up. She turned them over in her hands and smiled.

"I still remember the day I enchanted them," she said.

Turn to **628**.

480

The searching had taken a long time, and as Derilion turned to leave, she wondered if it'd taken too long. As if fate had heard her, there came the noise of a crying child from just ahead. Derilion stopped where she was, feeling sick to her stomach at the prospect of Obishaa appearing, hurt in some way.

Though there seemed to be something amiss with the cry, something not quite right. Derilion scanned around her and saw a crevice she should be able to hide in.

Roll 2D6 and test *Stealth*.

If the test is successful, turn to **559**, otherwise, turn to **267**.

481

Derilion ran for the exit, skilfully dodging the obstacles in the way. After a moment, the creature copied her, taking long strides in the same direction. Much to the hunter's surprise, the creature reached the door first, and, unable to stop, hit the wall, and fell to the floor.

Blocking the door, it turned its head and looked at the adventurer.

Derilion knew she must get past it but was unsure how.

Use the explosive powder	Turn to **590**
Try something from her backpack	Turn to **332**

482

Derilion walked into the next room. She could see three exits, but more importantly, there was a loud buzzing noise coming from nearby.

A voice in her head told her to get down, but she wasn't fast enough. A swarm of angry flying bugs, no doubt on their way to the remains of the Otistro, appeared.

Roll a 1D6 with the following results:

> 1-2 – Take 1 damage to *Health* from the bugs
> 3-4 – Take 2 damage to *Health* from the bugs
> 5-6 – Take 3 damage to *Health* from the bugs

No sooner than they appeared they were gone.

If the hunter survived, she had three exits to choose form.

Go straight ahead	Turn to **665**
Go right	Turn to **670**
Go left	Turn to **160**

483

Derilion headed left through the door, into a corridor that stretched out ahead as far as the light from her shield allowed her to see.

The walls were wet, and she felt water seeping up through her boots. The thought of the tunnel flooding scared her, especially when she came across a body floating face down in a puddle of water.

As she walked further along the corridor, the water flowed faster, and within a few seconds, it was over the ankles of her boots.

She was going to have to decide what to do quickly.

Walk forwards	Turn to **656**
Go back to the door	Turn to **677**
Stay where she was	Turn to **128**

484

"I don't have anything to trade," Derilion said.

"Really? I beg to differ," Othwig replied. "I think you have a lot to trade."

The hunter's hand rested on the hilt of her sword.

"That really will be of no use to you," the witch said. "Take one of my tests; your chances of survival are far higher."

Pull out her sword	Turn to **585**
Try to detect the best option	Turn to **67**
Take a test	Turn to **625**

485

Derilion must fight the Cuddower. As well as attacking with the club, the Cuddower attacks with its tail each turn (therefore having 2 attacks to the Lightbringer's 1). The damage Derilion inflicts does not affect the tail.

	Speed	*Accuracy*	*Damage*	*Health*
Cuddower	10	7	2	12
Cuddower's Tail	~	6	1	~

If she wins, turn to **152**.

486

The Death Maiden placed her staff against Derilion's temple.

Immediately, the hunter felt an icy chill spreading from its tip, smothering her skull. Derilion's vision narrowed, and, with dread, she knew her soul was being sucked into the staff, where she would remain forever.

487

Derilion quickened her pace toward the end of the tunnel, which ended with the stream flowing swiftly from left to right.

The hunter looked around for a way to navigate it safely. There was a small ledge which she could use to go left or right along the wall above the stream.

Alternatively, she could jump into the water and be swept to the right.

Head left along the ledge	Turn to **142**
Head right along the ledge	Turn to **676**
Jump into the water to go right	Turn to **6**

488

Derilion stood before the throne and looked for a space to hide. There wasn't a lot of room, but she knew she had to try.

Did she eat any of the food on the table?

If she did, turn to **630**, otherwise, turn to **395**.

489

Derilion showed her the glass jaw, but the girl didn't seem impressed.

"I can't do anything with that. It's the sort of rubbish a troll might like."

Trade scrolls	Turn to **237**
Trade the golden cuff	Turn to **577**
Trade something else	Turn to **21**

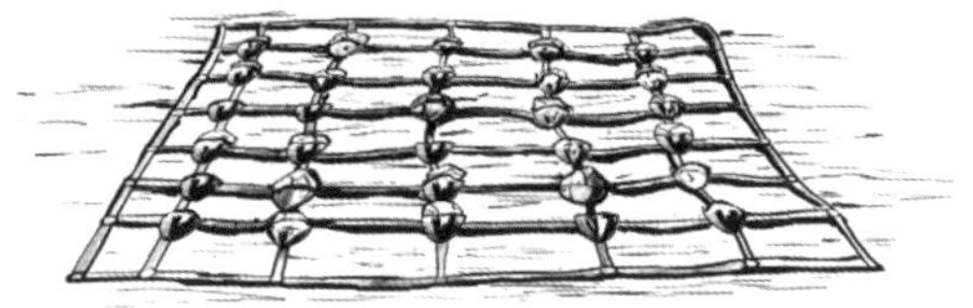

490

The Death Maiden cannot die, but Derilion knew she could disable it by cutting its limbs off.

	Speed	Accuracy	Damage	Health
Death Maiden	6	7	2	~

If the Death Maiden lands 2 blows on the Lightbringer, turn to **486**. If Derilion lands fours blows, turn to **43**.

491

Derilion shook her head.

"I don't have a silver ring," she said.

"Hm," the demon replied. "Let's see."

The demon turned and looked at the hunter with a searing stare. Derilion wanted to look away but fought the urge and met his gaze.

"You have been judged," the demon said after a few moments.

Did Derilion have the ring? If so, turn to **609**, otherwise, turn to **261**.

492

The scorpion's stinger hit the back of the hunter's hand. Tremendous pain shot up from the wound and Derilion fell to the floor in agony. The girl got up from her desk and walked over to her.

"Don't say I didn't warn you," she said, smiling.

The hunter felt her muscles spasm and then nothing but darkness.

493

Roll 2D6 and test Derilion's *Stealth* 3 times.

For every unsuccessful test, reduce her *Health* by 1.

Even after travelling so far across the room, there was still a little way left for her to go. She only had one choice.

Turn to **108**.

494

Derilion went to the dwarf and crouched over him. The blood was dry on his face and splattered onto his clothes.

"What happened here?" she asked him.

His eyes rolled, and he appeared to be drifting in and out of consciousness.

"Do you have… a gold cuff?" he whispered.

If the Lightbringer has a gold cuff and is willing to help, turn to **647**, otherwise, turn to **692**.

495

Derilion held her breath and swung the sword as close to her hand as she dared. It worked, the vines were cut and recoiled back. The hunter thought for a moment and came up with two possible options.

Try and set the door alight	Turn to **229**
Use some explosive powder	Turn to **41**

496

Derilion didn't want to be stuck in the wardrobe should the troll come to investigate. She tensed her legs and put a hand on one of the wardrobe doors.

Taking a deep breath in, she pushed it open and sprung out, drawing her sword. The troll continued to look at her, expressionless.

If Derilion had already met a troll, turn to **661**, otherwise, turn to **35**.

497

"I'm sorry," Derilion told her, as she picked herself up from the floor once again.

The woman looked sad.

"I thought you really had a chance there for a moment. Instead, you're just like the others."

The hunter shrugged and then went to leave the room (turn to **131**).

498

As she approached the lamp, the air around Derilion grew cold. The flame was a very light blue, almost transparent.

She tried to pick the lamp up, but instead of lifting it easily, she was barely able to raise it off the counter. Unable to carry it, the hunter wondered what she should do next.

Touch the flame	Turn to **194**
Look at something else	Turn to **148**
Leave the room	Turn to **29**

499

The words on the wall changed again.

"Thank you," they read. "I have no other way to move. Place your hand on the wall, and I will attach."

Derilion moved forward to place her hand on the wall.

Roll 2D6 and test for *Detection.*

If the test is successful, turn to **208**, otherwise, turn to **606**.

It felt to Derilion like she was falling forever, but when she opened her eyes, she realised she was lying on a floor and had been unconscious for a while.

Before her were five thrones, four of them occupied by Pajoli warlocks, the fifth empty. Initially, the hunter thought they were looking at her but then realised their eyes were closed as if in meditation. Between the Lightbringer and the thrones was a shallow pool of water.

Derilion attempted to move but was held to the spot by an invisible force.

"Where's Obishaa?" she shouted at the men.

"The girl is unimportant." These words came straight into her head without any of their mouths moving. "You have returned to us, and that is what is important."

"Returned to you?" the hunter asked, confused. "I've never been here before."

The men smiled in unison.

"Come and sit in the throne, and then you will remember."

Derilion felt the spell release its grip on her, and she was free to move. She looked around for an exit yet saw none.

Sit on the throne	Turn to **536**
Use her amulet	Turn to **541**
Demand to know Obishaa's location	Turn to **530**
Use something to attack the Pajoli	Turn to **85**
Stay still	Turn to **679**

501

Derilion retrieved a pouch of the explosive powder, wedged it in a stone she picked up from the floor, and tossed it into the hole. At least she didn't have to aim.

She counted as it dropped, trying to measure how deep the hole went. After ten seconds, she heard a 'whump' noise. She looked over the edge and saw a flame spreading rapidly up the hole.

Derilion stood back tight against the wall.

The flame shot upward in front of her, and behind it came a massive Insect Demon.

Fortunately, the explosion had damaged it.

	Speed	Accuracy	Damage	Health
Insect Demon	7	7	1	8

If the Lightbringer wins, turn to **135**.

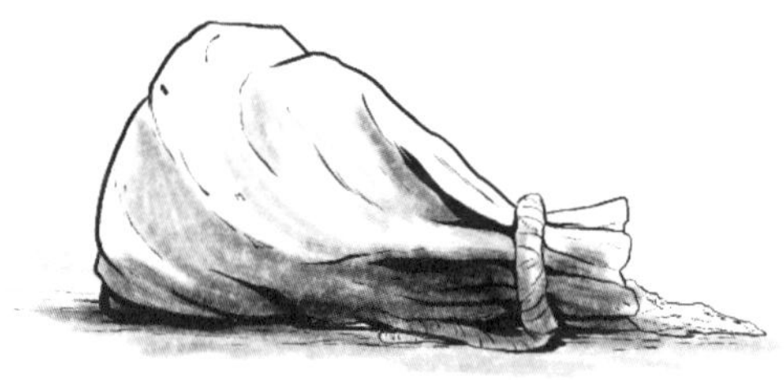

502

Unseen up till now, Derilion noticed a small girl was sat in front of the exit from the room. She watched as the hunter approached.

"Did you open any boxes?" she asked with no emotion.

If she did, turn to **406**, otherwise, turn to **325**.

Derilion approached the Cuddower with caution. Whether he was a statue or not, she knew one hit from him would be enough to kill her.

She placed her sword under his neck and pulled the arrow out with her other hand. Nothing happened at first, but then she could hear a cracking noise, and the beast's flesh softened. Derilion held onto his head.

"Don't move," she told him. "Or I'll cut your throat and take my chances."

"Very well," the Cuddower said. "Don't stick the arrow in me, and I'll help you."

"How do you open the door?"

"With a spell. You do know where you are, don't you?"

Derilion touched the arrow to the Cuddower's side.

"All right," he said. "I apologise. I'll say a spell and the door will open. Do you swear not to use the arrow again?"

"I swear, but I'll keep it with me."

"Very well. I wasn't that hungry, anyway." The Cuddower spoke words under his breath, and the door opened.

"Don't come after me," she said into his ear.

"I won't."

Derilion backed away carefully, and left the room, making sure the Cuddower didn't move (turn to **443**).

504

The Lightbringer skirted around the woman, giving her a wide arc on the way to the opposite door. No sooner had she passed, then a humming began behind her. The hunter turned, hand on the hilt of her sword and saw the woman had stood. Derilion recognised her immediately as a Death Maiden, an undead creature who sought out others to claim their soul.

"I have an offer for you," the Death Maiden said in a sing-song voice, raising a staff she was holding in her hand. "Kill the monster in the room beyond, and I will spare your soul."

It was an odd request, but a simple one. The hunter could either fight the Death Maiden (turn to **374**) or agree to her request and proceed to the next room (turn to **674**).

505

Derilion kicked the fire orange balls into the pool and watched as the water around them turned red. The Elemental screamed and withered slightly before her eyes.

Subtract 6 from its *Health*.

If the Elemental has no more *Health*, turn to **137**. If the hunter hasn't kicked four items in yet, she can try another (turn to **633**). If she has, she must face the Elemental (turn to **107**).

506

The hunter sensed the Cuddower was cautious. Its eyes flitted to the bow and arrow, and instantly she knew it was afraid of it. Derilion raised the bow and loosed an arrow at the creature.

Roll 2D6 and test for *Accuracy*.

If successful, turn to **356**, otherwise, turn to **363**.

507

Derilion stopped moving and began to tread water. She waited to see what would happen. In theory, the water-level would continue to rise the longer she waited, yet it stayed the same.

None of it was making sense.

She could continue to wait (turn to **388**) or swim to the end (turn to **682**).

508

The wardrobe was unlocked. Derilion opened the doors and saw it was filled with clothes for a person much bigger than her. Just above the clothes, she found two wooden staffs, but before she had time to inspect them, she heard the noise of someone approaching the door ahead of her.

Instinctively, she hid in the wardrobe and hoped whoever it was didn't need a change of outfit.

Turn to **255**.

509

Derilion walked past the woman who stepped back even more as the she went by. The hunter leant towards the net and placed the stone into one of the empty pockets.

While doing this, she realised she had an opportunity of taking one of the other gemstones she was now obscuring from the woman.

If she wanted to take a gemstone, turn to **566**, otherwise, turn to **215**.

510

Derilion moved as quickly as she could in the gloom of the chamber. She only had a few seconds to get as far away as possible, and she felt the fear trying to take her over.

She dodged past a body sprawled on the floor, but as she looked back to see how they'd died, her foot caught underneath something. Even as she tumbled, she attempted to shift whatever it was that had snagged her, but it was stuck fast.

Derilion fell hard, knocking her head against the stone floor. She fought to stay conscious; her eyesight now doubled by the blow to the head. She concentrated on what had tripped her and saw a sword coated in an amber substance.

It was then she realised the room had grown quiet again, and she began to raise her hands towards her head to protect it. It was too late. The amber ball hit her square in the face, and quickly solidified around her nose and mouth, making it impossible to breathe. She tried to reach her backpack to find something, anything, she could use, but there wasn't enough time.

As she was taking her last breaths, she could hear the creature dislodge from the ceiling, and fall to the ground next to her. Her last sight was of the Ambrite's nightmarish face, peering at hers, waiting for her to stop moving.

511

Derilion felt her body become lighter and watched as the woman effortlessly lifted her from the ground and threw her head-first into the net. She expected to hit the table beneath, but instead, she fell through the net, and for the moment before she disintegrated, she saw a strange land below her, with tall buildings on a scale she'd never seen, divided by wide grey pathways.

Her adventure ends here.

512

"Oh, yes," Othwig said, inspecting the moss. "Yes, that'll do just fine."

She took the moss (**-1w**) before the hunter could say anything.

Turn to **298**.

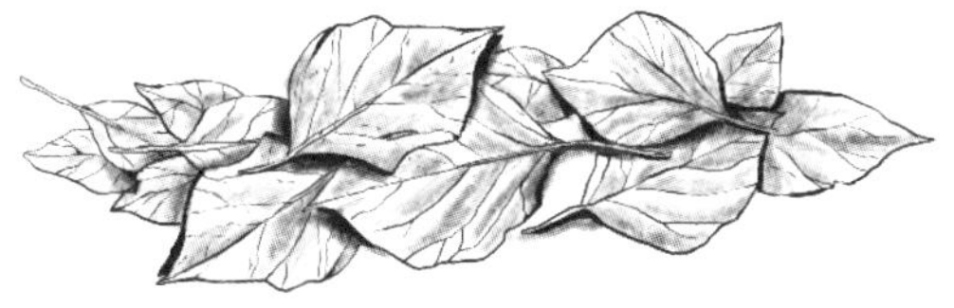

513

Othwig took hold of the necklace, took a substance from her belt and sprinkled it over it. Then she stamped her foot and clapped her hands three times.

"There, it is done," she said. "Be careful; the greatest tests are always yet to come."

"Thank you," the hunter said and turned and left the chamber.

Turn to **466**.

514

"All right," the troll said. It didn't sound like its heart was in it.

It swung its club and the Lightbringer raised Volkov to deflect it.

Roll 2D6 and test for *Accuracy*.

If the test was successful, turn to **182**, otherwise, turn to **19**.

515

"Here, take this," Derilion said, holding out the silver ring. The trolls stopped and looked at the piece of jewellery. Their brows furrowed and they looked blankly at each other, and then back at Derilion.

"Is that it?" they asked. "Next, I suppose you'll be offering us gold!"

The hunter felt stupid and scared. She tried to think about what else she had to offer.

Offer a golden cuff	Turn to **286**
Offer a glass jaw	Turn to **95**
Offer the trolls nothing	Turn to **465**

516

Derilion carefully picked her way around the right-hand side of the wall. Progress was slow; the further she went, the more debris got in her way. Most of it consisted of bones and clothes from previous adventurers. She tried to put them out of her mind.

She stopped for a moment to think. As far as she could see, there were two options. She could search the clothes (turn to **249**) or press on (turn to **167**).

517

The blacksmith shook his head.

"You're lying to me," he said. "Which makes me think you mean to use it. I'm sorry this couldn't end less violently."

"I don't know what you're talking about," the hunter replied.

"I can *feel* you have the carving."

The hunter saw the man transform in front of her into a large demon with armoured skin, easily twice her size.

"What are you?" she asked.

"It doesn't matter," he replied, drew breath, and breathed out a scorching fire which incinerated Derilion within seconds.

Her adventure ends here.

518

Without warning, Derilion swung for the Death Maiden's legs, cutting most of the way through her left thigh.

"You may not die, or even feel pain, but you still need your muscles to stand up," the hunter said.

The Death Maiden screamed and staggered away, but Derilion hadn't finished. She stepped forward and severed her right arm. The staff she was holding fell to the floor, still gripped with the better part of her limb. The Lightbringer picked it up and pressed it against the Death Maiden's head. The Maiden screamed a silent scream and collapsed to the floor, motionless. The staff glowed brightly and then vanished from the hunter's hand.

Turn to **43**.

519

The hunter continued along the corridor, encountering nothing more frightening than the odd rat scurrying past her in the opposite direction.

In the quietness of the caves, it was easy to forget so many other creatures inhabited them. Derilion stopped and drank from her bottle. As she raised it to her mouth, she thought she heard a noise coming from further down the passage. She waited, and the noise came again; a low moaning sound, as if someone was in pain ahead.

The Lightbringer proceeded cautiously, trying to keep to the shadows. Within a couple of minutes, she saw the source of the sound. Lying across the path in front of her was a woman dressed in robes and holding her head.

Two doors led off from the chamber; one ahead and another to the right with a lightning symbol carved into it.

Help the prone woman	Turn to **383**
Put her out of her misery	Turn to **14**
Step over the woman and go on	Turn to **504**
Step over the woman and go right	Turn to **634**

520

Derilion looked towards the closing door. There was no handle on this side; no way out. Quickly, she attempted to move her foot to block the door, but it merely pushed it aside and closed with a definite thud. She felt movement behind her and looked up. Above her an axe was mid-swing, being held by a dwarf who looked hungry.

"I'm sorry," he said, "I need to eat."

These were the last words she ever heard.

521

With incredible speed, the hunter whipped her leg away from the vines and was a mixture of amazed and relieved when it broke free. The door had been the death of the person behind her, she was sure.

For a moment, the thought of why these vines were growing here flashed across her mind. How did they get here? What purpose did they have? It didn't make any sense, and she didn't have any time to work it out.

Derilion looked at the door with hatred and came up with two possible options to move forward.

Use the explosive powder	Turn to **41**
Try and set light to the door	Turn to **229**

522

The hunter tried to keep her centre of balance on the rock. Just when she thought she was okay, the rock moved, and she fell heavily on one knee.

The trolls were awake and ready to fight in seconds, armed with large knives. They stood between the hunter and the door, making it impossible for her to leave.

Derilion held up her hands as a sign of friendship. It was unlikely she'd survive against both. As her mind whirled, she thought she might be able to barter her way out of the situation. She had several objects to offer, she mused.

Offer them a golden cuff	Turn to **286**
Offer them a glass jaw	Turn to **95**
Offer them a silver ring	Turn to **515**
Don't want to give them something	Turn to **465**

<h1 style="text-align:center">523</h1>

"What do you want?" the hunter asked.

"I can tell you where to find your ward - for a price."

Derilion's heart quickened. Perhaps this was the luck she needed.

"What is your price?" she demanded.

"The amulet you're wearing. I used to have one just like it."

Derilion wondered why he needed the amulet. It seemed a lot to give up, but then she knew the biggest gambles sometimes gave the biggest rewards.

Give him the necklace   Turn to **51**
Keep the necklace   Turn to **402**

<h1 style="text-align:center">524</h1>

The hunter wiped the blood of the werecat off her sword and replaced it in its scabbard. She felt sorry for the creature. It had probably been held in the crate for a long time and just needed to eat.

She looked at the remaining boxes and decided now would be the right time to focus on the search for Obishaa.

Turn to **502**.

525

The music slowed, and the two of them came to a standstill.

"It is rare anyone can keep up with me," the girl said. "I can offer you this ointment for your shoes. They will make your step lighter and faster."

"Thank you," the hunter said.

Derilion took the bottle and applied it to her boots. Add 1 to her *Stealth* and 1 to her *Speed*.

She moved onto the next room, feeling pleased with herself.

Turn to **548**.

526

Derilion shifted the dirt on a few of the patches and nodded. There was a definite pattern to them, and now she had seen it, she'd be able to search faster.

In no time at all, she'd found the true burying site. She dug and within moments her hands were brushing the top of what felt like paper. She dug the objects out and held them in her hands – two scrolls (**+1w each**), neatly done up.

The light was not good enough to read them, so after deciding whether to keep them or not, she moved on.

Turn to **480**.

527

Derilion carefully picked up the orb, turned to leave and froze on the spot. There, almost directly behind her, was the glass skeleton waiting, poised to attack.

The hunter looked to see if there was an obvious way to retreat, but she was hemmed in by all the ornaments and had no choice but to face the attacker.

Turn to **337**.

528

The tunnel continued. The ceiling got lower, and the walls narrowed. On a few occasions, Derilion thought she'd seen movement on the rock wall which had subsequently turned out to be nothing but shadows from the light the shield was casting.

Finally, a blank wall blocked her path forward. It had been a dead-end, after all. Derilion screamed with anger, cursing the wall, the caves and the Pajoli. She sat on the floor, exhausted.

Search the dead-end	Turn to **158**
Turn back	Turn to **323**

529

Derilion stopped what she was doing and listened. Heavy footsteps were approaching the door ahead of her. Whoever it was, she didn't want to meet them.

The Lightbringer searched the room for possible places to hide, but her options were limited.

Hide behind the throne	Turn to **488**
Hide in the wardrobe	Turn to **139**
Draw her sword and fight	Turn to **103**

530

"Where is Obishaa?" Derilion called again. She was getting angry now. She'd come all this way to save her.

"We sent her somewhere... else. A long way away. You don't have to worry about her."

"Is she alive?"

"Probably," they replied. "But the girl is unimportant. Why don't you come and sit on the throne?"

Use something to attack the Pajoli	Turn to **85**
Use the amulet	Turn to **541**
Stay where she is	Turn to **679**
Sit on the throne	Turn to **536**

531

Derilion found a packet of the powder (**-1w**) and took a couple of steps back. She launched it at the wall and ducked behind her shield.

The explosion knocked her clean off her feet, causing 2 damage to her *Health*. If she survived, she opened her eyes to see the debris around her feet and the runestone sitting in the middle of it.

Turn to **425**.

<h1 style="text-align:center">532</h1>

Derilion stepped forward, shield raised against attack. The Otistro was quick, though its immovability limited its range.

	Speed	Accuracy	Damage	Health
Otistro	9	8	1	12

If the Lightbringer won, turn to **545**.

<h1 style="text-align:center">533</h1>

Derilion breathed in and stood on tiptoe to try and make herself thinner. She adjusted her sword so it didn't stick out and moved her backpack to the front so she could better manoeuvre.

Even still, there were a couple of moments where she nudged an object and thought it might break something only to see it steady itself.

Finally, she stood in front of the orb.

Look into the orb	Turn to **627**
Smash the orb	Turn to **642**
Take the orb	Turn to **527**

<h1 style="text-align:center">534</h1>

The hunter peered into the remains. The shiny object appeared bigger than she'd first thought. Carefully, she wrapped her hand in cloth, reached in and pulled the object out. She brought the shield up to see it better and was surprised when she saw it was a simple crown made of a silver strand wrapped around many times (**+4w**).

Turn to **165**.

She moved carefully towards the sword, reaching out when she was finally close enough to pick it up. Her hand closed around its hilt, but something felt wrong. Derilion brought the shield closer to the sword and saw the weapon's blade was coated in a hard, resin-like substance.

She put all her weight into shifting the sword, but it didn't budge. It was then she heard a creature scuttling overhead in the darkness. The adventurer turned and raised her shield and sword to the unseen enemy.

Turn to **381**.

536

"I'll sit in the throne if you release Obishaa."

"Very well."

Derilion stood and crossed the shallow pool to the front of the throne. She turned and sat. As soon as she had, the scene around her changed, and she was within white walls of crystals. The same four warlocks were there, this time their eyes were open.

"Well, that was easier than we thought," a warlock said. He stood and, in his hand, held a staff with a glittering orb on the end. "This should be very easy."

He moved toward Derilion, who felt her mind being pulled into the orb.

"Not as strong as she would have been, but who are we to complain?"

Derilion struggled to no avail. The Orb consumed her mind and her power until there was nothing left. She had failed in her quest.

537

Derilion moved toward the door. Before she'd taken more than a couple of steps, there was a clunking sound behind her, and someone cleared their throat.

"That's quite far enough," said a voice.

Turn to **637**.

538

Derilion opened the door to the left and walked into the large room beyond. Did she recently talk to the blacksmith?

If so, turn to **252**, otherwise, turn to **361**.

539

The Lightbringer inspected the second coffin and found its lid was nailed shut. It seemed like overkill to her, and the pun made her smile. She could probably prise it open with her sword, if she had to, or she could leave via the left door or the one in front.

Open the coffin with her sword	Turn to **687**
Continue straight on	Turn to **537**
Exit to the left	Turn to **178**

540

With the final blow still reverberating around the chamber, the armour fell. Derilion wiped her brow and watched as the metal turned back into a liquid and disappeared into the floor. Another noise startled her to the left, and she crouched, ready to pounce. She was relieved to realise it was just a door opening in the wall. Derilion didn't need to think twice to go through it.

Turn to **91**.

541

Derilion reached for her amulet; surely, this was the moment to use it.

"No!" the hunter heard the Pajoli scream, and from somewhere within the chamber came an unsettling rumble.

The Lightbringer stood sword drawn, and shield raised.

Turn to **202**.

542

Derilion turned around and headed back along the corridor. She moved swiftly aware she had already taken too much time to explore the caves; every second she wasted was a second Obishaa was suffering.

The Lightbringer came to a set of steep stairs and descended, aware of the smell of death coming from below. At the bottom of the steps lay a body. Derilion put her hand to their cheek and was surprised when it was still warm; they had died recently.

Derilion searched the body but found nothing of value, so pushed on. At the end of the corridor, she saw a door overgrown with vines.

Turn to **680**.

Derilion took the carving out of her backpack and held it out to the blacksmith.

"Here," she said. "What is it?"

The smile faded on the blacksmith's face as he took the carving from her.

"It's designed to hold the soul of whoever carries it. It was originally used as a hiding place, but of course, it's also used as a prison."

"Are you sure you want it?"

"If I have it within my possession, then I can hide it better than most in these caves. Let me give you something in return."

Holut took a key from his pocket.

"This will allow you to unlock a very special door in the caves."

"Which door?" the hunter asked.

"You'll know it when you come to it."

Derilion took the key (**+1w**) and looked at it.

"Thank you."

The man shrugged.

"I hope you live long enough to use it," he said. "Oh, and this is important, don't open the chest in the morgue."

Turn to **613**.

<h1 style="text-align:center">544</h1>

The hunter stopped and listened and realised she could hear the faint sound of breathing coming from in front of her. One of the bodies was alive.

She stepped closer and saw the man's chest rising and falling as he breathed. Not sure why he would choose such a place to slumber, Derilion had several options.

Wake him up	Turn to **216**
Attack him	Turn to **72**
Search the boy	Turn to **198**
Search the woman	Turn to **458**
Head for the morgue	Turn to **144**

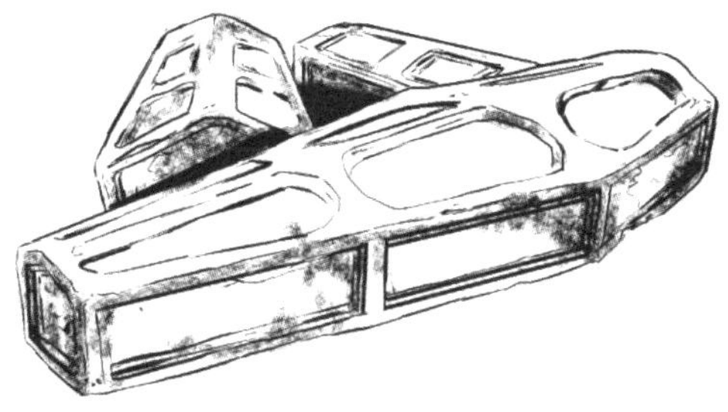

<h1 style="text-align:center">545</h1>

Derilion looked at the creature's lifeless body, confused as to why this mythical creature had come to live in the real world.

As she turned to leave, she heard scuttling from behind it, and to her horror, an oversized, half-digested, spider-like creature emerged from the Otistro innards and advanced towards her.

	Speed	Accuracy	Damage	Health
Spider	8	6	1	5

If the Lightbringer survived, turn to **289**.

546

"I've dealt with her," Derilion told the child. "Who are you?"

"Who are *you*?" she replied. "You're the one in my home."

"My name is Derilion," the hunter said. "I'm here to try to rescue my ward. She was taken by the Pajoli this morning."

The girl smiled, the corners of her mouth turning up slightly.

"Is your ward worth dying for?" she asked.

Derilion thought it a strange question. Of course, she would sacrifice herself for Obishaa. And still, from the child's perspective, maybe such a sacrifice didn't make any sense at all.

"Yes, she is," Derilion replied.

"Good," the girl replied. "For in this place, death is the most likely outcome."

Turn to **259**.

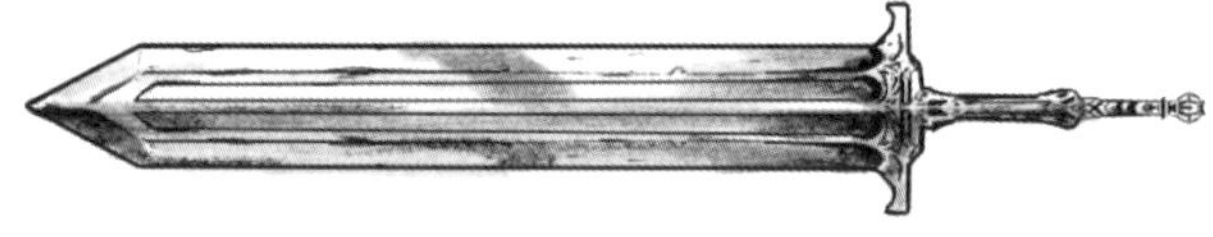

547

Enough was enough; her time was better spent looking for Obishaa. She walked to the door at the far end and twisted the rusted handle.

She was relieved to find it unlocked and went through it without incident.

Turn to **119**.

548

Derilion stepped into the next room. It was well lit compared to the others and had a slightly raised circular platform in its centre, though it wasn't that which caught her attention. What the hunter stared at was the seven-foot human-like figure standing in the middle of the platform.

It was a Slabac. Usually found near the coast, it had a hard shell over most of his body. One arm looked like a shield, while the other ended in a claw with three-finger pincers.

"I don't want to hurt you," it said. "But unless I kill another adventurer, I can't pass through this room, and I haven't come all this way to die."

Before Derilion had time to answer, the figure advanced at her.

	Speed	*Accuracy*	*Damage*	*Health*
Slabac	8	9	2	12

If the Lightbringer is about to land the killing blow, turn to **650**.

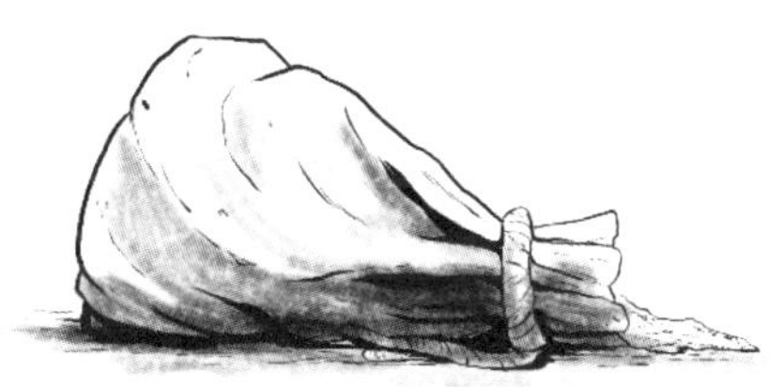

549

The hunter found what appeared to be a bag of three fire orange balls (**+3w**). She couldn't work out what they were made of, but they were heavy. After a moment, she noticed the man she thought was dead was stirring and decided to move away from the bodies as quickly as possible, and head into the morgue.

Turn to **342**.

Derilion took a small step closer to the vines and raised the shield to inspect them. Immediately, they moved away from the flame, scared of it. The hunter moved her shield around the door, watching as the vines retreated in a rippling effect. They were alive.

She looked at the body on the floor behind her and realised for the first time there was no obvious weapon that could have killed them.

She turned back to the vines and felt them looking back at her.

Kick the door open	Turn to **114**
Try and set the door alight	Turn to **229**
Use the explosive powder	Turn to **41**
Open the door	Turn to **364**

551

Derilion peered around the door, weapon ready and senses on high alert. All she saw, however, was another corridor leading away, with a separate branch off to the left.

Try and detect the best route	Turn to **36**
Go straight on	Turn to **183**
Take left branch	Turn to **209**

552

There was an underlying smell the hunter thought she'd encountered before. She held her breath while she tried to place it.

As soon as she did, she began to back out of the room, making sure she didn't turn her back. The smell was a sleeping gas. She'd been in a few taverns where the owner would attempt to use the same gas to attempt to rob you.

Fortunately, the Lightbringer made it safely out of the room and closed the door, turning the key in the lock.

She had two options, now.

The door on the right	Turn to **141**
Next set of doors	Turn to **253**

553

Derilion thought about her next move, knowing the fewer people she encountered, the better. She looked behind her; it wasn't a long way back to the other path.

She turned and took a few steps back towards the entrance but had to stop when she felt an unseen barrier blocking her way. She followed the invisible obstacle from one side of the entrance to the other. There was no break.

It seemed something didn't want her to leave.

Call out to them	Turn to **76**
Use *Stealth* to sneak up on them	Turn to **391**
Use *Speed* to attack	Turn to **629**

Try as she might, Derilion couldn't grasp the reason behind the fear she was feeling. After a moment, the chamber grew silent, and she knew it was ready to attack.

She felt the rush of air before the blow to the face. Something sticky coated her flesh, and even as she tried to claw it away, it was hardening.

The Lightbringer turned and started to run as fast as she could, but the substance hindered her sight, and she quickly fell to the floor, knocking her head against the stone floor.

The creature landed next to her. Through the amber substance on her face, she thought she could make it out, but wasn't sure. The Ambrite waited patiently as its latest victim's movements began to slow and finally stop. It looked at it for a while, and then slowly, carefully, made its way back into the darkness.

Derilion fetched the purse of coins from the backpack and held it out to the Cuddower.

"Have these," she said. "It's more than my life is worth."

The Cuddower frowned and then shrugged.

"What's the point of offering me those when I can just as easily take them off your dead body."

No sooner had the Cuddower finished speaking than he lunged at the hunter, hoping to catch her off guard.

Roll 2D6 and test for *Speed*.

If the test is successful, turn to **375**, otherwise, turn to **405**.

The scarf completely covered the mirror. Within a few moments, the other reflections returned to normal, and the hunter decided to move as quickly as she could through the room.

Turn to **312**.

557

The hunter drew in her breath. She wasn't sure why she was bothering to open the casket. It was not likely to heed anything of use.

Still, there was a chance it might, so she put her fingers under the lid and gently pulled upwards. It came up without resistance, and she looked underneath.

Unsurprisingly, she found a corpse wrapped in purple robes. She couldn't see anything of value, so she replaced the lid and thought about her next move.

Investigate the second coffin	Turn to **539**
Continue straight on	Turn to **537**
Exit to the left	Turn to **178**

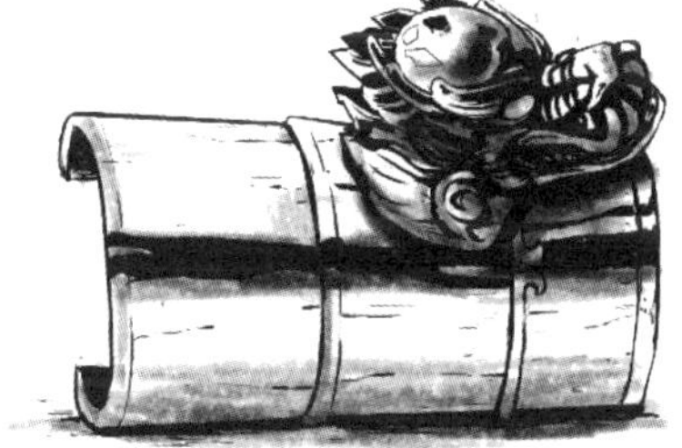

The hunter reached the bottom of the stairs, the stench of death growing with every step, till she had to cover her mouth and nose to stop her from being violently ill.

A figure lay a little way in front of the stairs, barely moving in the filth of the ground. Derilion went to them, knowing they were too weak to pose any threat, and knelt.

"Can I help you?" she asked.

The figure breathed one last deep breath, closed their eyes and laid still; the life now gone from their body. Their palm opened and something rolled across the floor into the darkness.

Derilion followed its path and retrieved the object - a round stone with circles running across it (+3w). She had never seen anything like it but thought if the figure had held onto it so much, it might be worth something.

Derilion searched the body but found nothing of note.

She stood and approached the door very slowly.

Turn to **680**.

559

Derilion fitted herself into the tight space, extinguished the shield, and waited completely invisible in the gloom.

The sobbing sound continued, and out of the darkness, a creature appeared, around five-foot-tall, its only facial feature a gaping hole where the mouth should be. It had four arms which were little more than claws, tethered onto long bones which it used to move quickly.

It was hideous, and Derilion did her best not to gasp at its appearance. As it grew closer, the adventurer could see spines protruding from its body, either a defence or an attack mechanism; maybe both.

She was relieved when it continued passed. The Lightbringer waited until it was long out of sight before deciding to move again, reigniting her shield as she did.

Turn to **231**.

560

Derilion put her hand around the door handle and twisted. It was unlocked, and she pushed it open, weapon ready.

The room in front was in darkness, and something felt odd about it. The hunter took a step closer, remaining outside but moving the shield towards the opening. She expected to see more, but the room seemed to eat the light. Derilion could hear the voice louder now.

"Stay away," it warned.

"I can help you," the hunter replied.

"Stay away."

It sounded almost convinced of its message, yet there was something underneath that concerned Derilion.

"Let me help you," she said and waited. The voice had stopped. "I'm coming in."

Derilion took a step forward.

"Where are you?"

No reply. The hunter took another step into the room and swung the shield in front of her. Derilion gasped.

To her left, curled into the corner of the room, an old woman cowered, her face turned away.

"I told you not to come in," she said and began to laugh.

Protect herself with explosive	Turn to **303**
Try and help the woman	Turn to **415**
Leave	Turn to **411**

"I'll take the charm."

The woman took the necklace in her hand and began recanting a spell in a language unknown to the hunter.

"There," she said. "It is enchanted. Now, your end of the deal."

She stepped aside to let Derilion through.

Turn to **509**.

562

The hunter came to a section with no useful handholds. Looking around, she realised she'd be able to go further by either moving higher or lower on the rock face.

Continue higher up the rockface   Turn to **26**
Continue lower down the rockface   Turn to **150**

563

On closer inspection, Derilion saw the door was already ajar. Carefully, she opened it further using her sword and watched as it swung inward.

Beyond the door was a strange sight. A brightly lit orb-shaped room with a thin wooden shelf running the circumference of the chamber, upon which sat various clay pots and glass ornaments.

Two objects caught the hunter's eye - a glass skeleton with a missing jaw and a large glass ball directly across from it. She took a step into the room, and the door slammed shut behind her. Derilion turned and tried to open it, but it didn't budge.

She turned back to the room. Hopefully, something in here would help get her out.

Use a glass jaw if she has one	Turn to **64**
Go for the glass ball	Turn to **191**
Investigate the room more	Turn to **422**

564

Derilion took one of the torches from the wall and tossed it into the hole. At least she didn't have to aim. She counted as it dropped, trying to calculate how deep the hole went. After ten seconds, she heard a whump! She looked over the edge and saw a flame spread across the bottom of the hole. As she watched, a large Insect Demon flew up towards her.

	Speed	Accuracy	Damage	Health
Insect Demon	8	9	2	12

If the Lightbringer wins, turn to **135**.

565

Derilion opened her backpack and put the book in (**+3w**). She pushed the white door shut, locked it, and kept the key with her.

With only one other option available, Derilion went through the stone door.

Turn to **197**.

566

Carefully, Derilion sneaked a green gemstone into her pocket (**+3w**) as she placed the other stone into the net.

Almost immediately, the woman pushed the hunter aside, and her initial look of hunger turned to confusion when whatever was supposed to have happened, didn't. She turned in fury to look at the Lightbringer.

"What have you done?"

She lunged towards the hunter, but her anger made her slow and clumsy, and Derilion had the chance to defend herself.

Push her off with the shield	Turn to **2**
Run her through with her sword	Turn to **444**

567

Derilion knelt and looked through the wet clothes but found nothing of value. She turned to have a look at the wall but could no longer see the hole or the stones which had contained Zalixa.

Confused, the hunter headed toward the stream.

Turn to **487**.

568

Derilion carefully made her way to the next set of doors. Fortunately, they were no more traps prepared for her.

The doors looked exactly like the last set, and as there were no other exits, she had to choose one or the other.

Choose the left door	Turn to **664**
Choose the right door	Turn to **477**

569

Derilion focused her mind as much as possible but couldn't pick up on anything. She cursed her stupidity at wasting time. She opened her eyes and must now face the Elemental.

Turn to **107**.

570

The potter's wheel was in a good state considering it had received a fair amount of use. Just to the side of the wheel, Derilion noticed a small bag of turquoise sand (**+2w**).

The hunter sat at the wheel and pushed the foot-pedal, making the centre spin. It worked as expected, and as it spun, she looked at the rest of the room, trying to decide what to do.

Investigate the pots	Turn to **134**
Investigate the kiln	Turn to **612**
Leave the room and go to the left door	Turn to **624**

571

"What brings you here?" the hunter asked.

"I'm stuck here, like everyone else," it said. "If I were you, I'd turn around and walk out now, while you still can. But I can tell by your attire that my words will fall on deaf ears."

It looked at Derilion for a couple of seconds before returning to reading. Perhaps if she took a different tack, she'd get more of a response. Or perhaps she should leave it altogether.

"I'm on a mission to help the Pajoli."	Turn to **382**
Say nothing and continue	Turn to **595**

572

Derilion closed her eyes and concentrated, pushing her senses out, trying to detect anything which would ease her concerns. She pictured investigating her surroundings, as if her soul was outside of herself, searching. She heard nothing, saw nothing, smelt nothing but the cave.

She opened her eyes and tried to step forward. Her leg didn't lift, and she had to steady herself on the wall. Derilion looked at her feet and saw the mud was creeping up her boots. She nearly laughed.

She pulled at her legs, but they were stuck firm. She watched the mud moving towards her ankles and knew there was no point in running. It covered the floor a good twelve feet in front and behind her. The only option she could think of was climbing her way out of it. She inspected the nearest wall for a foothold and found several.

Roll 2D6 and test for *Accuracy*.

If the test was successful, turn to **38**, otherwise, turn to **418**.

573

There was no other way of doing it, the hunter thought. She'd go as fast as possible through the middle of the mirrors and hope for the best.

Roll 2D6 and test for *Speed*.

If the test is successful, turn to **222**, otherwise, turn to **431**.

574

The hunter wasn't going to hang around to meet whatever had attacked the adventurers. She moved swiftly towards the other exit, keeping as far away from the wounded as possible. As she neared the door, she heard the 'thwip' of a crossbow string firing.

Roll 2D6 and test for *Speed*.

If the test is successful, turn to **366**, otherwise, turn to **700**.

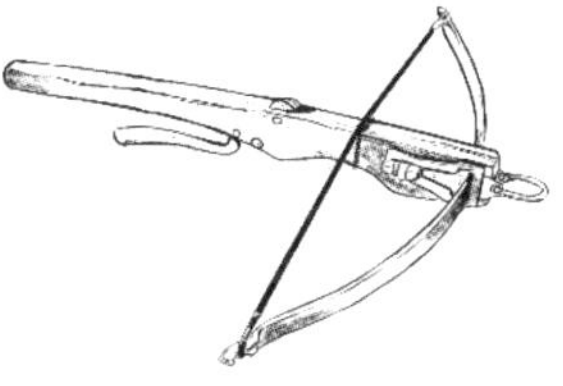

575

Alone in the chamber, Derilion felt very exposed. It wouldn't be so bad if she could see the enemy above her, but the darkness hid it entirely.

Something wasn't right, and Derilion knew she needed to work out exactly what.

Roll 2D6 and test for *Detection*.

If the test is successful, turn to **694**, otherwise, turn to **554**.

Derilion thought about what she should do next. She didn't know who Corzen was or why she was embedded in a wall. Still, she figured, if the Pajoli had done this to her, wasn't the enemy of the enemy, her friend?

"Very well," the hunter said.

"Stand back when you do it," Corzen thought.

Derilion took a couple of steps back and knelt behind her shield.

"I forgive you," she said.

At first, there was nothing, and then the slow, creaking, cracking sound as the woman separated from the rock.

Derilion watched. It was too strange an event not to. Gradually, a deep crack meandered along the rock in the vague outline of the woman's body. She could see Corzen straining to move, and finally, with an almighty bang, her left arm was free. The woman kept moving. Her left shoulder became free, then her right arm, then the left leg, each one greeted with the same deafening noise.

Finally, with one last push, she was out of the wall. Corzen stepped forward as the Lightbringer looked on.

"That was a brave thing to do," the woman thought. "I admire bravery. It's what got me in here in the first place."

The hunter moved around her. When she viewed Corzen from the side, the woman all but disappeared, and Derilion realised it wasn't her body that had been encased, just her image.

"Don't worry," Corzen soothed as she saw the fascination on Derilion's face. "I made myself like this. It was what they didn't like."

"Why didn't they just kill you?" the hunter asked.

"Because endless imprisonment was so much sweeter for them. But you have freed me. Thank you."

"I am on my way to retrieve my ward," Derilion said. "Would you like to join me?"

"A kind offer, but I need to see the world. Perhaps we will meet again on the outside."

Corzen started to walk away.

"Mind the mud," Derilion called to her. The woman looked back and smiled.

"Who did you think put it there in the first place. May I see your sword?"

Show Corzen her sword	Turn to **8**
Don't show her the sword	Turn to **461**

577

The girl appeared quite interested in the cuff, though it was hard for Derilion to tell either way. The hunter thought the child would be good at cards.

"Okay," she said. "I suppose I could use it."

"Tell me the information, and it's yours."

Turn to **460**.

578

The current was strong, and Derilion struggled to keep her head above water as she was swept along.

Unable to stabilise, she hit the left wall and felt the backpack snag briefly on one of the sharp rocks. It came free, and she finally reached the bank at the end and crawled onto it, drenched and out of breath.

She looked at her backpack and saw a tear. The last two items she put in had fallen out and were lost.

Turn to **197**.

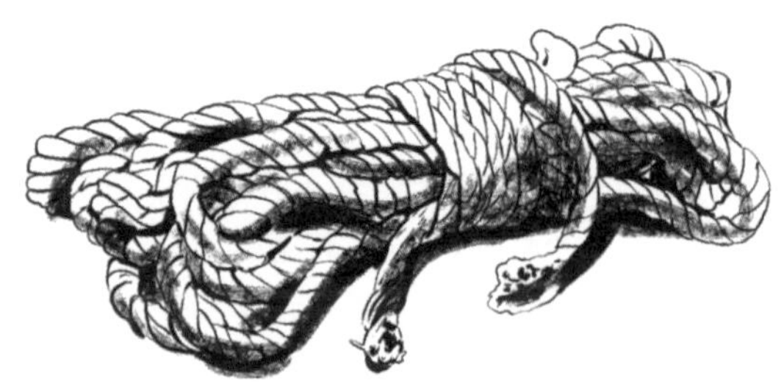

579

The creature looked at the gift and smiled.

"Perfect," it said. "They don't let me have metal."

The Lightbringer watched as the metal melted in its hand and reformed into a dagger.

The creature jumped at Derilion

	Speed	Accuracy	Damage	Health
Creature	7	8	1	7

If she defeats the creature, turn to **436**.

Derilion kept still. Something touched her foot, and when she looked down, she saw what appeared to be a giant worm going past her leg. She held her breath, as slowly, the woman appeared from the darkness.

Her arms and legs were thick worm-like limbs, constantly on the move. Her torso and head looked normal, though the hunter noticed movement under her plain tunic.

The woman had a concerned look on her face.

"Thank you, for not running," she said. "My name is Grom."

"What happened to you?"

"When I was a teenager, one of my spells went wrong, and it turned me into this. The Pajoli would have killed me, but I ran and hid in this cave. They didn't seem interested in pursuing me, so here I stay. What are you doing here?"

"I'm trying to find my ward; the Pajoli took her. Can you help?"

"Not much will work against the things you're going to face, but a simple stun charm will. Take this."

She handed Derilion what looked like a small ball of moss.

"Throw it at their feet as soon as possible."

Did the hunter put on the steel gauntlets?

If so, turn to **479**, otherwise, turn to **628**.

581

The stinger hit the metal gauntlet and bounced off. Derilion shut the lid of the box and put it back on the shelf. The girl turned around.

"That was a lucky escape," she said gleefully.

Investigate the lamp	Turn to **498**
Leave the room	Turn to **29**

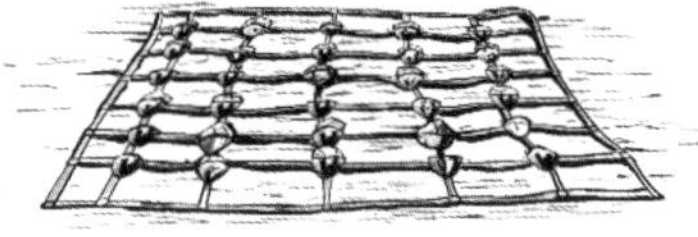

582

She approached the nearest mirror and peered into it. At first, the reflection was blurry, but the longer she looked, the clearer it became, and the area around the mirror grew hazy.

Too late, Derilion realised she was now inside the reflection.

Without hesitation, she walked towards the mirror, weapon raised. Almost instantly, a reflection appeared, ready to fight.

Attack the reflection	Turn to **393**
Try and talk to reflection	Turn to **28**
Keep moving toward the reflection	Turn to **605**

583

"I haven't got a carving," Derilion said.

"Very well," he said.

If she does have the carving, turn to **517**, otherwise, turn to **613**.

584

The faceless woman lay motionless on the floor. Derilion searched the room but found nothing of any value.

Some of the rock walls had images drawn in red, and the Lightbringer shuddered when she thought it might be the woman's blood. Most were of monsters, but whether the monsters were real or just a product of the faceless woman, it was impossible to know.

One appeared to show a large pool, with thrones all around it. This one was the most unsettling, but the hunter wasn't sure why.

After a few minutes, she left the room by the way she came in and continued along the corridor.

Turn to **232**.

585

The hunter pulled out her sword, and the witch laughed.

"What are you going to do with that? I'm not one of those mindless monsters, you know. I don't have to use strength to fight you."

With that, she dipped a hand into one of her pouches and threw some dust into the air. It fell onto Derilion's skin, and where it settled, her skin began to turn into wood.

The process was painless and quick. When the hunter could no longer move, the witch came up to her and smiled.

"Oh, if there's one thing I like, it's new subjects to experiment on. Know that you will die for a reason."

Her adventure ends here.

<h1 style="text-align:center">586</h1>

"Where's the noise coming from?" Derilion called to the man.

Without looking up, she watched as he flicked his hand towards her as if trying to swat an annoying fly.

Instantly, the hunter was knocked backwards with a blow which lifted her off her feet and slammed her into the cave behind, causing 2 damage to her *Health*.

Derilion gripped her sword, trying to fight the urge to attack him. After a moment, the rage passed. Around her, the noise increased again.

Turn to **57**.

<h1 style="text-align:center">587</h1>

A short while later, Derilion came across a door in the passageway. Nothing fancy, just a wooden door. The sort of wooden door anyone would have in their home. It seemed so ordinary it looked out of place.

She wondered if she should investigate or follow the corridor's gradual turn to the right. The door could be the right way, the only way, to save Obishaa.

The hunter put her ear to it and waited. There was some noise there, for sure, but it took her a moment or two to make out what the words were.

"Stay away. Stay away."

It made her heart run cold.

Enter the room	Turn to **560**
Ignore the room and continue	Turn to **232**

588

Derilion drank the green potion and waited, hoping for something to happen. Unfortunately, it didn't. Frustrated, the hunter looked at the Cuddower and then around at the small room and got an idea. In one swift move, she picked up the bow and arrow once more and loosed the arrow at the Cuddower.

Turn to **356**.

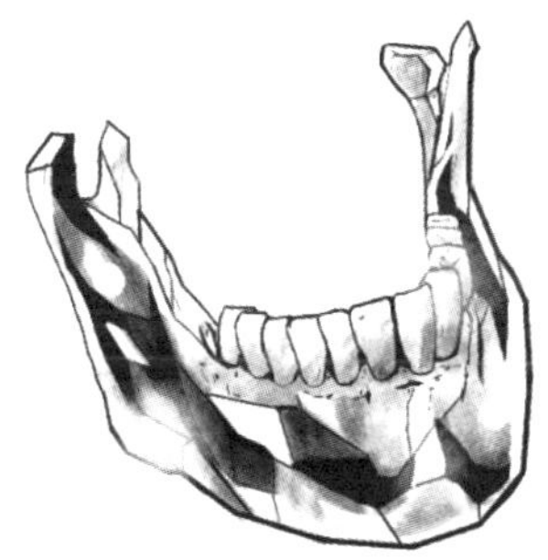

589

The Lightbringer inspected the bones closely. Most of them seemed garishly normal, but one, right at the bottom, resembled a human jaw made from glass (**+4w**).

Turn to **57**.

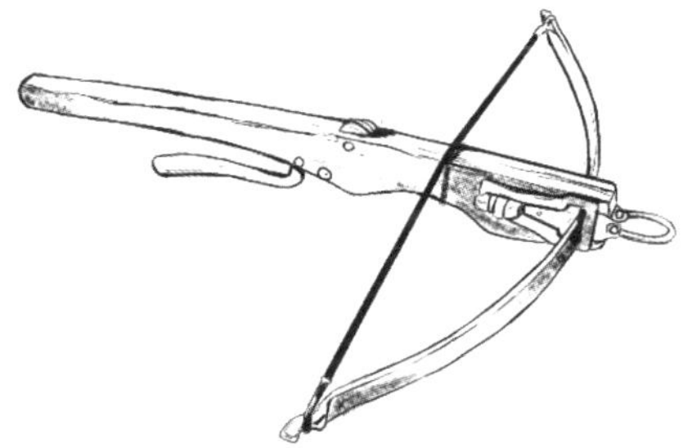

590

The creature was hard to miss. Derilion retrieved some explosive powder from her belt **(-1w)**, took aim at the creature's mid-riff and threw. It hit perfectly and exploded. The Lightbringer realised she'd have to find somewhere to hide from the falling debris.

Roll 2D6 and test for *Accuracy*.

If the test is successful, turn to **662**, otherwise, turn to **686**.

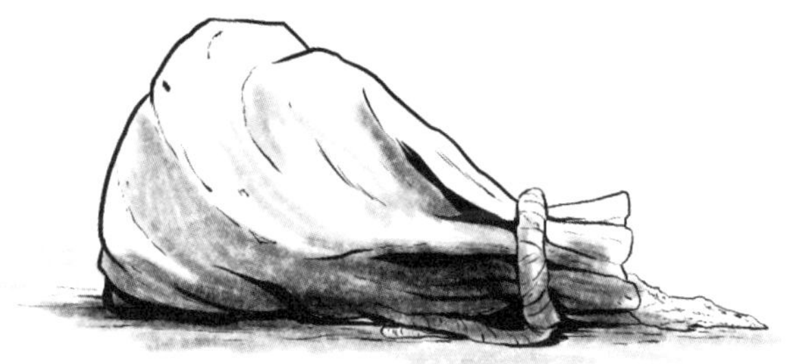

591

Derilion sucked at the wound on the back of her hand, spitting the blood she drew out onto the floor. Finally, she stopped, exhausted, and waited to see if her attempt had been successful.

When she felt no ill effects, she thanked her reflexes and cursed her stupidity. With a sigh of relief, she stepped forward through the door and into the next room.

Turn to **300**.

592

Derilion investigated the wall where the girl had been trapped. Every stone bore the same hex symbol, three wavy lines one on top of the next.

The hunter could take one of the stones if she wanted (**+3w**). Whether she did or not, Derilion moved on.

Turn to **487**.

593

The drip caught her face, just below her right eye, where she immediately felt stinging and tried to wash it out with water from her skein. She got most of it out, but it left her with a slightly blurred view.

Reduce Derilion's *Accuracy* by 1.

"Well, that's enough of that," came a woman's voice from behind.

Turn to **615**.

<h1 style="text-align:center">594</h1>

Derilion didn't like this situation at all. The fact the body showed no wounds was very strange. Perhaps magic had killed him, or a gas of some kind. If it was a gas, she had no way of protecting herself. Should she trigger it, she'd be forced to run, and running left her open to attack.

Carefully, she reached forward and turned the adventurer over. A thick, hard layer of amber covered his face, suffocating him. She'd seen the substance before, produced by a creature known as an Ambrite. She didn't want to stay here any longer. The Ambrite was likely nearby.

She could reach for the cuff (turn to **277**), head back to the wall and keep going (turn to **13**), search the adventurer for treasure (turn to **27**) or reach for the sword (turn to **535**).

<h1 style="text-align:center">595</h1>

Derilion reached the door and tried the handle. It was locked.

"I have the key to that," the creature said, offering it to the hunter in its hand. "Would you like to trade?"

Derilion looked at the key. It was made of bone, by the look of it, which seemed a strange substance to use.

She could offer the creature something for the key (turn to **33**) or take it (turn to **353**).

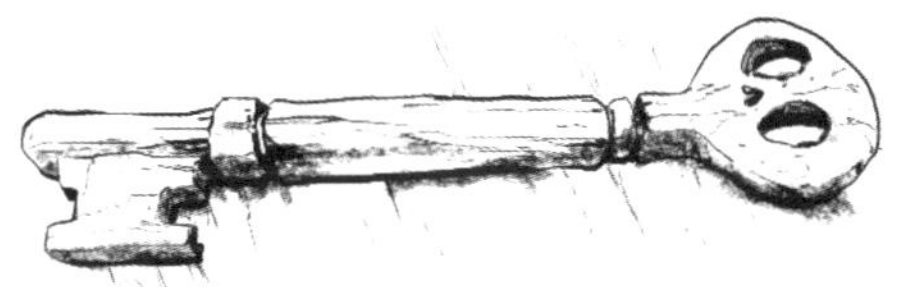

596

Derilion watched as the faceless woman unfurled her arms and legs to an inhuman size, pushing herself upwards until she towered over the hunter.

The hunter readied her sword.

	Speed	*Accuracy*	*Damage*	*Health*
Faceless Woman	6	8	2	12

If the Lightbringer wins, turn to **584**.

597

Derilion kneeled and bowed her head, in a move she hoped would show submission to the creature.

Turn to **44**.

598

Derilion missed the foothold, lost her balance and fell into the water below, knocking her shoulder on the rocks beneath the water, causing 1 damage to her *Health*.

Turn to **6**.

599

Roll 2D6 and test Derilion's *Speed* three times.

The Lightbringer took 1 damage to her *Health* for every unsuccessful test. Even after travelling so far across the room, there was still a little way left for her to go.

Turn to **108**.

600

Derilion walked the few miles into the village. As she arrived, the woman who'd asked about Huranee appeared looking hopeful. Derilion shook her head.

"I'm sorry," she said. "I didn't hear anything."

The woman broke down in tears, and the Lightbringer comforted her as best she could.

"What do you know about Crystalfall?" Derilion asked when she'd calmed down.

"It's a long, long trek from here, but you seem able enough to make it. Go east and find the town of Tombin, they'll be people there who can help you further."

The woman gave the hunter food and balms to heal her wounds. Restore the Lightbringer's attributes to her starting values.

The next morning, Derilion set out east in the direction of Tombin, hoping to find Obishaa.

Congratulations! You have completed Arcane Rites: Cult of the Pajoli. Look out for Derilion's next adventure – 'The Ascendence of the Witch'!

601

Derilion unsheathed her sword and struck the wall, hilt first. Softly at first, she hardened the blows, but even after several minutes hadn't put a dent in the wall. She could try something else or keep going.

Use the stone with concentric circles	Turn to **153**
Use some explosive powder	Turn to **531**
Leave and continue	Turn to **547**

602

"I'll take the explosive powder."

The woman gave a small smile and walked over to a wooden chest. Derilion heard it unlock and assumed the woman had done it using magic.

She pulled open a drawer, took out three sachets and closed it, upon which the mechanism sounded again.

"Here you go," the woman said, handing the sachets to the hunter (**+1w each**).

"Now, your end of the deal."

She stepped aside to let Derilion through.

Turn to **509**.

603

Derilion dropped the box, and the scorpion's stinger missed her hand by a fraction.

The little girl appeared beside her and picked the box up and put it back on the shelf.

"I did warn you, didn't I?" she said, before returning to her desk.

Investigate the lamp	Turn to **498**
Leave the room	Turn to **29**

604

She didn't know how long she had before it attacked, so as quickly as she could, Derilion swung the backpack around to the front. As she did so, the chamber went quiet.

The Lightbringer moved swiftly to the side as a ball of amber flew by where her head had been. She knew it'd be a couple more seconds before the creature could shoot again, and as she didn't know how far from the exit she was, she decided moving away would be safer than trying to engage with the enemy.

Roll 2D6 and test for *Speed*.

If the test was successful, turn to **372**. Otherwise, turn to **510**.

605

The hunter moved toward the reflection, which kept moving toward her. She tensed the nearer it came but was surprised when she was able to pass straight through it and into the normal room once more.

Her relief was short-lived, as standing in the centre of the room was an exact copy of her. This one, however, was no reflection.

Turn to **620**.

606

The hunter places her hand on the wall. Immediately the shadow began to cover her fingers, moving swiftly up her arm.

Derilion tried to pull away, but her hand wouldn't budge. Within a few seconds, the shadow had completely covered the hunter's body, consuming her.

Her quest ends here.

I AM NEITU
WILL YOU HELP ME?
IN RETURN
I WILL HELP YOU

607

As Derilion entered the now empty corridor, she heard a noise coming from the door with the lightning symbol. There was a click, and it gradually swung open.

With little choice, she moved through the doorway and began to walk, the way ahead lit by Volkov. She continued until the area before her was dark in spite of the shield. Slowly, the darkness began to move, forming words she recognised on the wall.

"I am Neitu. Will you help me? In return, I will help you."

Derilion had never encountered anything like it before.

Interrogate Neitu	Turn to **333**
Accept its request	Turn to **499**
Ignore the words and continue	Turn to **161**

608

"I don't need the enchantment," the Lightbringer said.

"Oh, right," the girl said. She turned and picked up the book Derilion had seen earlier. "This is a spell book. I know them all anyway, so you take this instead."

"Thank you," the hunter said, taking it off her (**+5w**).

The girl waved her hand in the direction of the door, and it glowed red for a moment.

"You're safe to go now," she said.

Derilion walked through the previous room, exiting through the other door.

Leave the room, turn to **404**.

<h1 style="text-align:center">609</h1>

"You lied to me," the demon said. "And for that, you are cursed."

Derilion felt her backpack grow light and realised the demon had taken all her belongings. Cross all backpack items off. The demon began to leave the room.

Attack the demon	Turn to **172**
Head left	Turn to **47**

<h1 style="text-align:center">610</h1>

Derilion decided the chest might hold something useful and approached it with caution. She couldn't see any locks adorning the front, though there were some runes atop of it, carved into the wood.

She didn't recognise the runes and couldn't read them either. Such runes could denote the chest contained magic of some sort, or, equally, they could be the idle doodles of an underworked craftsman.

If Derilion had a lens and wanted to use it, turn to **429**, otherwise, turn to **446**.

<h1 style="text-align:center">611</h1>

Derilion screamed at Ashingya, looking to see what reaction she had. Ashingya continued to circle, unimpressed.

The hunter thought she should attempt something else before the creature lost patience.

Kneel in front of Ashingya	Turn to **597**
Hide behind the shield	Turn to **275**
Turn her back	Turn to **683**
Wait and see	Turn to **640**

612

The kiln was in use, with several pots visible through the opening in the front. As she watched, she heard a faint scream coming from within.

"Get out! Get out!" a woman's voice screamed.

Derilion couldn't see anyone or anything inside. Whoever was making the noise didn't seem to pose any threat.

Then, with no warning, a flame shot out of the kiln, knocking the Lightbringer back, making her clatter into the shelves. She turned in time to see the vase with the word 'Ashingya' around its base fall to the floor and shatter with an ear-splitting boom.

From out of the debris of the pot, a swirling mist began to form in front of the hunter.

Turn to **169**.

613

Derilion watched as Holut stood and made his way into the morgue, exiting through the door to the left without looking back.

Needing to get going, the hunter walked into the morgue herself and looked around.

Turn to **342**.

614

Derilion started down the stairs, unhappy at not being able to see where it led. Volkov wasn't giving out enough light, and she didn't have another hand to carry one of the torches. She didn't put much pressure on the wall, just in case any traps were there.

About halfway down, she noticed a stone with a dark crack running around it. Carefully, she made her way by it and decided not to use the wall for the rest of the way.

Turn to **190**.

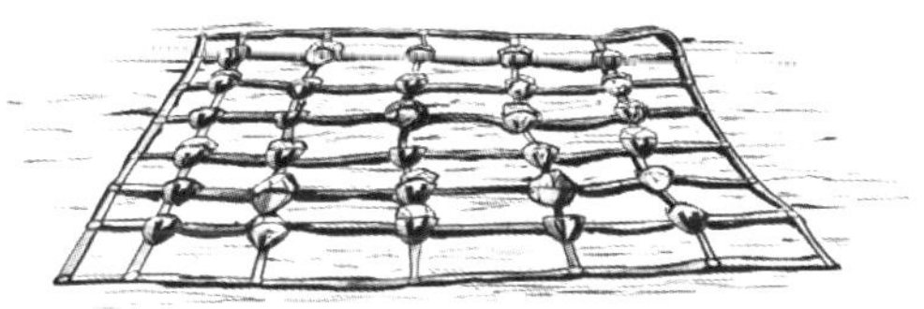

615

Derilion turned and looked at the woman who'd spoken. She was shorter than the hunter by a head and wore layers of grey robes.

"Who are you?" Derilion asked.

"The people call me Othwig, but let's not get too familiar. We both know you shouldn't be here."

Othwig smiled, but it was a tight, emotionless smile.

"I don't mean you any harm," the hunter said.

"With all due respect," Othwig said. "That's what people who mean harm say, too."

Attempt to trade with Othwig	Turn to **338**
Attack Othwig	Turn to **358**
Leave the room	Turn to **213**

616

The adventurer crouched, the shield covering her legs as much as possible. The scrabbling overhead continued, and Derilion was sure it was getting closer. Derilion looked around her. There were several places she could move to, though the ground was scattered with debris. If she was careful, however, she might move out of its reach.

Roll 2D6 and test for *Accuracy*.

If the test was successful, turn to **87**, otherwise, turn to **341**.

617

The assassin was still alive.

"Take this," she said, opening her hands and showing Derilion a small box filled with ash. "You will need this if you survive."

Derilion took the box (**+2w**).

"Please, give me one of my pills. They are in my belt."

Derilion looked to where the woman was pointing and saw the almost invisible compartment opening. She placed a finger inside and retrieved two small white pills (**+0w each**). The assassin opened her mouth, and Derilion put one of the pills on her tongue.

"Thank you," she said. "Keep the other. You might need it..."

The assassin's eyes glazed over, and the Lightbringer rested her back down on the floor.

Derilion headed to the exit.

Search the elven hunter	Turn to **136**
Head to the exit	Turn to **74**

618

The dancer smiled as Derilion started towards her brandishing her shield and sword.

"Fresh meat is so hard to find," she said.

The hunter prepared to attack, but before she could even register movement, the girl was next to her and Derilion felt the blood spurt from her neck.

She collapsed to the floor, and the last thing she saw was the woman's hungry eyes staring at her as she died.

619

There was no way Derilion was going to dance with her. The hunter pushed the girl's hand away and stepped back.

In an instant she had a knife in her hand and was coming at Derilion, moving in the same choreographed way. The Lightbringer had to move quickly.

Roll 2D6 and test for *Speed*.

If the test is successful, turn to **645**, otherwise, turn to **288**.

620

Derilion circled her double in the room, looking for a weakness. Her opponent did the same. There was no point waiting, the hunter knew. She raised her flaming shield and advanced.

	Speed	*Accuracy*	*Damage*	*Health*
Doppelganger	As Derilion	As Derilion	2	As Derilion

If the Lightbringer wins, turn to **312**.

621

Derilion's thoughts went to the chair; something wasn't right about it. She looked closely, picking it up to look underneath. As she did, she noticed one of the legs had been resting on a button on the floor.

It looked like a trigger for a trap, but she didn't know whether to leave the chair off the button or put it back on.

Leave the chair off the button	Turn to **113**
Put it back on the button	Turn to **42**

622

The hunter uttered the word, and the flame on her shield went out, plunging the cave into darkness. She now needed to navigate to the other side without walking into anything. It took longer than she'd hoped, but finally, she reached the door.

Turn to **312**.

623

Derilion tried her very best to keep her balance in the wardrobe, but unfortunately, wobbled and knocked one of the wooden sides with her elbow. She looked out of the gap again and saw the troll looking in her direction.

Stay in the wardrobe	Turn to **321**
Jump out, weapon ready	Turn to **496**

624

Derilion walked to the other door in the corridor and tried, in vain, to open it.

Turn to **7**.

625

"All right," Derilion said. "I'll take one of your tests."

Othwig's eyes lit up.

"Oh, thank you. I'm always looking for more test subjects," she said. "Well, all you have to do is sample the liquid or smoke from one of the benches. Choose either the left, centre or right bench."

Left bench liquid	Turn to **71**
Centre bench liquid	Turn to **305**
Right bench smoke	Turn to **111**

626

Derilion went to the door to the left and listened for any signs of movement beyond. It was always better to be forewarned of any dangers. She heard nothing. There was a key in the lock which turned, followed by a click. She pushed it inwards. Inside, hundreds of small blue lights hung in a darkened room, as if it were full of tiny stars.

Derilion thought through her options.

Enter the room	Turn to **685**
Investigate the other room	Turn to **141**
Choose the next set of doors	Turn to **253**

627

Derilion peered into the orb, trying to work out what it was. The surface was highly polished, and after a couple of moments, she could see a face forming on the surface.

Roll 2D6 and test for *Detection*.

If the test is successful, turn to **218**, otherwise, turn to **324**.

628

"Keep the moss dry," Grom said. "It won't work otherwise."

The hunter tucked it into a pocket high up on her tunic (**+1w**).

"Thank you," she said and returned carefully to the stream.

Turn to **676**.

629

The woman was concentrating on the net, muttering to herself. The Lightbringer thought, if she was quick, there was a good chance she could surprise her and take the upper hand.

Roll 2D6 and test for *Speed*.

If the test was successful, turn to **403**, otherwise, turn to **447**.

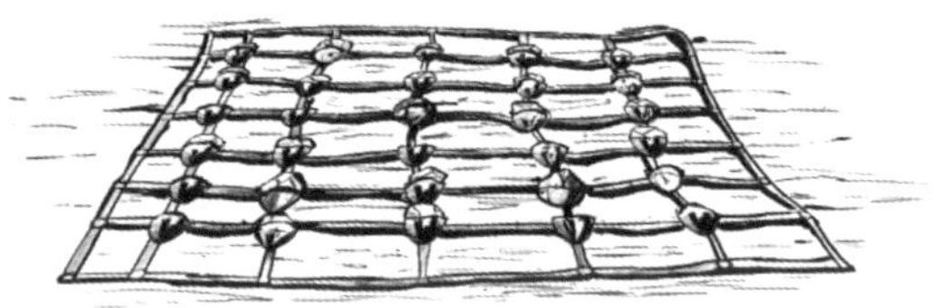

630

Try as she might, Derilion couldn't find a space where she could adequately hide. Knowing they were going to come through the door at any moment, and that there was no way she could avoid them, she turned to face whoever was coming.

Turn to **103**.

631

Derilion began moving along the wall. It was hard going, and she nearly slipped with the first couple of steps. She reached for the next handhold without really looking and was shocked when the stone came away in her hand.

Roll 2D6 and test for *Speed*.

If the test was successful, turn to **156**, otherwise, turn to **112**.

632

The hunter managed to hit the Insect Demon with her sword in a single swoop.

The creature roared, and Derilion ran back to get a better footing for an attack.

The Insect Demon stared at the hunter, a murderous look on its face.

She knew this was going to be her hardest fight yet.

	Speed	*Accuracy*	*Damage*	*Health*
Insect Demon	7	8	2	10

If the Lightbringer won, turn to **135**.

Derilion upended her backpack onto the floor and looked for anything she could use to poison the pool of water the Elemental was using as a power source.

She had time to kick four of them into the pool.

She could also attempt to detect two items that would weaken the creature, though there wouldn't be any more time to use anything else.

After she used the four items, she must face the Elemental. She can elect to face the Elemental at any time (e.g. if she doesn't have four of the items).

Attempt to detect two items	Turn to **452**
Blue Egg from the Trolls	Turn to **449**
Hex stone with concentric circles	Turn to **18**
Fire orange balls	Turn to **505**
Eye pendant	Turn to **223**
Phial of clear liquid	Turn to **206**
Box of ash	Turn to **203**
Yellowish leaves	Turn to **234**
Blueish leaves	Turn to **313**
Lead weight	Turn to **89**
Moss	Turn to **362**
Face the Diamond Elemental	Turn to **107**

<h1 style="text-align:center">634</h1>

As Derilion stepped over the fallen woman, she felt an icy grip on her leg. The hunter looked down to see the woman looking up at her, clutching her ankle.

Derilion struggled free and watched the woman rise from the floor. The hunter's blood ran cold; this was a Death Maiden, looking for a soul to replenish her own.

"Stay away," Derilion said firmly, holding her sword out to ward off any sudden attacks.

"I will," the Death Maiden said. "If you help me."

"What do you want?"

"Kill the monster in the room beyond, and I will spare you your soul."

What should she do?

Fight the Death Maiden	Turn to **374**
Fight in the next room	Turn to **674**

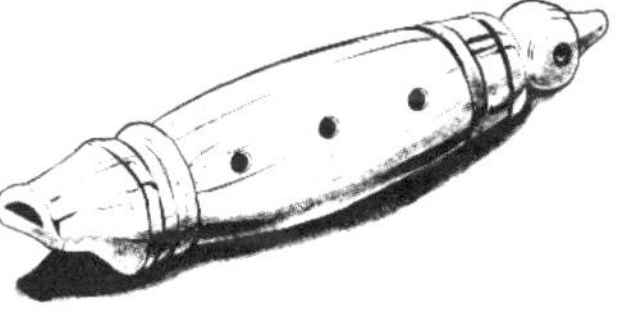

<h1 style="text-align:center">635</h1>

Derilion rolled quickly to the left, hoping to find some cover. Disorientated, rocks continued to hit her as she searched.

Try as she might, there was no cover to the left of the room, and before she'd had time to think of another plan, a large rock struck her firmly, and everything went black.

636

The hunter headed toward the exit, passing the chest and the slab with its sinister set of tools. From her left, she heard what sounded like a muffled voice coming from the direction of the coffins.

She paused and listened but couldn't make out what it was saying.

Investigate the coffins   Turn to **266**
Continue straight on   Turn to **537**

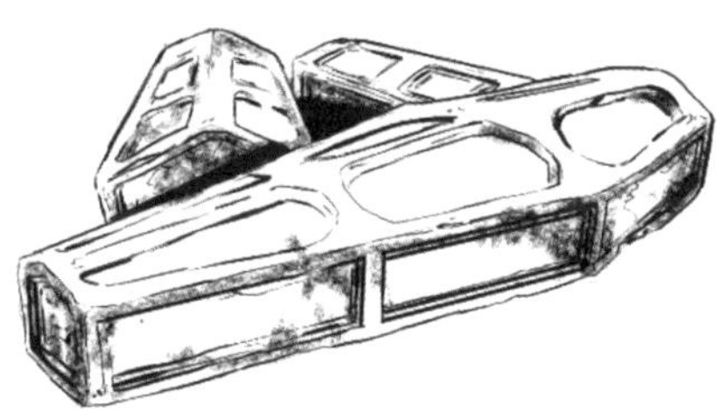

637

Derilion turned and saw the lid of one of the coffins was off, and a pale man in flowing purple robes stood in front of her smiling.

"You look perfect," he said, eyeing her up and down.

"Perfect for what?" she replied.

"You'll find out. Or rather, you won't."

He moved his hands in front of him, and she saw he was holding two of the crude tools. He meant to fight her.

Turn to **177**.

638

The hunter put the leaves into her mouth and began to chew. They tasted very sweet. She finished eating the leaves and smiled at Othwig, who seemed to be waiting for something to happen.

"There," Derilion said, "I have taken your test."

"You have, indeed. At least your death will be quick and painless. Take solace in that," she said.

It's the last thing Derilion heard.

639

Derilion stood in front of the crossroads. She had the option of continuing, heading left or turning right. In each direction, there was a door to go through. Something about the setup had a finality she didn't like. It felt like she would not return.

Still, she had a job to do, and she had to choose one of them.

Go left	Turn to **483**
Go straight on	Turn to **93**
Go right	Turn to **673**

640

The hunter continued to watch Ashingya circle her, keeping eye contact all the time. After what felt like an age, Ashingya stopped and spoke to Derilion.

"You are worthy," she said. "And I see you need enchantments. I can offer you a *Speed* enchantment if you need one."

If she needed a *Speed* enchantment, turn to **124**, otherwise, turn to **285**.

641

The troll tucked hungrily into its food, completely ignoring the hunter who stood in the middle of the room.

"I'll go then," Derilion said. The troll waved a hand as if to say 'leave', and the hunter carefully retreated out of the door.

Turn to **126**.

642

Derilion picked the glass ball up and weighed it in her hands. It felt hollow. Perhaps the key to escaping the room lay inside it. The hunter let go of the orb and watched as it hit the ground and smash into hundreds of pieces. Nothing happened. Disappointed, she turned to leave and came face-to-face with the skeleton.

Turn to **37**.

643

Derilion instinctively put her hand on the hilt of her sword, and the demon laughed a deep, slow laugh.

"If you want to die," it said. "I can help you with that. But I do not wish to harm you."

It sounded sincere to the hunter, but then that was their skill. She'd heard plenty of stories in taverns about how they'd conned people out of gold, treasure and sometimes even their souls.

Derilion looked around. There was a turning off to the right she could choose to go down instead of facing the demon.

Turn right	Turn to **47**
Fight the demon	Turn to **172**
Speak to the demon	Turn to **474**

644

Derilion focused her mind as much as possible but couldn't pick up on anything. She cursed her stupidity at wasting time, but as soon as she opened her eyes, she had a vision of a lead weight and fire orange balls.

If she had either of these items, she quickly kicked them into the pool and watched as the water around them turned red, and the Diamond Elemental screamed in pain.

Subtract 6 from the Elemental's *Health* for each object.

She must now face the Elemental in battle.

Turn to **107**.

645

Derilion adeptly dodged the knife and made for the door.

"I admire your speed," the woman said. "But if you do not dance, you cannot leave this room without paying a toll."

The hunter turned and once more, the girl was offering her hand. Was it worth the risk?

Pay the toll	Turn to **98**
Take her hand	Turn to **228**
Attack her	Turn to **618**
Leave anyway	Turn to **82**

646

Derilion focused on the job in hand. She brought her backpack around and held it to the side of her so that it went through first. That way, it might take any damage should there be a trap.

It wasn't a fast process. The hunter didn't want to knick or tear anything if she didn't have to. The wounds from fighting she couldn't help, they were an occupational hazard, but hurting herself would be careless.

A few metres in, the hunter stopped and concentrated, searching the walls for any triggers.

Roll 2D6 and test for *Detection*.

If the test is successful, turn to **473**, otherwise, turn to **330**.

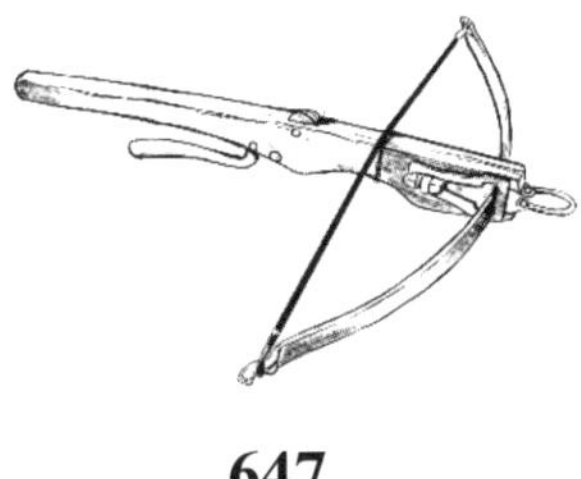

647

Derilion nodded and rummaged in her backpack for the cuff. She found it and passed it (**-4w**) to the dwarf.

"Can you help me?" he said, holding out his arm.

The hunter took it and put the cuff on his arm. Immediately, he grabbed her, and she felt herself growing weak. Something about the cuff was giving him the power to drain her energy.

Roll 2D6 and test for *Speed*.

If the test is successful, turn to **438**, otherwise, turn to **317**.

648

Derilion managed to stop herself falling further into the darkness. The crossing was too hazardous, she thought, and quickly returned to the room with the Cuddower. She had one option left; remove the arrow from the monster.

Turn to **503**.

649

Derilion walked around the hole, her back to the wall. The sides were smooth. She'd barely taken a few steps when an insect demon flew up towards her.

Roll 2D6 and test for *Speed*.

If the test was successful, turn to **632**, otherwise, turn to **464**.

650

Derilion pushed the Slabac away. It was almost dead.

"I don't want to kill you," she said.

"One of us must die for the door to open," it replied.

Give them a chance to live	Turn to **174**
Finish them off	Turn to **451**

651

Unsure of why the Cuddower was hesitant, and with nowhere left to run, Derilion took her sword and shield and advanced towards it.

Turn to **485**.

652

As soon as it left her backpack, the creature focused on the blue egg and caught it before it had time to hit the floor (**-2w**). As it studied it, Derilion collected the rest of her belongings, put them in her backpack and left the room, shutting the door behind her.

Turn to **624**.

653

Derilion sprinted towards the exit as the shower of boulders increased. One grazed her shoulder. Another landed directly in front of her, causing her to jump at the last minute.

As she landed, her foot caught on a fallen stone, dealing 1 damage to her *Health*. The hunter gritted her teeth and ran as best she could through the door to safety.

Turn to **143**.

654

The Lightbringer managed to find handholds good enough to grab onto, and though it was tiring, she made it to the other side of the bank and dropped down onto the ledge.

Turn to **197**.

655

The adventurer lay dying on the ground, his blood seeping over the stone floor. As the hunter prepared to land the killing blow, he looked up at her with hatred.

"They know you're coming," he hissed.

"Who?" the hunter demanded.

The man smiled and closed his eyes, his last ever breath escaping his lips. Whoever it was, Derilion was going to have to find out by herself.

The hunter searched him and found an opaque scarf around their neck (**+1w**). It didn't look very special, but it could be useful. She moved on, emerging into an area with three paths.

Turn to **639**.

656

As she walked further down the tunnel, the water rose again, until she realised it'd be faster to swim.

She pushed her panic away, and swam along the corridor, keeping her backpack high and out of the water.

She looked at the space left above her and didn't think she'd make it to the end of the corridor without being completely submerged.

Derilion's panic was rising; this wasn't the way she wanted to die.

Continue to the end	Turn to **682**
See if there was another way out	Turn to **507**
Go back and inspect the body	Turn to **168**

657

Something wasn't right about the Cuddower's behaviour, but Derilion wasn't sure exactly what. She took a step backwards and watched as the creature took one forwards.

Roll 2D6 for *Detection*.

If the test is successful, turn to **506**, otherwise, turn to **651**.

658

Derilion knelt and began to rifle through the pockets of the Sprites. The first two produced nothing, but as she turned to the third, its eyes opened, and it gripped her wrist, causing icy pain to shoot up her arm. The Frost Sprite muttered something and closed its eyes.

Reduce Derilion's *Accuracy* by 1.

She stood and moved off out of the chamber as quickly as possible.

Turn to **226**.

659

"Hello?" the hunter called.

"Help me," came a voice. "I'm so weak."

"Obishaa?" Derilion called. "Is that you?"

The hunter got no reply. She couldn't be sure it was her ward. It could well be another trick by the Pajoli.

Help the girl	Turn to **105**
Press on	Turn to **487**

660

Derilion landed awkwardly in the mud. She tried to keep her balance as best she could, but it was not enough. The hunter fell onto her back, and it's all the mud needed to get a better hold.

The mud held her to the floor, and as it crept up and over Derilion, she knew she had failed her ward.

661

The troll stopped, squinted a little and then shook his large head.

"Not you again?" it said. "Didn't I tell you what would happen if I ever saw you again."

"The caves don't have a lot of variety when it comes to paths," the Lightbringer replied. "We were bound to bump into each other sooner or later."

"You'd be surprised how many paths there are," it said, knowledgeably. "But that doesn't make your reappearance any more gratifying."

The troll took its wooden club from its belt and advanced towards the hunter.

Turn to **514**.

662

Rock and dust filled the room. The hunter hid behind her shield as debris rained down from above. When it cleared, the monster had gone. Derilion was relieved, but it was short-lived, as a mist was beginning to form in the room.

Turn to **169**.

663

Derilion ventured further into the room. The blue lights seemed to be just out of her reach above her. They went on forever. After a few seconds, the hunter started to feel disorientated.

She tried to turn around, but her legs gave way, and she fell to the floor, landing on her back.

She smelt the sleeping gas immediately. The Lightbringer cursed her stupidity as she sunk into unconsciousness.

Sometime later, she awoke but could not feel her body. She looked around her, and with a sense of dread, realised she'd become one of the floating blue lights in the room, her soul separated from her body.

This is where she'd spend eternity.

664

Derilion walked up to the left door and tried the handle. It didn't budge, and she assumed it was locked.

There was no key in the door or nearby.

Investigate the right door	Turn to **477**
Knock on the door	Turn to **433**
Kick the door down	Turn to **7**

665

Derilion moved with speed up the passageway in front of her, frustration growing inside. It was dark, even with the shield held out before her. The hunter tried to swallow her panic. This rescue wasn't going well, and her mind dwelled on the time it was taking her to find her ward.

The hunter resisted the scream she felt inside her. Better she channelled it into her next battle.

After several minutes the passageway did not look like ending, and the hunter was having second thoughts about whether to turn back or not.

Continue down the dark tunnel Turn to **528**
Turn back Turn to **323**

666

Derilion went to put the book back on the plinth, but it wouldn't leave her hands. She waggled them, but it was stuck fast. She threw her hands forward to no effect. If the book wouldn't go back, she'd have to take it with her.

Turn to **565**.

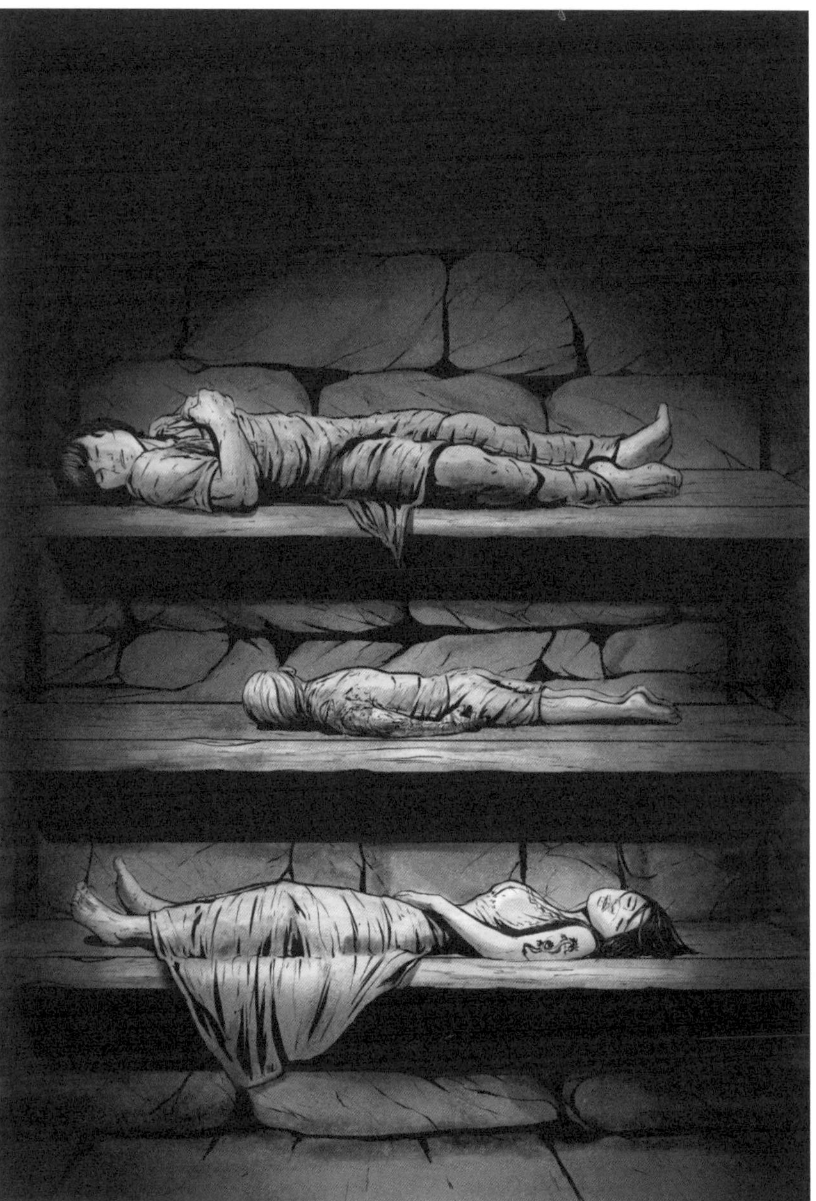

<h1 style="text-align:center">667</h1>

There were three differently dressed cadavers - a woman with flowing robes, a man with heavy leather overalls, and a young boy wearing everyday clothes. The hunter looked at the bodies, wondering why she felt strange about looting them. After all, she often searched the bodies of the enemies she killed.

Still unsure she looked through the doorway to the morgue itself but couldn't see much from her position.

Search the woman	Turn to **132**
Search the man	Turn to **164**
Search the boy	Turn to **96**
Head into the morgue	Turn to **144**

<h1 style="text-align:center">668</h1>

Derilion went back to the crate, bent and put the wand back into her hand. Almost immediately, a light flowed down from the wand into the woman. Derilion felt weaker, losing 3 *Health*. She watched as the woman blinked open her eyes and pushed herself up until she was standing.

"Thank you," she said. "I know why you're here, and I can give you an enchantment you need, though it will come at a cost."

"What cost?" the hunter asked.

"Whichever enchantment I give you will drain that particular attribute from you."

If Derilion chooses an enchantment, deduct 1 from that attribute's total. Whether or not she chose to get an enchantment, the woman replaced the box lid and walked off into the caves alone.

Search the other boxes	Turn to **45**
Head for the door	Turn to **354**

669

Derilion reached in and touched the person's face with the back of her hand. It felt cold. She was able to see more now. The figure was dressed in simple grey robes and held what appeared to be a wand.

The woman looked around Derilion's age, and the adventurer thanked the gods she'd managed to make it this far.

Search the other boxes   Turn to **45**
Take the wand   Turn to **34**
Head for the door   Turn to **354**

670

The hunter ducked right and followed the corridor around to the left. Thankfully, there were no more bugs here, and she was able to make her way quickly along the tall corridor.

After a minute, the passage opened out into a larger cave, easily the biggest so far. It was lit with torches around the edge and had a lived-in feeling.

Continue into the cave in front   Turn to **439**
Go back and choose another way   Turn to **698**

671

Derilion chose something from her backpack and offered it to Othwig. She watched as the witch raised an eyebrow.

"I'm afraid I don't need that," she said pointedly. "Please, take my test."

Turn to **625**.

"I could help you," Derilion said.

The Cuddower stopped and laughed.

"And how would you do that? By dying?"

"Perhaps there's some quest I can perform. Maybe a score to settle with someone?"

Much to the Lightbringer's surprise, the Cuddower stopped and thought.

"Now you say it, there is something you could do for me, but it's difficult."

"I understand."

The Cuddower took a ring from its finger and held it out to the hunter.

"Wear this, and I will let you go."

Derilion looked at the ring; it looked simple enough. No obvious runes inscribed on it. Yet, the creature was intelligent, and it was unlikely to be a task without penalties. If she didn't take the ring, she would have to fight the Cuddower.

If she agrees to wear the ring, turn to **225**, otherwise, turn to **485**.

673

Derilion chose to go through the right-hand door. The room beyond was dark. She waited for her eyes to grow accustomed to it, and as she did, she heard the door shut behind her.

The hunter turned and saw there was no handle on this side. If she were to come back this way, she'd have to work out how to get through it.

After a few moments, she was able to make out a door on either side of her.

Head left   Turn to **404**
Head right   Turn to **423**

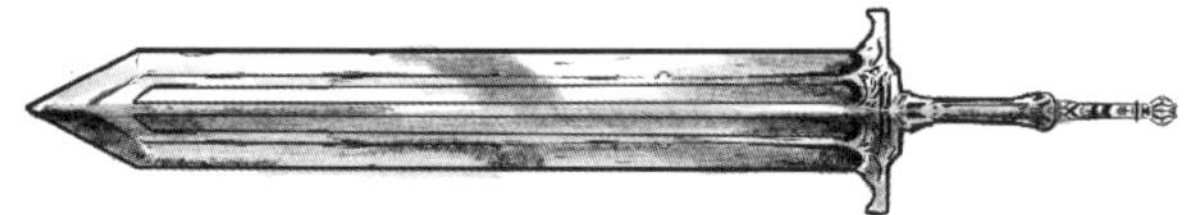

674

"All right," Derilion told the Death Maiden. "I'll fight the creature in the next room for you."

"Good," the Maiden said, hunger in her eyes. "Bring them to me alive."

Derilion nodded and approached the door, weapon ready. She placed her left hand on the metal knob and twisted, expecting it to be locked, but found it wasn't.

The door swung open, and the hunter stepped inside.

Turn to **129**.

675

Derilion suspected the corridor might be under an enchantment, making people think it's flooding the further they ventured down it. She tested this theory by walking a few steps, noting how the water appeared around her. She then took several steps back, and it disappeared.

Such a spell, she knew, required a specific rune-stone to be left here, which, if she found, might be of benefit in her quest.

Search for the rune-stone	Turn to **5**
Continue along the corridor	Turn to **547**

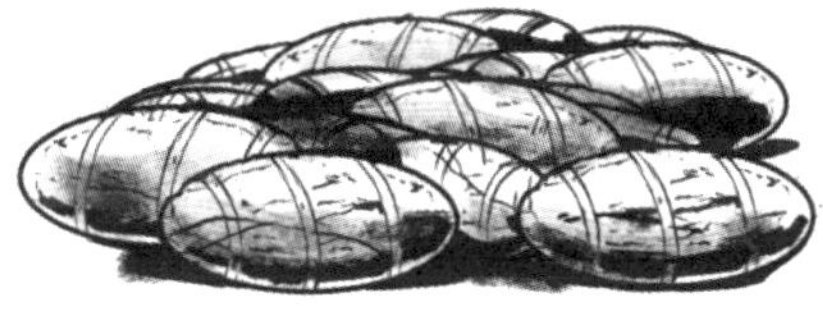

676

Derilion looked at the options. She could either move along the wall or wade through the water.

Neither were particularly attractive.

Go along the wall	Turn to **327**
Go via the water	Turn to **6**

She made it back to the door, but it didn't appear to have a handle this side. She used her sword to try and prise it open, but the door was stuck fast.

Derilion turned and looked along the corridor once more, to see all but a few puddles of water left, and her feet felt almost dry.

Turn to **675**.

"Wait," the girl said, standing up and approaching the hunter. "As you managed to resist taking anything, I will enchant your necklace with a *Stealth* enchantment, if you need one of those."

If Derilion needed a *Stealth* enchantment, turn to **368**, otherwise, turn to **608**.

"I'm not going anywhere."

"Very well," the men said. "You want to see proof of who you are."

An image appeared between the hunter and the men. A young girl, of around Obishaa's age, sneaking out of the cave entrance.

"This is you escaping our caves when you were young. We were going to kill you, but instead, we let you live, and cast a returning spell upon you."

The image shifted, and now Derilion saw the child sleeping with a witch standing over her, enchanting her.

"We figured you would be more useful to us when you were older."

"And now, here you are."

"So, why don't you join us?"

Refuse to sit	Turn to **302**
Sit on the throne	Turn to **536**

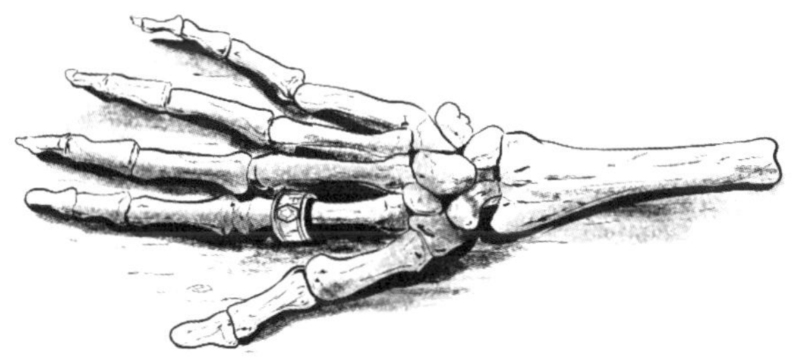

680

Derilion stopped and looked at the door. It wasn't covered in vines as she'd first thought, it was *made* of vines, knotted tightly together, hiding whatever lay on the other side.

The leaves moved gently in whatever breeze penetrated this far into the cave system. The hunter thought through her options, aware of time ticking by.

Try and push the door open	Turn to **364**
Inspect the vines closer	Turn to **550**
Kick the door open	Turn to **114**

681

Derilion threw the powder and ducked behind the body of the Cuddower. The explosion was deafening in the small space, and the hunter thought the cave might collapse. She put the shield above her, expecting the worst.

She was surprised when nothing hit it. After a moment, the dust settled, and she looked over towards where the door had been.

Turn to **443**.

682

Derilion kept on swimming, and the water kept on rising. Soon, she was swimming completely underwater, and as the time ticked by her panic increased.

Unable to hold her breath any longer, she swam as quickly as possible towards the door at the end.

Roll 2D6 and test for *Accuracy*.

If the test was successful, turn to **318**, otherwise, turn to **379**.

683

The hunter turned her back to shield her face from the swirling dust and tried to think about her next move.

Turn to **44**.

684

Try as she might, Derilion was unable to make a dent in the vines on the door. Then she had an idea – perhaps if she attempted the vines nearer her hand, the smaller shoots, it might make a difference. She'd have to be accurate, though. She could easily lose a finger if she cut too close.

Roll 2D6 and test for *Accuracy*.

If the test was successful, turn to **495**, otherwise, turn to **284**.

685

The hunter took a couple of steps into the room. She was suddenly aware of just how silent it was. Something was odd about the place, but she couldn't pinpoint what.

Roll 2D6 and test for *Detection*.

If the test was successful, turn to **552**, otherwise, turn to **663**.

<h1 style="text-align:center">686</h1>

Rock and dust filled the room. The hunter hid behind her shield as debris rained down from above. Fortunately, Volkov took most of the impact, but a rock caught Derilion on the side, causing 2 damage to her *Health*.

When it cleared, the monster had gone. Derilion was relieved, but it was short-lived, as a mist was beginning to form in the room.

Turn to **169**.

<h1 style="text-align:center">687</h1>

The hunter bent down, placed her sword under the coffin lid and, using all her weight, began to prise the lid open. She heard a faint voice coming from inside the coffin.

"Watch out, behind you," it said.

Roll 2D6 and test her *Speed*.

If the test was successful, turn to **283**, otherwise, turn to **117**.

<h1 style="text-align:center">688</h1>

Derilion couldn't find anything on the boy, at first. Then she investigated his burned arm and saw he was gripping what appeared to be a piece of glass.

Carefully, she opened his fingers and caught the piece of glass before it hit the floor. It was a lens (**+1w**), meant to fit into an eyepiece.

Before she could find out more, she noticed the man was stirring and decided to move away from the bodies and into the morgue.

Turn to **342**.

689

Derilion wanted to get out of the morgue as quickly as possible.

She had the choice of leaving via the door in front of her or the one to the left.

Leave by the door on the left	Turn to **538**
Leave by the door straight on	Turn to **548**

690

The hunter approached the right bench carefully, the smoke threatening to choke her. Derilion stopped a couple of steps short and watched. After a few moments, the hairs on her arm stood on end, and she started to feel hot inside.

"That'll be enough of that," came a woman's voice behind her.

Turn to **615**.

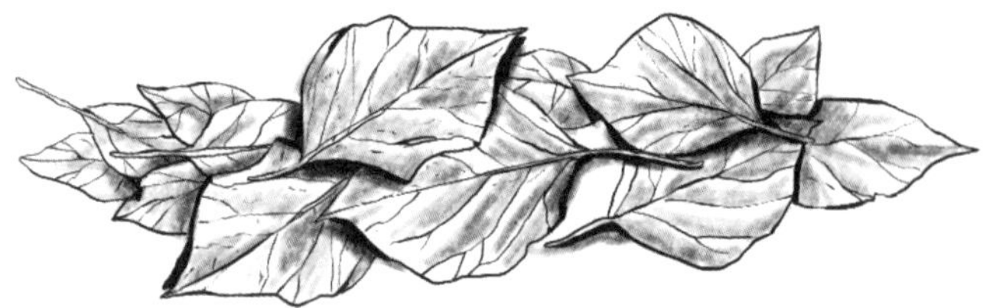

691

Derilion watched in horror as the explosive flew past the faceless woman's shoulder, hit the wall just behind her and ignited. There was an almighty flash, a roar and the cave wall exploded, showering them both in heavy rocks.

Roll 2D6 and test for *Speed*.

If the test was successful, turn to **417**, otherwise, turn to **80**.

692

Derilion shook her head and watched the anger grow in the dwarf's face. Enraged, he pushed her away. He must have been faking the wound.

"Why aren't any of you any good?" he growled. "All I want is the cuff."

He drew his axe, ready to fight.

Turn to **122**.

693

The floor looked too regular and clean for the hunter's liking. She crouched to take a closer look at the stones nearest to her and noticed regular gaps between them.

She found a rock and threw it across the stones. On the third slab, the stone flipped violently, hurling the rock towards the creature. Derilion knew it would require a lot of skill and patience to get across the stones unscathed.

Carefully, using her sword to test each one, she managed to trigger every trap and made it across safely. Behind her, she heard the creature sigh, clearly unhappy she wasn't its next meal.

Turn to **165**.

694

From up there. Derilion realised, it had the element of surprise, of course, but it also had the high ground, able to attack its enemy's weakest spot, the head. Swiftly, the adventurer brought the shield up to protect her head.

Turn to **155**.

695

Derilion said a short prayer and grabbed the Pulreney vase, gripped the stopper and pulled it out in one swift movement. For a moment, nothing happened, and the hunter thought it an anti-climax, but then the vase shattered.

Derilion stepped back and watched something emerge from the vase. Starting small, it grew rapidly until a seven-foot-tall stone creature stood before her. Derilion scrambled backwards, attempting to get out of the reach of its arms. It stood with its back to her but was between her and the doorway.

She thought her sword would be useless against the creature. Perhaps she could use some explosive powder if she had some.

Otherwise, she could try to creep around it using *Stealth*.

Use *Stealth*	Turn to **270**
Throw explosive powder	Turn to **590**

696

It took Derilion a couple of moments more, but then she recognised what she was seeing. The figure was dancing to the music in the room. She wore a dark flowing dress with tattered sleeves.

The girl looked serenc as she moved in patterns that seemed to be second nature to her. The hunter wondered how long she'd been dancing in this room. As she watched, the dancer made her way to Derilion and offered her hand.

Take her hand	Turn to **228**
Refuse her hand	Turn to **619**
Leave the room	Turn to **131**

697

Derilion was pulled through the narrow passageway and into the room beyond. There was a low rumbling behind her, and she was able to turn her head to witness the pathway back to the door collapsing into a deep chasm.

The pull on the hunter softened and then disappeared. She stood alone in the room for a moment, then went to the bow and lifted it from its cradle.

From the other direction, an uneven door opened in the rock and a Cuddower, a large six-legged animal, climbed through. He was smiling, holding a spiked club, and moving his heavy tail back and forth.

"Thought you'd take my bow, did you?" he said.

He wasn't in range yet, and Derilion tried to think about what her next move should be.

Talk to the Cuddower	Turn to **672**
Search for something in her backpack to help	Turn to **281**
Replace the bow	Turn to **316**
Prepare to fight	Turn to **657**

698

Derilion returned to the room where the flying bugs had attacked her earlier and dispatched the last few with her sword.

She had two exits she hadn't tried.

Go left	Turn to **160**
Go straight ahead	Turn to **665**

699

Derilion began to dislodge the stones using her sword, being careful not to damage either her weapon or the girl trapped in the wall.

After several minutes there was enough of a gap for Zalixa to step out into the corridor.

Turn to **188**.

700

Something pierced the back of Derilion's neck. The hunter just had time to turn to see the dwarf with a crossbow pointed at her before she breathed her last.

Members of the
Adventurers Guild

Jenifur 'JeniSkunk' Charne
Ralf Steinberg
Oliver Traxel
Darryl W.
Gonçalo Rodrigues
Andrés.
Andy Miller
Kevin David
Simon Scott
Charles Revello
Ian Livingstone
Steve Jackson

Your help was greatly appreciated